# Prologue

## MICHAEL

I stepped up to the lectern and nodded at the jury of twelve.

"Ladies and gentlemen, nothing the District Attorney has just told you is evidence. It is purely argument. He wants you to believe Douglas Kurtin wanted his wife dead. But there isn't one shred of evidence of that. He wants you to believe that Douglas Kurtin went to his house that night even though his wife had a court order keeping him away. But there is no evidence of that. Oh, yes, the woman next door, the Peeping Patty. She says she saw a man who looked like Douglas Kurtin sneaking around the house. But remember her answer when I asked, 'What part of the man looked like Douglas Kurtin?' Remember what she said? She said, 'He had huge hands like Mr. Kurtin's.'"

I paused and allowed the smiles and nods to happen. They did. So far so good.

It was my third trial in the month of August and I was truly exhausted. Plus the stuff with Danny, my wife, was dragging me down. She was living apart from me and our kids because the stress of being part of our family had become too much for her. Plus, my investigator, Marcel, was on hiatus in Europe, visiting his mother and paying his respects at his father's grave. It felt like my right hand was missing; and maybe it was, with Marcel away.

There were nights I would lie in my bed wondering how different my life would have been if I'd gone to medical school instead of law school. I had been accepted to both, with a major in economics and a second major in biology. But I'd chosen law school because it was only three years, and medicine looked no less than nine years away. Staring at the ceiling, I asked myself what the big damn rush had been to get out of school? The angst of youth, I decided. The need to get out and make some money and raise some hell. Which I did for my first fifteen years, until the ARDC of the Illinois Supreme Court pulled me aside one afternoon in my office and said I needed to lay off the sauce. Or they would jerk my license. I haven't had a drop since. Well, maybe a solitary beer here and there, but the limit is one, whatever the occasion. Unless I'm put in a situation where I'm feeling like the little kid I once was. That might get me hammered.

I turned back to my jury as these thoughts passed through my mind in an instant.

"The detectives all say the same thing: that Douglas Kurtin confessed to beating his wife to death. Nothing could be further from the truth. He didn't say, 'I killed her,' and leave it at that. He said, 'I killed her by emotionally neglecting her all those years I was on the road.' That's what he actually said. The tape you heard just wasn't the whole thing. There are huge pieces missing out of it. Douglas told you that and the state didn't see fit to put on a witness to contradict him."

It was true. My guy testified and the state didn't come back with a rebuttal witness.

Somebody screwed the pooch and would get raked over the coals for that one. Unless the jury said my guy was guilty. If they found him guilty, none of that would matter. The assistant district attorney would be celebrated by everyone in the office. High-fives and "attaboys," from everyone.

"Bogus," I said distastefully. "That's what the state's case was--bogus. No one ever found the weapon used to bludgeon poor Mrs. Kurtin to death. And remember the testimony of her boyfriend? That they'd had a fight by telephone that day and that's why he wasn't there with her? So what do the cops do? They never get a warrant and search his house and car. For all we know there was a blood trail, bloody clothes, maybe scratches or wounds on his face or hands--but we'll never know because the Keystone Kops didn't follow up with him. No, they immediately focused on Douglas Kurtin and no one else. He was guilty of killing his wife from the first minute the first detective viewed her lifeless body.

"Now let's look at what we do know. We know Doug's secretary, Mary Katherine, said they worked until after nine that night. According to the medical examiner, Sally Kurtin was murdered in the late afternoon. So she was already dead by the time Doug and Mary Katherine called it a night. Then there's the receipt from the Quik-Stop where Doug gassed up on his way home at nine-thirty-two p.m. That puts him almost an hour from his old home, given traffic conditions.

"So none of this holds water."

I went on for another five minutes, smothering any remaining embers from the fire the District Attorney tried to ignite with the jury.

After the trial and our not guilty verdict, Douglas Kurtin remained behind in the courtroom and watched me pack my two pull-along briefcases. Then he took up one briefcase by the handle and I took the other. We loaded onto the elevator. We were alone. I looked up at him. Tears filled his eyes.

"I did it, you know," he said to me through his tears.

"I know it," I said. "It's all right."

"What about you, Michael? You just set a guilty man free. How does that make *you* feel?"

I leaned against the wall, the briefcase standing on its bottom side, waiting for me to drag it back to my office. I thought long and hard about the question.

"How does it make me feel? It makes me feel like I just talked my way out of a jam with my old man again. He was a hitter. I'm twelve years old, in serious trouble, and I fix it with my lies. You walk out a free man and I walk out a little boy who's safe again. Safe until the next time he sets foot in a courtroom."

He wipes away his tears with his fingers. "Jesus, man, how do you live with that?"

I was tired, I missed my wife. The win left a hollowed-out, very brief, moment of feeling okay.

"How do I live with that?"

"Yes, I mean Jesus, man."

"I live like a man with one foot on his father's neck and one foot in the real world. That's how."

"Jesus, man."

"Yes."

That night, I did get hammered. A taxi took me home.

That lying little boy had come near. Leaving a man who murdered his wife walking around free.

I woke up without a hangover, rolled over, and smiled luxuriously.

The kid sure had a way with juries.

# Chapter 1

CARLOS

If you're ever running from the cops, there is a golden rule: do not--don't--board a commercial aircraft. If you do, you will get made. You might say, "But I've got fake ID; they won't know." Don't believe it for a second. Look at your driver's license. That's you. Know who else has that picture? TSA and the NSA have pictures of each and every licensed driver. Any ID you show the airlines or the TSA checkpoints will be processed by facial recognition software and your real identity immediately established.

I took my own advice and rode the train from San Diego to Chicago. Along the way I saw deserts, Rocky Mountains, prairie land, and cornfields stretching from horizon to horizon. Most of the way I slept, except for one stretch a couple of hours west of Chicago where we stopped and a bounty-hunter/detective type got on board and took the seat across from me. He was wearing black jeans, Roper's, and a black leather jacket over a T-shirt . His eye caught mine and he nodded. Then he turned to hand his ticket to the conductor and that's when I got a peek of a big black gun up under his arm. It was time for me to reconsider things. I got up as if going to the bathroom and left my *Chicago Tribune* in my seat. "I'm not finished reading it," I said to the man in black.

He didn't look up at me but he said, "Check."

Instead of stopping at the bathroom at the back of the car, I went out into the walkway and into the car behind. Four more times I repeated this and then I locked myself in the bathroom and refused to come out. Repeated knocks and complaints finally shamed me into showing my face and an anxious-looking trio of passengers stared daggers at me as I found a seat further back yet. Now my back was turned to the way I had come and I was scrunched down in my seat, my head barely showing above. Even so, I knew the guy could find me any minute and I knew he was probably looking even then.

But who was he? Had someone spotted me on the train and made a call? But how would that even work? I had participated in the First Commercial robbery while wearing a mask.

Nobody saw my face, I mean nobody. So how would the authorities even know who to look for?

Unless Phaeton had turned me in. Phaeton was the late-comer to my crew that hit the First Commercial Bank. I didn't know him at all and it turned out he was trigger happy. He gunned down a customer in the bank and we all had to make a run for it. So, who else would turn on me but Phaeton? That son of a bitch! Of course that's what happened. He turned state's evidence in return for immunity. Why would he do that? Because he knows I'm going to eventually catch up and kill him. He did it to save himself from me. So now I could safely assume that every law enforcement agency in the country had my picture out to every road cop and undercover dick within the first hour.

It was time to disappear.

We pulled into Chicago, into the long, covered arrivals and departures tunnel, and I went right just beyond the sliding doors and headed up the small incline to the men's room. I quickly ducked inside and went down to the far stall and locked myself inside. Then I sweated profusely for the next fifteen minutes while I ignored guys knocking on my stall and cursing as they moved on.

Then I came out into the station. Up two flights of escalators and I was looking at street side. Outside it was just past nine p.m. A long line of taxis was stationed curbside waiting for someone like me to come along. I jumped in the backseat of the next vacancy and told the driver to lose anyone who followed us at the next right turn. I passed a hundred-dollar bill over the seat to confirm my request. He floored it at the next right--turning right on a red--and we shot down to the end of the cross-street, bucked across three lanes on our left, and hung a left at the next corner on a stale yellow. Then we timed the next four lights and zipped through, driving aimlessly for the next half hour.

Finally, the driver said, "You want Hyatt?"

Feeling freed of any followers, I happily answered, "The Hyatt is perfect."

Once inside, I walked right back out the entrance and then waited by the doorman for several beats before turning and hurrying back inside. Up to the registration desk, plopping down my prepaid Visa, then up to the fourteenth with just one bag, my trusty backpack from Sears in San Diego.

Later that night, I changed clothes and quietly entered the twenty-four-hour dining room. The grilled cheese and soup went down easy, chased with iced tea and pecan pie. While the food was very welcome, I was glum. It had been a long ride, starting out in San Diego and winding up in Chicago, and I was no richer for it. My scheme to steal enough money to buy my daughter's medicine was going nowhere fast.

In the Hyatt gift shop I asked about prepaid phones. I chose a cell phone loaded with 400 prepaid minutes. Then I returned to my room and changed into sweats. No robbery today. That would come tomorrow.

Thirty minutes later, I called a 619 area code number and spoke to the woman who answered the phone.

"What about Amelia?" I asked. "Any change?"

"Resting in ICU. Nothing's changed."

"No worse?"

"She dies without her meds. You heard the doctors."

"It isn't fair. She's only eight."

"Who said life was fair?"

I hung up and climbed into bed.

I swallowed hard. The room was dark and unfamiliar. Outside, somewhere down the hall, a woman laughed a shrill intoxicated laugh.

I couldn't say when I had last been that carefree.

* * *

The next morning, I crept down the street to a Walgreen's. It would have everything I needed. Men's hair color products were tops on my list. I made my selection and looked for a haircut kit. The cashier gave me a bored smile and never really looked at my face as I plopped down two twenties and walked on past. "Keep it," I said back over my shoulder, and went outside. It was an early fall day in Chicago; the air was crisp and the daylight had that clear autumn look. Back to the hotel I hurried along. I had thought of grabbing a hat back at the store but to my way of thinking that just gave someone a target to follow.

Back inside my room, I first gave myself a flattop haircut. Then I stripped out the color and dyed it blond. Same with the eyebrows. I got online; I ordered new clothes unlike any I'd ever worn. They would be delivered the next day to the phony name on my Visa card right here in my hotel room. So far, so good.

The next day my clothes arrived and I dressed in light gray slacks, a white turtleneck, a navy blazer, and black alligator grain shoes. Next I slipped on my new Malcolm X hipster non-prescription eyeglasses--the Carlos Pritchett I knew was suddenly no more. Seriously, I didn't recognize myself.

Everything I owned then went into my new fat leather briefcase, gun on top.

Now I was ready to visit my personal banker.

# Chapter 2

CARLOS

When it was over, the Chicago victims all said the same thing. He was neither tall nor short, thin nor pudgy, well-dressed nor street-person--according to the people who viewed him from the wrong end of a gun. To those employees of the bank on Wacker Drive he had no memorable features, no tats, no scars. He was a man no one would notice. Until he drew out his gun.

I pointed it at the "personal banker" sitting across the desk, first. No one else in the bank was paying attention, so the confrontation went unnoticed.

"What time is the time lock?"

The personal banker--a very young man wearing a white shirt that looked to be two sizes larger than he needed--recoiled in his chair. His arm swung up from the arm of his chair and nervously massaged the dark mole on the side of his face. "Jesus," he whispered. "Don't fail me now."

"Did you hear me? What time's the lock?"

"Uh--nine o'clock. Four minutes ago."

"Who has keys?" I asked.

"Mr. Kelso and Mrs. Wochner."

"Take me to Mr. Kelso. Now!"

The personal banker swept around his desk and double-timed to a locked door at the end of the lobby, a door with buttons below the knob. He punched it several times and the door swung open. I followed him through, my gun pressed against the personal banker's neck.

Down a short hallway we scurried, then entered the office at the far end. The name inscribed on a small gold panel to the right of the door frame said WALTER S. KELSO, MANAGER. I followed the young banker through the door without knocking. The man behind the desk was pink and bald and cradled a phone between his left shoulder and ear. When he spotted the gun, he immediately dropped the phone and reached both hands into the air. His fingers twitched and his lips trembled.

"Mr. Kelso, this man wants the key to the vault."

I pushed the personal banker aside. I pointed my gun in the direction of the bank manager. "On your feet, Mr. Manager. We're cracking the vault."

The manager collected himself enough to stare daggers at the young banker. Only the kid would have known who had the vault keys and he was the one who had obviously brought this crazy person into Kelso's office for the key. He was angry and terribly frightened, both emotions causing his face to run through a diorama of expressions from frightened to angry to terrified to hopeless.

"I've got the vault key that goes in first. Mrs. Wochner has the second key. It has to go in second or an alarm goes off."

"Fine. Let's go collect up Mrs. Wochner. You," I said to the personal banker, "you bring her to the vault. Tell her Mr. Kelso needs her key. Don't screw this up or Kelso dies and I come and find you and kill you and your wife and your kids. Understand?"

"Understand. Bring Mrs. Wochner with her key."

"Exactly. And don't be stupid. If you're stupid I'll beat you to your home address and kill everyone there."

"Don't be stupid. Got it."

I waved the muzzle at the manager.

"I'm putting this gun inside my pocket. I'll have it aimed at you the entire time we're out there. Don't do anything stupid, Mr Kelso. Agreed?"

"Or you'll kill my wife and kids?"

He had managed to calm himself and he smiled. It was a nice smile, the kind of smile your pharmacist might give you when he hands over the little paper bag. "I'm glad you understand."

Mrs. Wochner arrived. She was heavyset, dressed in a gray suit with red vest and holding a cup of coffee she was nursing. The vault was opened and the personal banker with the manager and Mrs. Wochner passed inside as indicated by me. That morning's cash delivery was spread in stacks across the table in the center of the vault.

"Where's the dye charge?" I asked the manager.

"There's no charge in the vault cash. Only in the teller's drawers."

"Then we won't bother the tellers for their cash, will we?"

It was rhetorical.

"Now," I was opening my briefcase, "fill this."

"You know you'll have the FBI after you," said the manager in a plaintive voice as if remembering the money was his personally.

"Don't start," I warned. "Remember about your wife and kids."

"Got it. I was just saying."

"You were trying to intimidate me. Tell your FBI I don't intimidate easily."

The manager and his assistant filled the briefcase. When they were done, it held all of the vault cash.

"How much?" I asked, indicating the briefcase.

"Two-hundred and fifty-thousand. Minus the drawers."

"Leaves?"

The manager shrugged as if this kind of thing happened every day in his bank, a kind of nonchalant, thousand-dollar shrug.

"Leaves two hundred thousand. Easy two hundred."

"What if I gave each of you a grand?" I asked the threesome. "Would you like that?"

The three employees didn't look at each other.

"Okay, well, it was just an idea," I said. "The hell with it then."

"How are you getting out of here with a briefcase full of money? Aren't you afraid someone will notice?"

"No, I'll look like some businessman wearing a suit and carrying his briefcase. Maybe a lawyer."

"Not with a turtleneck," said the personal banker. "You'll need a necktie. Here, take off the turtleneck and trade with me. Take my shirt and tie."

Kelso frowned at him. But we made the trade; he was right, the shirt with the collar and necktie looked more businesslike.

"One more thing. No alarms. Or what happens?"

The personal banker had the answer. "Our wives and kids will be killed by you."

The manager glared at his employee. He shook his head.

"Exactly. So, no alarms."

"You know we can ID you," said the personal banker. "And your face is on the CCTV feeds."

I shook my head. "Don't worry about CCTV. I've disabled it. Now let me tell you why I don't think you'll want to ID me."

"Doubt that," Mrs. Wochner said, her eyes fearful. She startled herself when she spoke. Her face registered total disbelief that she had said anything at all while a robber brandished a gun inside the vault.

"That may be," I said, "but let me at least try. I don't want to rob banks. But I have a very sick daughter and need money to keep her alive."

"Then why not come into the bank and get a loan like everyone else?" asked Mr. Kelso.

"I tried that. No bank would agree to loan me money for medicine."

"Why not?"

"For one thing, I made the mistake of telling my bank that the drugs were experimental. That killed the deal right there."

"Why?"

"Because the loan officer said the bank wasn't into gambling. They considered experimental drugs to be a form of gambling. Anyway, they turned me down. So I tried asking family members and friends for help. That went nowhere. My wife and I don't have enough equity in our house to borrow against. So I bought a gun and here I am."

"What's wrong with your little girl?" asked Mrs. Wochner.

"She has Hepatitis-C and it's getting worse. There are experimental drugs on the market that might cure her. I have to give her that chance."

"Is she dying?" asked Mr. Kelso. He looked crestfallen. Sick children affected him terribly, even making him want to turn away and hide his tears when he heard about such things. Here was a man who rescued pound puppies and kept carrier pigeons. The idea of dogs being put down caused him unending grief just to think about it. The idea of a little girl so sick with a possibly curable disease was enough to push him over the edge. Unbeknownst to his employer, the bank, their manager, Mr. Kelso, was more humanitarian than cold-hearted banker. He wasn't cut from the usual profit-motive cloth like most bankers. He was different. And now he was interested in my little girl's plight. I definitely had his attention.

"She will die without a cure. Her disease is especially virulent. She's lying semi-conscious in a hospital right now as we talk."

"How much money do you need?" the personal banker asked.

"Two hundred thousand," I said, raising the bag they had just helped me fill. "This right here will save my little girl's life."

"Thank God," said Mrs. Wochner.

"You must get away," said Mr. Kelso."

"I hope it's enough," said the personal banker.

"Yes," I said, "I think there's enough here to get it done. So I'm going to ask you: When the FBI questions you, please don't ID me. If they put me in a lineup, please don't ID me."

"That's asking a lot," said Mr. Kelso. "That would be very dishonest. None of us wants trouble with the law."

"Just think of my little girl, then. Think of her slipping away without the medicine. Doesn't that come first in your heart?"

The three bank employees looked at each other. Was he kidding? We might not want to ID him?

"Look. I know I've scared you with this gun and I've ruined your day. I'm sorry for that."

"We three need to talk," said Mr. Kelso. His two employees nodded their agreement. There was much to discuss.

I knew they could cross me once I was outside. But there was nothing I could do about that. On the other hand, maybe I had reached them by explaining my circumstances. Only time would tell. I was ready to slip back into full-blown anonymity as soon as I turned the corner outside.

Which I did. Once I made the corner I suddenly walked confidently, half as fast, smiling and meeting the eyes of other walkers. I looked nothing like a man who had just taken down a bank for two hundred thousand dollars.

But I had.

* * *

The FBI hit the ground running, but the three bank employees couldn't provide them with a description of the robber. They agreed only in this: when he pointed the big gun at them his hand didn't shake and his voice didn't quiver. He was equally unruffled when he cleaned out the bank vault; he even allowed Greta Wochner to use the restroom when she told him she had a bladder problem. No one felt threatened and no one needed medical attention.

How was he dressed? Well, said the bank manager: something like gray Dockers or faded jeans; said the personal banker: a blue or brown knit pullover; said the door guard: a navy or black windbreaker; said the quartet of tellers on duty: hair color ranging from light brown to raven black. Eye color was just as big a mystery as the rest, except for Greta Wochner, who actually became agitated when the others guessed blue or brown eyes. She was adamant they had been green, "Piercing, but kind."

So, the FBI went to the bank's CCTV and prepared to isolate a still photograph that they could disseminate in hopes of a quick sighting at some gas station pump or fast food aorta clogger. Except, to their astonishment, the CCTV had been disabled. It had recorded exactly nothing. This was a sealed, locked unit with its own power supply and locking mechanism that neither bank officials nor employees could operate. The unit could only be accessed by the off-premises manufacturer which, of course, was bonded, licensed, and thoroughly vetted by the FBI when it had approved the contract for CCTV. The company was immediately notified by the FBI of the empty hard drives and they were asked to access their backup drives on their server farm in Omaha and make the video feed available to the FBI's Chicago office without delay. Except...there was no backup video. The feed had been disabled throughout. Only a person skilled in bank security systems would know how to do all that. Even more troubling, the failsafe wireless system that should have warned of the unauthorized access that left them empty-handed had also been bypassed.

My experience installing bank security system was paying huge dividends. Two hundred thousand huge, in fact.

FBI brains whirred and clicked. Computers raced to find similar incidents over a ten state area the past six months. Nothing. So the geography and calendar were expanded to include the entire U.S. for the past year. One other incident where the CCTV had been rendered useless: San Diego.

The Mexican and Canadian ICE teams were notified that all vehicles were to be searched. They were to look for large sums of cash. They were to look for a single male driver, with only soft details. Roadblocks were set up on all main roads and on interstate highways leaving Chicago. O'Hare was suddenly bustling with FBI agents dressed in everything from shorts and T-shirts to business suits to Levi's and hoodies. Earpieces were plugged in and communications linked all points of egress. Buses were searched.

The next morning before dawn, I hooked my backpack on my shoulder and hiked out to the Interstate. With my thumb in the pre-dawn sky and a constant stream of L.A.-bound truckers who might enjoy someone to talk to, it didn't take twenty minutes to score a ride. My host was operating a late-model Freightliner hauling a load of Frigidaire freezers to Anaheim. Whatever; the driver was friendly and even offered me hot coffee from his huge thermos. We talked NFL and bass boats all the way to Yuma, Arizona, where the topic switched to the drought and wildfires. I was mellow just riding along; we were making good time but then, just as we were about to cross the Colorado River, we came upon a roadblock. The cops were forcing everyone out of their cars and trucks and even rummaging through suitcases and bags.

I looked around desperately. There was nowhere to run, nowhere to hide. We were surrounded by scorching desert for a hundred miles all around.

I climbed down from my perch in the Freightliner as directed by the officer. I left my backpack in the sleeper compartment. However, the police dog alerted on the cab and he was lifted up onto the passenger seat, where he immediately alerted on the backpack. His handler retrieved the backpack and handed it off to a second officer, whose eyes bulged when he unzipped it and viewed the bundles of cash. I and my driver were taken into custody. We were placed in the rear seats of two different police vehicles and left alone until the FBI agents arrived. At that point the questions began in earnest. The truck driver told them he'd picked me up in Chicago. The Fibbies had counted the money in the backpack: $215,575. Money the hitchhiker was refusing to explain. Within the first hour, the FBI strongly suspected they had apprehended the mystery man who robbed the First Chicago Bank and Trust.

The Fibbies decided that Chicago would have first dibs on prosecution. So, I was handcuffed and ankle-chained and flown to O'Hare. I was then transported to the jail on California Avenue, where I was booked. I was allowed one call; I called my wife.

"Find me the best lawyer in Chicago," I told her. "And hire him."

"What about money?"

"I'm no good to Amelia if I'm in here. Get me out and then I'm after it again."

"Will do. She's even worse tonight than she was this morning. The sweats have started."

"Oh, my God."

"But there are new drugs, I've just been told. FDA-approved drugs just now on the market that can cure her."

"How much?"

"A hundred thousand. And she might need them twice to get the cure."

"I'm working on it."

"I hate this. I hate what you're doing, yet I want you to keep doing it. It's making me crazy."

"I'm working on it. The money will be supplied in time. I promise you and I promise Amelia."

"You're a good man, Carlos. Your daughter's life depends on you."

"Call the lawyer. Bail will be high. Use the money in Tijuana."

"Will do."

"I'll see you soon."

"Amelia says she loves you."

My eyes clouded over and I turned my face away from the next man waiting for the phone. I pinched my closed eyes. I handed over the phone and was pushed along toward the common area by the guards. I didn't resist and I didn't care.

My mind was two thousand miles west.

The clock was ticking but now the money was going out instead of coming in.

My next move would have to be magic.

# Chapter 3

THE FBI

FBI Special Agent Norland Davis put together the data feed for the perp lineup. Except this wouldn't be an actual lineup with real people. This would be a serial paging through images on a tablet. The images he would show them on his tablet would just have to do.

He arrived at the Chicago bank just after it opened, two mornings after the robbery. He assembled Mr. Kelso, Mrs. Wochner, and the personal banker, inside Mr. Kelso's office. He arranged them around the banker's desk and placed himself in the middle, the tablet on the desk before them. It was propped up on its keyboard cover and all agreed they had a good view of the screen.

As the FBI is wont to do, Agent Davis began the perp lineup by paging through a half dozen images that were of FBI agents themselves in varying stages of dress, varying styles of dress, varying hairstyles and facial hair, and varying looks at the camera. As expected--and to the agent's relief--the bankers made no move to ID or ask about any of the planted faces.

Then he swiped his finger across the screen and up popped the image of Carlos Pritchett.

Carlos' picture was head and shoulders only, and the lighting and staging appeared to be booking photos from the jail on California Avenue in Chicago.

"How about number seven?" asked Davis. "Does this one look familiar?"

Mr. Kelso folded his arms and raised his head. He was scowling. "No. It's not him."

"Mrs. Wochner?"

"Well, this one looks like a genuine criminal, no doubt about that. But this isn't the man who robbed us."

The agent pursed his lips and looked at the personal banker. "Son?"

"It's hard to say. I think the eye color and hair color are all wrong. No, this isn't the guy. Do you have more for us to see?"

Agent Davis hit the HOME button on the tablet and exited the perp walk. He was upset. The picture of Carlos had been taken just hours after his arrest in Arizona, when he had been returned to Chicago and booked. Were these people really that stupid? How could they fail to identify the actual perp?

"Those are all the pictures," the FBI agent said.

"Was the real guy one of the ones you showed us?" asked Mrs. Wochner. She was definitely feeling the role now. She was playing it to the hilt. It felt like her high school production of *Rebel Without a Cause*. She had played Jim's mother and the memories were very pleasant. This morning's part she was playing felt equally nice.

Agent Davis scowled and narrowed his eyes in disgust. "Yes, he was one of them."

"Oh, my," said Mrs. Wochner. "Can you tell us which one he was?"

"No can do," said Davis. "We might need to do this again. I'll get more pictures and come back."

"I don't think that will help," said Mr. Kelso. "It all happened so fast that none of us really had a good look at the guy."

"Happened very fast," said the personal banker. "We've been taught by the bank never to look directly at or into the eyes of a bank robber. It's too much of a challenge and can get you shot."

"Great," said Davis. "How nice they taught you that."

"No need for sarcasm here," said Mr. Kelso. "We're all doing the best we can."

"You don't need to talk like that," Mrs. Wochner agreed. "We're all adults. We're not children."

"I honestly didn't see him that well," the personal banker went on. "Mostly I was walking ahead of him. Then when we were in the vault I just didn't raise my eyes. Bank regulations--"

"Yes," said Davis, "I know. Don't look him in the eyes. That's what you were taught. Well, that's just great."

"Why not just use the security camera pictures?" Mr. Kelso suggested.

Davis blanched. "Not available."

"What do you mean?"

"The CCTV was disabled. None of you knows anything about that, do you?"

"No need to be flippant," Mrs. Wochner said. "You're making me uncomfortable, Agent Davis. I'm going back to my desk." With a flounce, she stood up and hurried out of the room. Seconds later, the personal banker followed. Now, Davis was alone with Kelso.

"Well?" said Davis.

"I don't know," said Kelso. "But you've got all three of us on record saying we don't recognize any of your pictures. You're welcome to return with more and we'll try again."

"I don't think so," said Davis. "The pictures you looked at couldn't be any clearer."

"Well, if that's all, I'm getting back to work. Lots to do today. The powers-that-be want a full report by close of business. So please excuse me, Agent."

"Sure."

Davis was folding the tablet inside its cover. He then slipped it under his arm and turned away.

"Amateurs," Kelso heard the agent say under his breath.

But Kelso ignored the man. He had too much on his plate to go there.

# Chapter 4

MICHAEL

I received the call from Carlos the Ant's wife at 8:03 Monday morning.

"Michael Gresham speaking," I said into the phone.

"My husband is in jail in Chicago. He goes to court this morning at eleven. Can you help him?"

"What's he charged with?"

"Armed robbery? They say he robbed a bank. But he had to. Our daughter is dying and needs money, for the love of God!"

I let her hurry on with the story of her daughter's illness and her husband's efforts to cure her with medical care purchased with stolen money.

"Carlos has bank robberies in Illinois and San Diego. I don't know anything about the details. Most of what I do know, I got from the newspapers online."

"So you're calling me about the Chicago case?"

"Chicago isn't all, Mr. Gresham. He's also done stuff in California, like I said, and maybe Arizona and Nevada, I'm not sure."

"If that's accurate, you probably need more horsepower them my small firm can offer, Mrs. Pritchett."

In hopes of helping her see the magnitude of what Carlos was embroiled in, I gently asked whether they could actually afford my services. She didn't hesitate. They would do whatever it took. She said she was able to wire me $15,000 for a retainer—borrowing from a friend she was keeping for use in an emergency. I told her it would be a start--on the Illinois case only. We traded a few more details, including cell numbers and emails. Then she told me more about their daughter's illness and the father's love for his family. He would stop at nothing to save his child, she said.

"All right," I said, "put the bank wire into effect and I'll walk over to court and see about your husband."

"Oh my God, Mr. Gresham. Thank you! The money is on the way in ten minutes."

"That works for me."

"How much will your bill be for the whole case?"

"In Chicago only?"

"Yes."

"Depends on what's necessary. If there's a trial, maybe two-hundred-and-fifty thousand dollars. If there's a plea, maybe only fifty thousand. We'll just have to see."

"All right. I'll hang up now and contact my bank."

"Thank you for calling. Goodbye."

"Goodbye."

We hung up. I have a huge caseload, so I pulled files and dictated orders and memos for my staff while checking my watch now and then. I gave it two hours before checking with my bank. Then I went online. The deposit was confirmed deposited and so I pulled on my suit jacket and stepped out onto LaSalle Street on the Chicago Loop. Traffic was heavy, mostly cabs and UPS trucks. Pedestrians were everywhere, as it was half-past ten and many people were out and about on work errands. I worked my way over to the curb where the flow was lighter and headed for the Dirksen Building, Chicago's U.S. District Court.

Inside the Dirksen there was a twenty-minute long security line. The public removed its belts and shoes and flopped its briefcases and bags and purses down on the noisy conveyor belts while bored, unfriendly security people worked the crowd through like cattle to the slaughter house. Finally, it was my turn and I flashed my bar card and was hustled through. Around the corner to the elevator bank. One elevator whooshed open and I hurried on. Then I was up, up and away. Just like Superman. I burst through the double-doors of courtroom 801, just as Carlos Pritchett's case was called for initial appearance. Talk about timing.

"Michael Gresham for the defendant," I smiled at the judge, officially entering my appearance in the case. I turned to the man at my right, standing at the lectern. "And you must be Carlos Pritchett. I just got off the phone with your wife. We're good to go."

His face brightened. He nodded and stuck out his hand.

We shook hands and turned to face the judge.

"Mr. Gresham," said Judge Verkriz--who happened to be my favorite federal judge--"has your client received a copy of the complaint filed in this case?"

"I don't know, Your Honor. Could we trail this case and allow me to speak to my client in the conference room? I promise I'll return here a more effective advocate."

Judge Alfredo Verkriz smiled. "Certainly. This is the only initial on this morning's calendar, so we'll be in recess for twenty minutes."

The judge and courtroom staff slowly vacated the courtroom while Pritchett and I, in the company of two U.S. Marshals, disappeared inside the conference room. On the inside wall of the hallway, the room had no windows, so the marshals had no problem just waiting outside the door while the discussion got underway. The President of the United States--his official portrait-- looked down on us as we began.

Carlos Pritchett was still dressed in his gray slacks, white shirt, tie, and navy blazer. The man's face looked familiar but I couldn't say why. Not at first. And the bleached hair. He looked out of place in a suit and more like a surfer out of a Beach Boys song.

"Mr. Pritchett, your wife has wired a retainer to my bank account. Did you give her authority to do that for you?"

"I did."

"May I see the complaint? That would be the pink sheet in your stack of papers."

Pritchett handed over the entire sheaf of documents. I scanned the complaint; it contained nothing unusual--other than the fact a U.S. citizen was being charged by his government with armed robbery with a life sentence or two waiting in the wings.

"You're charged with robbing a federal depository at gunpoint. Did you do it?"

"I did. I've robbed two federal depositories at gunpoint, in fact."

"You seem like a reasonable man, Mr. Pritchett. And it says here on your face sheet that you have a college degree in electronics. Whoa, you even have a master's in digital security. Nice, that. So why would a man with these credentials rob a bank?"

"I wanted money."

I had to smile. "Willie Sutton said it. He robbed banks because that's where the money is."

"I rest my case, Mr. Gresham."

"Okay, but why else would you rob a bank?"

"My daughter is dying. Hepatitis-C. At first, the meds worked but then these hedge fund scammers raised the price to where we can't afford to keep buying what she needs. Now I hear there's a new drug that can cure her. But it's two hundred thousand."

"What about insurance?"

"Our insurance company refused to cover the hospitalization and refused to cover the drugs. I had no savings, my wife doesn't work, so that left a nickel plated revolver, my knowledge of bank security systems, and several vaults full of money. Lots of money. In four weeks I put together a hundred thousand. You have fifteen thousand of that now. You'll probably want the rest."

"How much did you score in Chicago?"

"Never got to count it, but it doesn't matter. The cops grabbed it when I was arrested."

I drummed my fingers on the gray rubber table top. I was thinking.

"I'm wondering what excuse the insurance company used for denying coverage."

Pritchett nodded and looked into my eyes. I got the sense he was telling me the truth.

"It had to do with the application for the policy. My daughter's name is Amelia Lynne Pritchett. She's officially gone by 'Lynne,' which is my wife's mother's name, for school registration, stuff like that. In the policy application my wife wrote down 'Lynne Pritchett' as our daughter's name. Her first name, Amelia, had been left off, and Grand Canyon Insurance and Annuity now claims that because the insurance application didn't specifically include our girl's first name, she isn't covered by the policy they issued to our family. They say they never would have covered Amelia Lynne Pritchett."

"Why wouldn't they have covered Amelia?"

"They say that given her history of anemia, they never would have covered."

"Did you reveal the iron deficiency on the application?"

"This application was three years ago, before Obamacare. She was fit as a fiddle then. No indication of anything being wrong besides anemia. The docs gave her iron tablets for that."

"So why not get Obamacare now? Wouldn't that solve the problem?"

"The new drugs are experimental. They aren't even covered."

"So I'm confused. How do they say that if they had had her name they would have never covered her? That doesn't compute."

Pritchett rocked forward in his chair and slammed his fist against the table top.

"Goddam cretins! We've been round and round on this until I want to shoot someone. I'm that angry."

"But you haven't shot anyone."

"I haven't shot anyone at any bank. But the claims manager at Grand Canyon Insurance? He has it coming. If my daughter dies I'll finish him. I promise you that."

I shook my head. "Please don't tell me that. If you really mean it, I have to turn that information over to the police. Which will make you hate me and which will cause you a huge amount of hurt. Tell me you're just blowing off steam."

"I'm just blowing off steam."

"Okay. Well. Let's talk about bail. Judge Verkriz typically sets bail in armed robbery cases at one million dollars. Illinois doesn't have bail bondsmen. But we do have the ten percent rule, which generally allows a defendant to pay ten percent of the bail to get out. So you'll need a hundred thousand to spring loose."

"My wife is wiring you money for bail."

"Well, don't tell me the source of those funds. I don't want to know."

"It's from her brother," he said, ignoring me.

"Let's do this. Once you're out, come to my office. I'm in the bank building right around the corner. No need to call first, I'll get you right in."

"Will do."

"Carlos, how much time before the medication money is gone, worst case scenario?"

"Maybe five days."

"And you need two hundred now?"

"Yes."

"But they took everything from you when they arrested you. How will you make that up?"

"I don't know. We've hit up everyone we know."

"One other thing. We'll need to make one condition of your release that you can go to California to visit your daughter. She's where?"

"UCSD Hillcrest Hospital. San Diego."

"All right. Any questions for me?"

"Nope. Let's go to court."

"Here we go, then."

It lasted all of eight minutes, our time before His Honor.

Judge Verkriz ignored the U.S. Attorney's call for no-bail and instead set Carlos Pritchett's bail at five-hundred thousand dollars. So he would need fifty-thousand cash to get himself released. I called my office and learned that his bail money had arrived in Chicago. Now it was only a matter of time until my staff could get it posted in the wife's name for her husband.

I told him I would meet him back at the jail. We would talk while he was being processed out.

He gave a wry smile as the marshals wrapped stainless steel around his wrists and double-locked the bracelets with the key.

"Gentlemen," he said to them over his shoulder, "your bird is about to fly."

They ignored their prisoner. They'd heard it all before.

But he did and he didn't actually fly. Yes, he was bailed out of jail in Chicago, but California had a hold. He was remanded back to San Diego to face charges there.

# Chapter 5

MICHAEL

I had managed to bail him out of jail in Chicago, but California had a hold on him. Instead of coming to my office to talk, Carlos was whisked away and returned to San Diego, the scene of the robbery and shootout at First Commercial. I learned all this after the fact when he didn't show at my office after making bail. But it didn't really surprise me, either. Like Illinois courts and law enforcement, California plays hardball, too. So I decided I could only wait for him to surface in California and call me.

The next day, just after noon Central, Carlos phoned me from the San Diego Central Jail. It was a collect call, and Mrs. Lingscheit accepted and put him right through, interrupting a talk I was having with my wife and law partner, Danny. Carlos begged me to take on his defense in California. Several charges were filed against him, he said, including armed robbery and murder. He told me that he'd had his initial appearance in San Diego court and that this time there would be no bail, which of course didn't surprise me. Worst of all, he informed me that his daughter was near death. Was there anything I could do to intervene there? Was there anything I could do to spring him so he could obtain medicine for her? I told him to call me again in two hours.

Outside my office window, bordering on the upper stratosphere in downtown Chicago, I looked out over Lake Michigan and struggled with my response to him. Two forces tugged at me. On the one hand, my own home life had been seriously impacted over the previous year by my wife's disappearance and reappearance after an automobile accident. Plus, I had two kids of my own, each more demanding of parent time than the other. If I left Chicago for the West Coast I would be leaving Danny alone and not yet completely herself. On the other hand, Carlos needed help and he trusted me. More important, I had very strong feelings about the underlying drama of the daughter's need and the parents' shortage of funding and lack of insurance. While I wasn't licensed to practice law in California, I knew that filing a *pro hac vice* motion with the court would go a long way and would get me under the wire so I could appear in court there and defend my client. Courts bent over backwards to ensure criminal defendants got the lawyer they wanted. This case would be no different, I was sure, but still I checked out the *California Rules of Court* 9.40 and found I could appear in California with an application, a check, and local counsel.

Then he called a second time, and again Mrs. Lingscheit accepted charges.

"Mr. Gresham, have you made a decision?"

"Carlos, I'm working on that. Let's get this out of the way up front. My fee for defending a robbery-homicide is five hundred thousand dollars. Can you make that work? Or is all money earmarked for your daughter."

He didn't hesitate. "All money is going to our daughter. I was hoping the fifteen-thousand my wife sent would get us down the road with you."

"And it does, certainly. Just not all the way down the road. Murder cases are horrendously time-consuming and, knowing that police officers died in the firefight you engaged in, I'm certain the case will go to trial. You're probably talking fifteen or twenty trial days at a minimum, depending on how much jury selection time the court will let the lawyers have versus the court doing it all. You're looking at a million dollars in legal fees and expert witness fees in California alone."

There was a pause, then he ignored the cost. "What, the court might pick my jury and not me?"

"Happens every day. Sorry, but that's how it goes."

"Well, I don't like that a damn bit. I want to pick my own jury."

"And we shall, to whatever degree the court allows. Plus we'll push for more participation by the parties."

"Okay. So, what else?"

"Look, you've paid me fifteen-thousand. I'm going to have travel, food, and hotel expenses. I'll be wanting to travel home most weekends to spend time with my family. That adds up. Fifteen-thousand isn't going to cover my defense fee and my travel time. It doesn't even cover Illinois, much less California."

He didn't respond immediately. He understood what I was saying was absolutely true. Family men insist on spending time with their loved ones and I was no different. Especially with Danny suffering from PTSD from her accident. There were also dissociative identity facets that were extremely difficult for her--and me.

Then, "It's the best I can do. And you're the only attorney I trust. And my daughter is slipping away and I need your help with that. Tell me what to do, Mr. Gresham."

"Do? I don't know your entire situation. For example, is there any other family that could help you out?"

"My wife's dad might, at least he might have thrown a few thousand at our problems, but that was before I got arrested. Now he's telling my wife to leave me and come home to him and her mother. She won't, thank God. She loves me and she knows why I did what I did. I don't know where else to turn. I only have you."

So... the spotlight was on me. His daughter's predicament came to rest squarely on my shoulders. I couldn't just stand by and allow her to go without meds and die without fighting for her. The dammed up feelings inside of me about my own family problems burst just then and tears came to my eyes. How I would love for someone to step in and untangle *my* family's problems. I knew just how Carlos felt. I couldn't say no.

"All right. I'm in. I'll be out to see you in a couple of days. In the meantime, talk to no one."

"All right, Mr. Gresham."

"And call me 'Michael.'"

"Okay, Michael. God bless you, sir."

We hung up. I reflected and could only shake my head, already regretting what I'd just done.

"But he's trying," I said through my cloud of emotions. "He's definitely trying."

So now I was defending Carlos the Ant on two fronts: Chicago, armed robbery, and San Diego, armed robbery-homicide. The cases were going to cost me several hundred thousand dollars out of my own pocket just for expert witness fees and reconstruction efforts. There would be an allegation of special circumstances and that alone could cost Carlos his life if convicted—not that California had been executing people but the death penalty was still on the books. His exposure to potential execution would be based on the felony-murder rule during a felony committed for financial gain.

It was becoming increasingly clear that my defense of Carlos would define success as managing to save him from being put to death. Just as clear was the fact he had, indeed committed a robbery and during the course of that robbery there was a homicide. People died.

Whether Carlos personally pulled the trigger on them or not made no difference. That was the beauty of the felony-murder rule--for prosecutors. It made no difference if you were only driving the getaway car; you could be found guilty of felony murder and put to death. That's why crews like Carlos' crew had to absolutely trust each other not to commit a murder during an armed robbery. But it had happened in Carlos' case; something had gone terribly wrong.

I didn't know at that point that "something terrible" was named Phaeton.

But I was about to find out.

# Chapter 6

Two days later, I was in San Diego. There were witnesses to interview.

I got a call from Danny the first night I was away. My wife of eight years was having huge problems.

"Michael," she said through her tears. "I need to see you."

"All right, Danny, we can make that happen. Bring me up to date. I haven't heard from you in a week and last time we talked you were all sunshine and lollipops. What happened since then?"

She sniffled. "I don't know. I just am--I'm having a hard time coping."

"Did somebody say or do something to you?"

"Yes."

"Tell me what happened, please."

"I was returning a sweater that pilled. It was a Nordstrom's and I went to the Michigan Avenue store. There wasn't any parking so I left my car on the street."

"There isn't any parking on the street, I don't think. Was it a restricted zone?"

"I parked going the wrong way. That was because I made a left turn across traffic to get there."

"That's a parking violation in Chicago. But not a very serious one."

"Well, when I came out of the store, my car was being towed. He had it up on one of those trucks. I ran up and knocked on his window. He rolled it down. I was crying by now but I told him I was only in the store about twenty minutes and they should have just written me a ticket."

"But it didn't do any good. He probably didn't care what you said."

"That's just it. He laughed and drove off with my car on his truck. I could see him still laughing in his rearview mirror. Damn him!"

Now the tears were flowing again, as well as the anger. Never a good mix for Danny. It was no secret that Danny had been having emotional problems. Officially she was suffering from

PTSD and there was also talk about a dissociative identity disorder. But the main one the doctors focused on--while I was in with her--was the PTSD. She had gotten a medical marijuana card and it was helping, she told me. At least it got her off the strong medications that were screwing up her thinking. There was nothing to do at times like this except be with her.

"Can you come by and see me?" she asked.

"Of course I can, but I'm in San Diego as we speak. I'm here on a case."

"What about the kids? Who's watching them?"

"You must not have called home. Your mom is with them and Cindy is too. Both are staying over and making sure all is well. Your mom takes Dania to school and picks her up. Cindy makes their dinners."

"Good, Michael. I really need to see you, honey."

We were living apart because one of her key stressors was her family. She felt she had been a failure at mothering and at being a wife and it became too much for her to cope. So we were having a doctor-prescribed time apart. Was it working? I'm sure I didn't know.

"I'm glad you called me," I said.

"Please, Michael. Come get me."

"I'll come see you. I'll call the airlines now and get a reservation."

"Okay." Her voice was very small and sounded more distant than the mere miles between us. There was more, much more buried in there and I was powerless in the face of it. When I hung up, I wanted to start crying too, but I knew I couldn't. She needed me and I had to make arrangements and get back to Chicago. So I went online, got a ticket on the redeye to O'Hare, and I was in the air an hour later.

It was much cooler in Chicago than San Diego, as I knew it would be. I brought along a leather coat and was wearing a sweater, too, as I went out to the car rental lot and picked up my car. Then I headed in the direction of Evanston at a pretty good clip. Thirty minutes later, I was knocking on her door.

Danny was living in a condo that we had found for her that was less than ten miles from our home. She lived alone, of course, with home health aides that came on a regular basis to check on her meds and her eating and tidy up what was evidently insurmountable to her because her condo was always in disarray. There were also nurses who came once a week and did vitals and blood draws and wrote everything down.

She opened the door and immediately reached out both arms and wrapped them around my back. Then we hugged, a huge, long hug that allowed me to inhale the familiar scent of her hair and feel her slender body pressed up against me. In spite of myself, I became aroused. I say in spite of myself because my mission there was really to just be with her and try to moderate her emotional temperature. Not to arouse her.

So I pulled away a trifle and invited myself inside.

I dropped my overnight bag on the floor while I removed my coat and, as I did, she hungrily lifted up my sweater and ran her hands up my chest.

That was it. We were in the master bedroom and making love minutes later. It was incredible lovemaking because I had missed her so terribly and because she was so open to me. I cherished every minute of our joining close together.

Then we sat up in bed, nude, and she reached to the floor and pulled her T-shirt on. She lit up a cigarette from her bedside stand.

"I thought you gave that up," I said.

"It isn't tobacco. It's a pre-roll. Pot."

"Oh, it's your medicine."

"It is, Michael; it helps a lot."

"I didn't mean it didn't help. I'm glad you have something that works."

"Something that isn't some kind of crazy-making drug like they were giving me before."

"Yes. I'm glad," I repeated. "So, overall, how are you doing? Is your doctor saying you're any closer to getting to come home?"

Her face fell. She took a deep drag off her joint and held it down. Then she exhaled in a rush and reached over and took my hand.

"We don't talk about me coming home. But I can ask if you want. I miss you guys like crazy but right now I'm afraid I'd just cause problems around you all. What I want most, I can't have yet. But I'm trying, Michael, honest to God, I'm trying. You believe me, don't you?"

"I do. And thanks for telling me all that. Hey, did you get your car back?"

"I had to take a cab down to the impound yard. Then I had to pay cash to get my car out and had to pay the parking ticket. It was embarrassing and I felt utterly stupid."

"No one's keeping score. I'm sure lots of people get towed. Chicago is a big city where no one really gives a damn when it comes to stuff like that. I'm just glad you got it back and you're okay."

"That's just it, Michael, I'm not okay."

"What's that mean?"

"My doctor is thinking about putting me on a mental health floor. In a home of some kind, maybe."

"You mean it's getting worse?"

"Well--"

She looked off into the distance and I could actually feel her withdrawing from me.

"What is it? Please tell me, honey."

"He thinks I'm suicidal. I told him I'm no such thing, but I guess some of the stuff I told him I was feeling after my car was towed--I guess that set him off."

"What kind of stuff? Can you share it with me?"

She nodded. "I just felt like I had let you and the kids down again."

Now she was starting to cry. She raised her hand and put it over her face and then completely let loose, her shoulders heaving as she was wracked by sobs.

I turned to her and took her in my arms. "Easy does it," I said softly, "I'm with you and the kids are with you. We all think you're pretty great whether you got towed or not. We don't care about stuff like that, Danny. The kids just love you no matter what and I do too. This is unconditional love you're getting from us."

Which made her weep all the more.

Ten minutes later--ten difficult minutes--she began to collect herself and was looking down at the tissues that were damp and wadded on her bedspread. The sight made her giggle, and I knew we were beyond the worst of it.

"Thank you for coming to see me, honey," she said. "I'm going to be okay now. I can't believe I let such a little thing become such a huge thing. Oh, God, now I'm feeling embarrassed."

"No need. We've all done things just like that. We're human and our feelings aren't always logical. In fact, they're never logical, at least not in my case. So you can forget about letting something you might say is little becoming huge. I can relate, seriously. No matter what, I love you and I'll always love you. So just let it go, just do it for me, okay?"

She looked sideways at me. "Yes. But thank you for coming, anyway. Now I can sleep tonight with you here. It'll be the first good night's sleep I've had since the last time you spent the night."

"I'm glad you're okay with me. That's very encouraging."

"Hey, are you hungry?"

"Not really. Tell the truth, I'm very sleepy."

"Me, too. Shall I turn out the light?"

"It's fine by me. I can hardly wait to sleep with you in my arms again."

She paused. "What about tomorrow?"

"I'm leaving early. My watch is set for six. Gotta get back to SD."

"Damn. Okay. Then let's not waste a minute."

Off went the light and she backed up across the bed into my embrace.

We were still like that when my wrist alarm went off at six the next morning.

It had been a wonderful night. At least, as wonderful as they could get anymore.

As for me, I'd take what I could get. I loved my wife more than anything and I never felt I was doing enough for her.

At seven o'clock I was headed back to the airport.

# Chapter 7

*4 Weeks Earlier*

Before I robbed my first bank, I was just like you. I had a significant other, a mortgage, two car loans, a kid, an IRA I couldn't touch for twenty years, and credit card debt eating up a good chunk of my take-home--I was Mr. Average Citizen. So why did I turn to robbing banks?

Short answer: that's where the money is.

Seriously, Willie Sutton aside, I robbed my first bank because of Amelia.

Amelia's eight years old, a collector of frogs and turtles, an astronaut candidate interested in migrating to Mars, a trusted confidante with those on the other end of her endless texting, and a girl who contracted Hepatitis-C on a Girl Scout campout in New Mexico. There was a stream with dirty water and my Amelia got down on her knees and sampled it. No one knew livestock waded upstream, leaving the water unfit for drinking. That's all it took.

It took them awhile to diagnose her. Hep-C is one of those diseases that masquerades as several other things. By the time they had it nailed down, Amelia was very sick. Into the hospital she went. That's when we learned about Convergent Pharmaceuticals--a company pillaged in a hostile takeover by hedge fund managers. They raised Amelia's drug costs from $12.50 a pill to $1250 a pill. All in about six weeks.

But I had good insurance--or thought I did. So I turned it over to Grand Canyon Insurance and Annuity, a mid-cap operating out of Bel Air on Sunset Boulevard across from UCLA. GCIA had its own inner drama playing out--a too-fast growth cycle requiring additional high-priced office space, a too-fast hiring rate requiring upper-level managers with their topped-out salaries, and an onslaught of claims from people like me trying to function in a world where only the wealthiest qualified for top-drawer health. People like me had copped cheap insurance from places like GCIA as a cushion, a guarantee that we wouldn't die because we weren't covered. So what does GCIA do when our request for payment comes in? They deny our claim. They denied mine because Amelia's name was nowhere on the application for insurance. My wife had filled out the form and called her Lynne Pritchett instead of using her full name, Amelia Lynne Pritchett, and GCIA glommed onto this and used it to cut us loose without covering Amelia's care.

I tried the usual "average citizen's" fallbacks: a second mortgage? Nope, they would only loan about fifteen grand. Amelia needed two hundred thousand to buy the drugs that would cure her. A Roth IRA worth $35,000--but if you cash it in there's the early-withdrawal penalty and taxes up the ying-yang. Of course we could sell our two cars but they were financed and upside-down. So I made a list of five banks where I thought my good credit would carry the day and visited each one. The answer was the same at all five: they would loan me fifteen thousand but wanted a second on my house. Fifteen grand wasn't going to cut it. Amelia's drugs would plow through that in ten days. I needed two hundred grand.

We tried Joanne's brother. My wife's brother is a surgeon. He would love to help, but his group had just purchased an office building in Seattle and his borrowing power was used up.

So I turned my attention back to the banks.

Because that's where the money was and because I was employed as a bank security system installer. That's right, I knew everything there was to know about bank security systems-- and a hell of a lot more. I knew safes, I knew bank protocol for armed robbery, I knew FBI armed robbery procedures, I knew the difference between a Hamilton safe and a knockoff-- everything a desperate father needed to know to make withdrawals guaranteed to knock any bank's double-entry accounting system into a tailspin.

But what I didn't know was the best way to rob one of them in broad daylight at gunpoint.

So I turned to my cousin, Fredo Macaretti, who had just done a dime at San Quentin for robbing a bank himself. On parole, at first he didn't want to talk to me. But I begged and pleaded and got down on my knees and told him about Amelia; I could afford her medications for only eleven more days.

My plight touched his heart and he relented. He gave me the recipe for robbing branch banks where I might score ten thousand any day of the week. I thanked him and promised to share my first ten thousand with him and he made me open my shirt and prove I wasn't wearing a wire before he threw me out. "Never say things like that to me, ever! I ain't going back to Q for helping some schmuck take down a bank. I'm not in on this with you and I won't accept any part of your take."

He sounded like he knew he was on tape and was speaking to the police, disavowing my foray and proving he wasn't part of any conspiracy.

Fine, okay, it was just meant as a thank you. If he didn't want a grand or two tossed his way out of gratitude, I got that. I told him I wouldn't be back and he said that's right, I wasn't welcome. And that's how we left it between us.

So there I was, loaded with know-how and determined to move ahead.

The thought of my little girl having something awful happen to her was just too much for me. A stronger man might have persisted and made something legal happen that solved everyone's problems. But I wasn't that stronger man. I was the weaker one.

Mr. Average Citizen now had to do something he wouldn't have ever believed he would do.

Next thing I knew, I was the owner of a used Glock nine millimeter and was headed for a bank branch not ten miles from my house in San Diego.

It was time to improve my balance sheet.

# Chapter 8

CARLOS

I worked alone on my first job. When I walked through those double doors and turned my head away from the cross-field cameras, my knees were rubbery and sweat was rolling down my back. Somehow I made it up to the teller line and waited as others went first. Then it was my turn.

She was a young, Hispanic woman, maybe thirty years old, small diamond ring, gold cross hanging from a thin chain, and, looking up, saw me and asked how she could help me. I passed her my note demanding money. She didn't hesitate. She coughed up her drawer and passed the note. The other tellers cleaned out their drawers. I hurried along with a night deposit bag and stuffed it full. It took all of three minutes. Nobody moved because the note said I was wearing a suicide vest. Then I escaped around back where I had a Yamaha crotch rocket parked and waiting to fly onto the 5 freeway. A motorcycle? Joanna would kill me if she caught me on a motorcycle. She would also kill me if she knew I had robbed a bank.

Long story short, I made it home and went straight into my garage and lowered the door. I put the money bag on my work bench and started counting. $7600, give or take. Enough to keep Amelia going another six days. It wasn't near enough. And, it was time to face the music: I had to tell my wife what I'd done.

Much to my astonishment, Joanna wasn't furious when I told her about the bank. But she did get angry when I told her about the motorcycle. That was over the line and she made me promise to never ride it again. "I want you in one piece," she said. "No motorcycles, please." I wanted to ask her, "What about bank robberies?" But I didn't. She had made a decision about that, a decision we never discussed, and in her silence she assented. I was free to rob if it was going to keep our daughter alive. Of all the people on the earth, Joanna was the one who I thought might love Amelia even more than I loved her. Keeping her alive was all that mattered. "The rest is details and commentary," she told me, and I thought I knew what she meant. We called out for Chinese and ate Kung Pao chicken and read our fortunes. Mine didn't say anything about getting rich.

Three branches were hit in San Diego. Each time, I grew bolder. On the third job, I disabled the security system before going in and I forced my way into the vault and cleaned out the reserve. Enough money was taken to move into the big time, just like Fredo had said I should do. I returned to my cousin even though he had ordered me not to come back. This time I had one hundred thousand to spread around. I only needed one more good job and I could quit. I gave Fredo ten G's and he gave me a name. The name was *Ramsey*.

I wasted no time. With seventy-five grand, I purchased a bank job from the man named Ramsey. The bank job included schematics--water, electric, sewer, and alarms, as well as employee records and Federal Reserve transactions. Ramsey conceived a trick to gain entrance to the vault. I assembled a crew out of names Ramsey provided. We all met several times and a plan began to develop. Chris the Cutter labored seven nights in a row on the roof of the bank where sparks flew and a giant incision deepened almost all the way into the vault. The final cut would be saved for the day of the robbery. Why not just finish the job at night and forget the day job? Because the bank used a wireless alarm system that we couldn't disable during the night. Only after the vault was keyed during the day was it shut off. I said a silent thank you for Ramsey's wireless schematic, which probably saved us all from a stretch in prison.

Then I assembled the crew, explained the heist, and stole a van. With everyone aboard, we drove to within a block of the the bank with the hole in the roof. It was Friday.

The Navy had three aircraft carriers in dock so the bank was swollen and fat with paycheck money. We had gone full-fledged armed robbery because we knew there would be armed guards.

My hands were shaking when the Wheel shut off the motor. I stuffed them under my armpits so no one would notice. Then I peered out of the stolen van at the First Commercial National Bank. I suddenly felt very small. But I remembered the guns. I wrapped my arms around my automatic weapon, a TEC-9 with laser sighting. Of course I had gone into the desert east of San Diego and run five-thousand rounds through the gun. It felt familiar and powerful in my arms that day, which helped calm me down.

I pulled my ant mask over my balaclava. The mask had two large feelers sticking out of the forehead and they waggled when I turned my head. Did you know ants can smell with their feelers? I don't know why, but this factoid wouldn't leave me alone as we sat there waiting for our last guy to show. Every time I turned my head, the feelers tattooed the window glass. When was he coming? What if a cop pulled in behind us? Four men wearing rubber masks sitting in a stolen van with machine guns? How was that going to work?

I watched the heat rising off the asphalt. San Diego was in the grip of an August hot spell and the day was stifling already. I inhaled what was maybe the final air of the free man and exhaled slowly. I felt Fredo's San Quentin cell swallowing me up, closing around me, and watching me die of old age. I gripped the gun even tighter.

All of San Diego knew the fleet was ashore. The vault would be bulging. Ramsey had the reserve cash at ten million, maybe fifteen. Enough for the whole crew to walk away and never look back.

Jerry the Gnome kicked the back of the van's half-wall. 'What's the holdup?" he yelled to the front. I turned in my seat.

"We're waiting on Phaeton."

"Who is he again?"

"Just out of Q. Ramsey found him. Comes highly recommended if you can keep him from shooting a place up. That's the skinny."

The Gnome snorted. "I'd rather have Bunny. You sure he won't dance?"

"Like I told you before, Bunny resigned. He's staying safe with the wife and kids. I don't blame him. He's got enough put away there's no need."

Just then the van's rear window was knuckle-rapped. A squirt of urine escaped into my underwear but I bulled ahead and swung my gun around, leveling it across the seat in the direction of the noise. The Gnome gingerly opened the rear door and peered out at the man wearing the UCSD sweatshirt and silvered sunglasses. He had a mass of gray hair pulled back in a ponytail and a braided rubber band. He bowed down to the Gnome. "I'm Phaeton."

The Gnome lowered his Remington pump shotgun. His forefinger snapped the safety on. "Get in!"

"Put him up here," I called back to the Gnome. "We need to talk first."

Phaeton went around the white van. It said *24 Electric* along the sides in jagged, lightning bolt letters. I checked the sidewalk and street before climbing out the passenger side; the mask would be hard to explain to anyone just happening by. Not to mention my automatic weapon. I motioned Phaeton in then I took the passenger seat. Our knees touched; I reflexively moved my knee away from the stranger's. Maybe that was my intuition warning me. Maybe not.

"Thanks for letting me in on the takedown," said Phaeton. I smelled garlic and bad teeth. I moved my head away.

"You've done this before?"

Phaeton smiled and scratched his knee. "Piece of cake. I've got the tellers, from what I'm told."

"Just keep their hands on the ledge where you can see them. And keep them spread legged. The alarms are foot-operated in here."

"You know that how?"

"I know that because I paid a seventy-five large for the schematics. I've got everything, walls, electrical, water, even sewer."

"What kind of safe?"

"Hamilton. Montgomery door."

"Monkey door. Ingress?"

"Timer at nine o'clock. Two keys after. But we've got a man on the inside."

"How's he on the inside?"

I looked at the newest member of his crew. "My, aren't we the inquisitive bunch today?"

Phaeton shrugged. "Hey, I just want to be able to pick up and finish it off if someone manages to get shot by a guard."

"Two guards. One up front, one in the safe."

"A guard in the safe? What the hell?"

"It's a Hamilton."

"So it's ventilated."

"You do know your safes," I said and couldn't help but smile. Maybe the guy was okay after all. "Nice to know."

"What do they call you, the Ant?" asked Phaeton. My feelers were dancing about every time I moved my head.

"I like that!" The Gnome shouted in his Arkansas drawl. "Carlos the Ant!"

Phaeton shuffled his feet. "Works for me."

"Why not?" I said. "Why the hell not?"

"Will you Semtex your way in? Is that how you got a man inside?"

"Not when there's a guard inside the vault. The one thing I will not abide is someone getting killed. We kill a guard, we've definitely got the FBI after us."

"You use a gun you're got the FBI after you."

"Only if your hometown is Islamabad."

"What did Ramsey tell me about the roof?"

I smiled--I was very proud of this part of the caper. "We've got a plywood shed we built at night on the roof of the bank. It's painted black. It shields our cutting torches at night. You can't see it from the street, too low."

"What kind of torch?"

"Oxy-fuel."

"With a hut?"

"Why, does that bother you?"

Phaeton pursed his lips. "I don't know about that. Where'd you get the plywood?"

"Home Depot."

"They've got video at HD. The Fibbies will trace the plywood back and find you on video. Doesn't that worry you?"

I couldn't help but throw my head back and laugh. "You actually think someone in my crew made the buy?"

"Who did?"

"Never mind. But she wasn't one of us."

"She. Oh."

"We're fifteen minutes away from cutting through the top of the vault. We'll be there right after the door opens."

Phaeton checked his watch. "How long?"

"Eight minutes after. Three to cut through, five to spring the door."

"Why didn't you just cut through the ceiling at night and take the money and run before the sun came up?"

"Wireless alarm. Couldn't disable it until the vault door was keyed after eight."

"I got it."

"Good on you."

"Then what?" he asked.

"Then Chris drops down inside and opens the monkey door from the inside. That's a five-minute job."

"Good enough. And I've got the teller line when the door opens?"

"You've got the tellers and the cash drawers. Didn't Ramsey spell all this out for you?" I was just a little pissed. The guy had been told by Ramsey exactly where he fit in. I was angry that Bunny had opted out at the last minute. But everyone on the crew always had that right, no questions asked. Still, I hated operating with an unknown like Phaeton. I promised myself that if the guy missed even one beat that I would personally blow him away. But that would come after, privately. Then I caught myself. I had gone from notes to guns in just a few weeks. Now I would seriously consider shooting someone? I answered my own nagging voice: *You're damn right I would.*

"What are *you* doing?" Phaeton asked.

"I'm in the vault with a drill Chris drops down through the hole in the roof."

"So you're popping the safe deposit boxes?"

"Exactly."

"And Chis is emptying the boxes?"

"I am," said Chris in his low voice. He was in the middle seat. "If that's all right with you, pal."

Phaeton spread his hands. He didn't look around. "Hey, I'm only asking. You might be glad I did."

"How's that?" Chris wasn't smiling, I could tell. He was a bleached-out surfing bum with dreams of moving to Hawaii and hooking up with Laird Hamilton's crew before he was thirty. But Chris wasn't all surf and sun. He had a mean streak; his tone said he already hated Phaeton.

Phaeton wasn't put off by Chris, not for a second. "I'm asking just in case SWAT blows you off the roof with a Remington. I don't know. So, what about other alarms? Teller alarms? They'll have a dozen or more."

"We're cutting the teller alarms plus phone wires. We're doing it a block away, our man's on the pole."

"Who's that?'

"Utility company guy. Five grand and I own him."

"Sweet."

I leaned back. The nerves were going away and excitement was coming on. "Any other worries?"

"What's with the dwarf mask?"

"That's the Gnome. He's got the front door with his pump twelve. Now, you know how to drive a TEC-9 machine pistol?"

"Charge and pull the trigger. I've used them many times."

"Chris," I called to the back of the van, "hand up Bunny's TEC."

The gun was passed forward and handed off to Phaeton. He racked the charging handle, ejected the magazine, then locked it open and checked the chamber. One in the chamber. He ejected the round and caught it in midair. Satisfied, he re-inserted the magazine and released the slide. "We're good here," he said. "An old open-bolt conversion. Guaranteed jam-o-matic. What kind of pistol do I have when I toss this away?"

"No backup weapons. If it jams, it's a hang fire. Rack it and clear it. You seem to know the drill."

"So much for shooting the good guys."

"Yeah," I said in my fiercest voice, "and if you pull that trigger while I'm in the same city with you, you better damn well kill me too. Because I am drawing down on you. Feel me?"

"Yeah.

"You shoot anyone and it's on you. You deal with it, not I."

"Understand."

I handed him a monkey mask. "Here. You're the chimp today."

Phaeton shook his head. "Does this mean I get to fling some shit at someone?"

What an asshole. I scowled. "You do and you're on your own, buddy boy. I thought I covered that."

Now I spoke to the crew in the van.

"Now, if we see a helicopter, we're fucked."

"Agree," said both Chris and Randy the Wheel. The Wheel had the driver's seat, the top wheelman on the West Coast. He'd been with Chris for five years, since the day Chris was paroled.

"If we see SWAT, we're fucked," I said.

"Agree," said everyone.

"If I say 'Go,' you will drop whatever you're doing, walk out through the front door and casually get into the van. Same seats. You will not delay, you will not argue, you will not make a scene. Everyone?"

"Agree," said everyone including Phaeton.

"And if you fire your weapon you are no longer welcome here. Last time I'm going to say it. Feel me?"

"Feel," said everyone.

"Okay. Chris, get on up to the roof. We're waiting exactly ten minutes for you to get up and do the last inch. Then you're going through the drywall and dropping down inside the next time a jet takes off. We wait exactly three minutes and then we go. Everyone ready to fund their retirement plan?"

"Ready."

"Ready."

"Yep."

"Lead the way, Carlos!"

At that moment, a 777 rumbled by overhead and thundered off between Ocean Beach and Pacific Beach. I waited until the aircraft began its gentle turn out over the Pacific, and then punched the sweep hand on my watch. The seconds ticked by, then the minutes.

Chris left the van and headed for the alley around the corner. A fake utility truck was waiting there with a cherry picker.

I punched the stopwatch.

It was time to go.

# Chapter 9

CARLOS

My crew climbed out of the van and ran for the bank, me leading the way. As we romped through the doors, customers and employees scattered like quail before hunting dogs. Surprise: there were two guards at the door instead of just one. One was raising his gun when he saw our masks. The Gnome cold-cocked him with his Glock and jammed his shotgun under the other guard's chin. The guard gingerly removed his revolver and two-fingered it over to the Gnome. Then the guard was forced down on his knees and his hands were PlastiCuffed. The customers all ran for the far end of the main lobby and huddled there, arms raised and color draining from their faces. We had been noticed.

Phaeton vaulted the tellers' counter and PlastiCuffed the money-changers one after another. He moved them back against the wall, away from their alarm buttons.

I swept through the lobby with the muzzle of my TEC-9 sliding back and forth across the crowd. One woman fainted. An elderly gentlemen raised his hands and fell to his knees, babbling prayers while others cringed away in fear and the certainty that the end was upon them. The truth was, I hated weapons around civilians because the possibility of someone doing something stupid was so high, but this time it was unavoidable.

The Gnome's mask slid down his sweat-bathed face and three sailors in whites saw his balaclava; two turned away, but the third glared at him and his mouth moved silently, cursing. The Gnome stepped away from his post at the double doors. His twelve gauge was carried hunter-style with the stock under one arm and the barrel in the opposite hand. The third sailor turned away and raised his arms. Meanwhile, I was hoping against hope that no one came to the door before we were finished, but if they did, the Gnome would stand aside, hiding the gun behind his back, and smile and greet them. Then they would be told to join the other customers at the far wall. Police arriving would be a whole other ballgame. If that were to happen he was to show them his gun and then step to the side of the door. That way he could at least kill the first one through if they stormed us. Killing numbers one and two and possibly even number three would create chaos, help block the door, and give us a chance to run for the back exit.

Phaeton vaulted back over the tellers' counter and yelled at the people inside the roped-off tellers' line.

"Nobody fucking move!" he cried at them, and no one moved. The main group just looked away instinctively, not wanting to challenge the big dog with their eyes. But there's always got to be one holdout. This time it was a thin man with a pockmarked face, carrying a motorcycle helmet. He shook his head and waved as if to brush the threat away.

"I'm an Iraq vet," he told Phaeton in a quiet voice. "You're gonna need more guns than you guys got before I break a sweat."

Phaeton leveled his gun at the man but the customer didn't flinch. "Go ahead. Then you've got the FBI up your dumb ass. We both know that, so fuck off!"

Phaeton flicked his safety off. It made a loud, metallic click. His trigger finger brushed against the trigger guard. "Give me a reason, mister vet-er-an. Go ahead!"

The customer shook his head in disgust and turned his side to the gunman. He busied himself with studying the wall behind the tellers' windows, withdrawing from the confrontation. Phaeton looked amused and finally managed to move his eyes off the target. One woman complained that she had wet herself and needed to use the restroom. Phaeton approached her from behind and stuck the barrel of his gun between her legs. He lifted her skirt up to the top of her thighs. Her underwear was, in fact, sopping wet.

"Sorry," he told her, "but you've gotta stay here. Besides, urine is sterile."

She shuddered and stepped spread-legged away from his gun.

Another teller shouted, from the far end, "The bank doesn't have alarm buttons for us. They said there was too much risk if a robber caught us using one. So they took them out. You're safe."

The military veteran turned back and was again eyeballing Phaeton with a sneer.

"Tough guy, huh?" asked the soldier. "Won't let the lady go dry herself in the toilet. What an asshole!"

Phaeton's expression changed from a merely anxious look to a look of pure rage. He whipped the TEC-9 to his shoulder and leveled the muzzle at the soldier. His hand shook where it gripped the barrel, an unwanted quiver that Phaeton immediately regretted, because the soldier noted it.

"Nervous? Your hand's shaking, Mr. Tough Guy. My guess is: this is your first time with a crew. Am I right?"

"Shut the fuck up!" Phaeton shouted. He inserted his finger inside the trigger guard as a warning to the soldier that he just might fire. Now they were in a standoff.

Five minutes passed, enough time for Chris to cut through the ceiling inside the vault and let himself down inside. I was waiting for him to open the vault. Chris turned to the inner workings of the Montgomery door. He set the final unlocks. Then, with a flourish, he turned the handle and pushed the door open from the vault side.

Immediately I joined him inside and lifted the heavy drill that Chris had lowered and left dangling from a rope. I jammed the drill against the nearest safe deposit box and squeezed the trigger. The vault erupted with a high-pitched scream of hardened metal on hardened metal. But the lock was no match for the tool and it gave way, allowing me to scoop up the contents and dump everything into a large duffle bag. I continued working in this manner, going from box to box to box.

Chris, meanwhile, joined the customer contingent outside the vault along the far wall and smiled at the people there, reassuring them that no one was going to be hurt if everyone would just remain calm. He called for their smartphones. In just seconds a pile of smartphones lay on the floor before them. The phones buzzed and jingled and played short tunes as callers attempted to reach the owners.

Phaeton was patrolling back and forth along the customer rope. As he did, the soldier who had called him out still hadn't taken his eyes off the robber. Phaeton knew this and it was making him nervous, knowing that the guy had him one up. His hand *had* been shaking on the gun, the soldier had been right about that. Which made him look weak, and Phaeton could not accept looking weak, not to anyone. He suddenly stepped up and leveled his gun at the soldier's face. This time, his hand wasn't shaking. He was totally calm and feeling mean and aggressive. Phaeton grinned and pretended to pull the trigger, pretended the muzzle recoiled up toward the ceiling so the soldier would be sure not to miss the pantomime. Chris saw all this and called me out. "Carlos, out here! Trouble with Mr. Asshole," he said and nodded at Phaeton. I saw the game Phaeton was playing and shouted, "Hey! Numb nuts!" I ran for him.

Phaeton startled and his finger, still inside the trigger guard, went all the way. A three-round burst erupted from his gun, stitching the soldier across his chest. Blood blossoms immediately sprung out of the man's chest and he slumped to his knees, his hands grabbing at his wounds, then he fell sideways onto the floor, dead. Phaeton looked on in disbelief. I exploded in a rage, coming up behind and swatting the back of Phaeton's head with an open hand.

"Fuck face! What did I tell you!"

"I--I--I--"

"You just got us all killed!" I cried. "You just jabbed the needle in our arms!"

In a white-hot rage, I leveled my automatic weapon at Phaeton but hesitated. It would be the totally wrong thing to do, killing him right then and there, although I wanted nothing more than to squeeze off a round into the guy's head. He deserved it, had it coming, and none of the others would disagree.

The only thing that saved Phaeton just then was the problem his death would create for me, as I would then be dealing with a dead body that could lead the FBI directly to us. I didn't have any idea how many phone numbers and contacts Phaeton had left behind in a trail of clues leading to me, but I wasn't willing to find out.

I swung my gun away from Phaeton's head and pointed a long, firm finger at him. I was so angry I couldn't even speak words. But it wasn't lost on Phaeton. His face said he knew I meant to kill him and knew he had to get away right then and there.

So he turned and walked right on by me and there was nothing I could do to stop him. He came around the line of customers behind the rope, and casually walked to the front door of the bank. He tossed his gun aside. Now he simply twisted the lock and pushed his way out without looking back. He knew, at that instant, that he was immune, that he couldn't be shot and killed by any of the crew, and he was taking advantage of those precious moments to leave.

I ran over to the door and caught a glimpse of him running for the corner, to a cab queued outside a hotel. He climbed in the back seat, threw greenbacks at the driver, and I guessed he told the guy to head for the Mexican border. At least that's what I would have done. The cab jerked away from the curb. It lurched up to the green light and squealed around the corner, bound for the I-5 southbound.

I checked my watch. We were screwed. We had been inside the bank only seven-and-one-half minutes, but the gunshots would bring trouble within the next four minutes. So I alerted the others and everyone headed for the front doors. We had managed to open only twenty of the safe deposit boxes and we had no idea whether any of the loot even had any value. For all we knew we might have a duffel bag lightly filled with automobile titles, wills, useless deeds, and bonds that could easily be traced.

"We're out, Chris," I said to my friend as we followed the Gnome through the door. "We got nothing."

"I know," said Chris. "That crazy son of a bitch just had to shoot someone. We're going to find him, pal."

"*I'm* going to find him. I'm the one got him onboard with us," I panted as we dashed to the van where Randy the Wheel waited.

Just as we all got settled in the van, the street erupted with a swarm of police vehicles. Marked and unmarked cars rolled in behind and in front. We worked the charging handles on our automatic weapons but I knew we were dead. Cops Unlimited had us boxed in. But my guys never flinched, I'll give them that. Safeties were switched off and high-threat targets located.

Right up on our tail was an unmarked vehicle driven by Detective Danny Medina. He threw open his door and crouched behind, his Beretta raised in both hands. His partner Underwood bailed out of the passenger door and remained standing behind it, his Glock raised like his partner's. They only had to wait for the van to unload and arrests would be made. If the robbers decided not to fight. Huge if.

Inside the van, Chris pointed his automatic weapon at the first detective out, Medina, and fired a short burst through the police vehicle's door. From his side of the van the Gnome did the same, firing through the passenger door of the detectives' car. Both detectives were flung backward by the spray of bullets, onto the pavement, where they lay, motionless.

"It's on!" cried Chris, and he threw open the rear door of the van. Other police cars were blocking any exit ahead of us and now they blocked us on the street side as well. We were left with no choice but to flee on foot. Chris stepped out of the van onto the asphalt and swung his weapon at an oncoming black and white patrol car speeding up the center of the street. I jumped down out of the passenger seat, moving right and to the rear of the van. Then I was on the asphalt beside Chris and we pressed our backs together and Chris started firing in a very controlled manner while we worked away from the van, up onto the sidewalk, now ducking down behind a mailbox and continuing, bent double, working our way toward an alley.

Randy the Wheel bailed from the driver's side of the van and was immediately caught in a maelstrom of automatic weapon fire from the SWAT team that had worked up to the head of the van. He twisted as the bullets tore into him, at first immune as the Kevlar vest he was wearing took most of the shots, and he made it partway back inside the van but then came the head shots and he was down and gone a second later.

The Gnome remained frozen in the van, his mask pushed atop his head and his weapon cradled in his arms. He lurched to his left and looked beyond the vehicle's windshield. A dozen or more blue uniforms were approaching, moving from car to car, guns extended and drawing a bead on the van, searching out any movement. Then he turned to his right and appeared to consider for just a second catching up to me and Chris. I witnessed all of this as we backed into the alley. But movement from just beyond the two dead detectives gripped the Gnome's attention and he realized he couldn't make it without being cut to pieces. He turned where he sat and wedged his head against the backside of the second row of seats. Through the back doors I could see he was lying flat on his back. Maybe he would surrender, I remember thinking, but then I remembered who we were talking about. The Gnome was a Q alumnus too and wouldn't ever be taken back. Suddenly the SWAT guys were standing and looking inside the van, aiming guns at him. He took up his TEC-9 and lifted it to throw it out the rear of the vehicle. As he did, the officers interpreted his movement as aggression and they began firing. He was stitched by crossfire from his toes to his head and was instantly dead. Among the police there was no discussion. They had done as they were trained: they had survived while overwhelming the threat with gunfire. While they might have misconstrued the dead man's intentions, they had survived and that came first in all confrontations.

Just as we made the entry to the alley, Chris caught two rounds in the abdomen. Someone was firing armor-penetrating rounds. Maybe they all were, as far as I knew. Chris pitched forward onto his knees, holding his free hand over the gushing wound and looking down in astonishment as a coil of intestine pushed against his hand, trying to work free.

I grabbed Chris by the arm and attempted to pull him out of harm's way. But as Chris froze there, on his knees, astonishment on his face, a second burst of machine gun fire opened him from navel to forehead and he died before he hit the concrete. Taking the extremely small opportunity that Chris's death afforded, I turned and ran for the nearest dumpster.

I managed to duck down behind a double steel wall and at the same moment I swung my weapon around and fired off a long burst. The bullets effectively sprayed down the alley and the advancing officers at the far end ducked back behind the buildings along the sidewalk. At that exact moment, I duckwalked below the steel horizon, then dashed to the next dumpster on the same side of the alley, a distance of twenty-five yards.

Again I raised my weapon around the wall of steel and fired off a covering burst. My gun jammed at that instant but I had presence of mind enough to lock back the slide, free the hang fire, and release the slide so the gun re-chambered the next round it would fire. Again I swept the oncoming police with a long burst. This time, two of the men jumped from the alley to safe positions behind the dumpsters and the officers at their sides jumped in behind them. I saw the opening and ran for the other end of the alley, picking my way around yet a third dumpster before dashing out onto the far sidewalk.

Charging into the street like a desperate bull, I accosted a woman in a Dodge Durango and ripped her from her vehicle. I slid behind the wheel and immediately threw the truck into reverse. Within seconds I had careened from side to side back up the street and suddenly found myself in the next intersection, instinctively turning left and accelerating away from the onslaught. Police dashed into the street seconds later, but the traffic and pedestrians between me and their guns kept them from firing. Shoulder mikes were keyed and superiors advised of the my movements.

Then it all grew quiet as the normal flow of traffic resumed. Suddenly, in the next instant, police vehicles came screaming by at either end of the street.

The chase was on but it was too late. I was on the southbound 5 driving the speed limit and looking nonchalant. At the next exit I shot off, hung a fast right at the light, and ditched the Durango. I casually walked into a Jack-In-The-Box and dropped a quarter in the pay phone. A cab picked me up ten minutes later and I was gone, no money, no loot, but running free and that was all that mattered.

# Chapter 10

My name is Leticia Cross and I do not go lightly.

I was in trial as the First Commercial robbery was underway. I had Pat DeWald on the witness stand, awaiting my cross-examination. DeWald was a fool, among other things, because if you are the defendant and I am the district attorney, the one thing you do not want to do is testify in your trial. If you do, I will fuck you up.

DeWald made that mistake. It was a rape/agg-battery case. He testified (clearly against his lawyer's advice) that he was nowhere near the stairwell where Melinda Bustamante was raped and tortured on Christmas Eve. In fact, he said, he wasn't even in California. I knew better. I grew up in the North Park ghetto in San Diego where Melinda was savagely attacked. I knew what went on there every night. I stood up from counsel table and approached the lectern. My fingers were twitching; I was so ready for this slime.

"Mr. DeWald, you testified you were in Tucson on Christmas Eve last?"

"I was. Visiting my sister. She'll collaborate my story."

"You're sure you didn't see Melinda that night in North Park?"

"I'm sure I didn't see Melinda that night. Or any other night."

"Were you present when the police officers executed a search warrant on your apartment the next day?"

"No, I was still in Tucson on Christmas Day."

"But your lawyer has told you what things the police seized from your place?"

"Yes, he's told me."

"You're aware that they seized a pair of Converse basketball shoes?"

"Yes."

"You have denied those shoes belonged to you, according to the statement you gave the police?"

He shrugged. "What can I say? They weren't mine."

"Did your lawyer tell you I had those shoes tested for your DNA?"

"I don't recall."

"Do you recall him telling you that the crime lab report says your DNA was found in the inside toes of those shoes?"

"Yes."

"And you still deny those were your shoes?"

"I might have borrowed them to wear a time or two."

"The reason I ask, those same Converse basketball shoes also testified positive for swimming pool acid. Does that sound like something you might know anything about?"

"I'm sure I don't."

"Well, according to the detectives and doctors, whoever raped Melinda that night wasn't satisfied with just the assault. They also poured acid in her eyes so she couldn't identify the man who attacked her. Does that sound like something you might have done?"

"Of course I didn't do that!"

"Well, the jeans that were also seized from your closet floor, those also had acid on them. And the fly had semen on them. Do you recall being told your semen was on those jeans?"

"Maybe."

"Do you know how your semen got on those jeans?"

"I'm sure--maybe--"

"Are you in the habit of ejaculating on your jeans?"

He blanched, turning white then red.

"Of course not."

"But those jeans had your semen and also, here's the good part: They also have the same swimming pool acid spattered on the trouser legs as the acid the doctors removed from Melinda's eyes. Does that sound like something you'd know anything about?"

"Definitely not. Can I have some water?" He said this to the judge, who pointed to the bailiff, who produced a glass of water for the witness. DeWald lifted, chugged, and wiped his mouth with the back of his hand. Then we moved along.

"So let me get this straight. You were in Tucson while this miracle occurred: shoes, with your DNA in the toes, went to the apartment building without you. Then your jeans joined those shoes. While they were there, the shoes and jeans assaulted Melinda and left your semen in her vagina and on her face. Your semen also found its way onto the fly of your jeans. Now comes the second miracle. Without any help from you, those shoes and jeans then poured acid into Melinda's eyes, blinding her for life, just so she couldn't identify the man who raped and tortured her. Where does an ordinary man like you, Mr. DeWald, buy shoes and jeans capable of performing such miracles? Or should the jury simply believe that those shoes and jeans didn't go alone, that you went with them? Doesn't that sound more believable than the miracle theory of events?"

"I--I--"

"You raped Melinda Bustamante on Christmas Eve last, did you not? And blinded her?"

"Someone else must have worn my clothes."

"Someone else wore your clothes! And they ejaculated your semen on the fly and left your DNA in the toes? Who is *this* miracle worker? Do you have some names?"

He looked around like a rat about to be munched alive by a big tomcat.

"Can I confer with my lawyer?"

"Why?" I managed to say before the judge could respond, "does your lawyer know about miracles too?"

"We'll take a five-minute recess."

He was convicted. The jury was out for just fifteen minutes. You know where to find Pat DeWald today? Life without possibility of parole at State Prison, where Junior Washington took him under his wing his second night. Junior is Pat's pimp now. He trades Pat around for cigarettes and fresh fruit.

Junior was homecoming king at my high school and I was queen. He'll do anything I ask, still.

It's Junior's cell where Pat's eyes stare out of a jar. Rumor has it, Junior dug Pat's eyes out of their sockets with a spoon he smuggled out of the mess hall. But that's just rumor.

Like I said, you get on that witness stand and testify and I will fuck you up.

I do not go lightly.

* * *

I was returning from court when the call came over my radio.

"Leticia Cross," I said, "Deputy District Attorney."

"San Diego PD Dispatch, Deputy Cross. There's been a robbery at Currant and Ninety-ninth. First Commercial National Bank. Please proceed to the scene."

"Roger that," I spoke into the mike. "My ETA is eleven minutes."

"Report to Special Agent Jon Hanover."

"FBI? Why do they want a district attorney if it's federal?"

"The case will be referred to SDPD. Hanover is there coordinating, and calculating FDIC involvement. The U.S. Attorney won't be prosecuting. That will fall to the San Diego County District Attorney."

The feds wanted to know how much they were on the hook for because federally insured funds had been stolen. Couldn't blame them for that.

"Roger that. I'm spinning up and on my way."

I was stopped a block away from the bank by a uniform. I flashed my DA's badge and a path was cleared. I drove to within maybe a hundred feet of the bank. No one noticed as I double-timed to the entrance and stepped inside.

Hanover was there in the middle of the lobby floor, barking orders. A group of customers was still cowering along the far wall and officers were distributing bottles of water to them as the frightened victims took turns using the bathrooms. Statements would be taken from each and every one before the day was over. I approached Hanover from behind and called out his name.

"Agent Hanover, Deputy DA, Leticia Cross."

He knew me, or at least knew of me, because there were no introductions, nor was there a need, as he turned and momentarily sized me up. I'm a black woman, five-eight, braided hair in a pageboy style, with a nose and eyes resembling Beyoncé when she was with Destiny's Child, I am told. Not hard to look at, my ex-boyfriend liked to say, piss on him.

"Ms. Cross, so we meet again."

"We've met before?" I asked.

"I attended the DA's Christmas party last year. I watched you and the two other DDA's do the Black Andrews Sisters' rendition of *Winter Wonderland*. I'm still laughing over it."

"Well, I'm glad you liked it. So I take it the FBI is going to pass on this mess?"

"I'm going to coordinate," said Hanover. He shook a cigarette out of a crumpled pack and lit up with a Zippo and great aplomb. *No Smoking* signs meant nothing to this man. And who in their right mind was going to tell the FBI they couldn't smoke anyway? The bank was electric with gratitude that he was there. You could tell by the way the bank officials deferred to him when they came up to speak. He could have been spray painting Justice Department graffiti on the windows and no one would have said anything to him.

"So what do we have here? Any similars?"

I was asking whether other armed robberies on the books had any similarities to this one. He shook his head.

"Not so far. But we've got a dead guy over yonder." He jerked his head toward a small clump of officials wearing Coroner's coveralls. Dead guy, indeed.

"Why kill one man?"

"Why not? Maybe it was a sport killing like a sport fuck. You follow me?" He was toying with me; I didn't flinch.

"No, I don't follow you. Why don't you explain that?"

He grinned. "Sure. A sport killing--"

"Yes, yes. I guess I didn't realize that random murder was on the same level as random sex. Live and learn, I suppose."

"I suppose."

"All right, everyone!" he shouted out, clapping his hands. "Gather round, please, all law enforcement!"

Detectives and uniforms meandered over and formed a tight circle around Hanover. I recognized several plainclothes officers but the majority were all unfamiliar. Robbery-homicide isn't my usual beat; I just happened to be in the area after court. At that point in time I doubted the case would remain with me. As far as I knew, I was simply covering for some other unlucky Deputy DA who would have a mess on her hands--homicide, bank robbery, several dead outside in the street, bad guys and good guys alike. It was going to take a small army of Deputy DA's just to get all the indictments and charges put together that this case was going to demand. I was happy to just be passing through.

"People," said Hanover to his group, "these guys are professional thieves. The cutdown through the roof is just a half-bubble short of genius. We saw this done recently in New York and apparently good news travels fast, because now we've got it happening out here. These guys must be networked or something."

"What kind of cutdown?" I asked. I wanted to get some notes for the next-in-line in my office. Some proof I'd done a good job at the scene and had asked the right questions.

"They built a shack on the roof of the bank. Painted it black on the outside and sealed the inside seams with duct tape. No light emissions so they could run their cutting torch at night. They used an oxy-fuel unit that sliced its way through eight inches of the hardest, densest steel made by man, the steel in a Hamilton vault. These guys knew what they were doing, because the Montgomery door on these babies is virtually impenetrable. The company guarantees vault integrity against a two-thousand pound bomb dropped from a B-52."

I scribbled a note on my Spiral pad. "2000?" I wrote. "Seriously? Or making joke?"

"So let's nail down stories. All customers get recorded. All interviews by Ms. Cross here. Uniforms go outside and assist with scene control. We have multiple homicides out there."

"Four officers dead," said one of the uniforms. He was a tall, slender man with sergeant stripes. There were tears in his eyes as he spoke. "It's a blood bath out there."

"All the more reason for you to take the other uniformed officers outside. Go now."

A little more than half the police officers inside the bank left to go outside and lend a hand. Then Hanover continued talking to the detectives and CSI's.

"These guys might have made off with cash, I don't know yet. But we know they unloaded maybe twenty or thirty boxes. That means jewels and other valuables are going to start turning up at pawn shops. So fan out, hit the pawns, enlist all the help you need, make sure they have CCTV and it's operating."

"Cash count?"

"We're working on it now. We're thinking a teller drawer or two got scooped. Maybe more. Which will put marked bills into circ. Check all casinos and racetracks, especially the horses. If they get a bill then you get the CCTV and make me a face. We'll get it out immediately. Who else is here?"

"Bryce Sisson, San Diego PD."

"Welcome, Detective Sisson. Are you the ranking?"

Sisson did a quick inventory of the other faces. "Looks like I am. Are you running with this one or punting?"

"I'm running the show but punting the investigation to you, detective. Tell me what you want and I'll make sure you get it."

"I counted four homicide dicks outside setting up. I'd like to send four more outside so each team has one death case."

"Do it, then."

"McAuliffe and Mendoza, why don't you take your partners and pick up the remaining deceased? I'll take the remaining pool and work the bank job."

Both named detectives, with their partners, headed for the door. They hadn't been homicide but they were now. Which was fine; I had very little to do and so I was simply making notes. Then Hanover turned to me.

"DA Cross, I've been on the horn with the U.S. Attorney's office. They're kicking it downstairs to the DA. I've been in touch with the DA and you've got the gold ring, it seems."

A chill shot down my spine. I had been given the entire mess? Was there something happening in my career file I hadn't been told about? Like a huge promotion? This was an enormous chance for me to prove my mettle on a very high profile case. I moved closer to Hanover.

"Inside and outside cases both?"

"Yes, inside and outside. Your boss is putting together a team of Deputy DA's and investigators out of your office to pitch in. But it looks like you're running the show."

So, it was true. I was too stunned to speak. No one would have expected to see me come away with a case this big. Those were usually reserved for the twenty-year veterans, which I definitely was not. I'd only been with the DA six years at that point. Wonder of wonders. My mind kicked in and started racing. I called my office and got the DA herself on the line. We discussed and she advised me she had two more DDA's on the way to give me a hand. Was there any chance I might get to choose my own deputies instead? No, she said, no chance of that. So we hung up and I approached Special Agent Hanover.

"Looks like I'm it," I said. "You're answering to me since the U.S. Attorney declined."

He wiped a drink of bottled water from his mouth with his sleeve. "Good enough. What do you want first?"

"Statements are good, but I'm more concerned with video. What do we have?"

"Video was cut a block away. Someone climbed a pole and took it down."

"Seriously? A block away?"

He studied me.

"Yes, seriously. This crew is very good."

"Then why do we have a dead civilian? Good crews don't kill civilians. It's not good for business."

"My guess? Someone got in a pissing match with a customer. He decided to win the argument the old-fashioned way like they did over in Tombstone."

"We had an OK Corral shootout?"

He grimaced. "We sure as hell did once they went outside, wouldn't you say? I don't know how many souls Wyatt Earp and his gang sent heavenward, but I bet it wasn't many more than our guys here in San Diego."

Hanover tapped another cigarette out of his pack and lit it off the first. No one offers anyone a smoke anymore. Not that I would have accepted. But here was a guy who was all about himself and his job. He was going to be difficult if not impossible to control. I would need to make sure I kept up with him, number one, and make sure I played it by whatever book he wanted it played, number two, if I was going to emerge at the other end victorious. I stopped in mid-step as I was approaching the customers. This case could actually cost me my job. It had just sunk in. I was working with a guy who wouldn't hesitate to call for my head if I didn't handle this just so. Communication was going to be key. If not hourly then at least a couple of times a day we'd need to talk. I'd make sure we did.

Just then, Hanover called me back over.

"Leticia, the outside officers would like some guidance. Do you want to speak with them or should I?"

"Why don't you?" I replied. "You've done bank robberies before, probably lots of them. This is my first."

He looked at me before turning away on his heel. "Sheesh!" he said in great burst of exhaled air as he began making his beyond the makeshift interview area with its church basement style of chairs and tables.

I shrugged as he walked away.

Screw it. I was only being honest.

Now I saw how far honesty would get me. It was time to tighten the screws and adopt the image of someone who knew what they hell they were doing. Before today, I worked robbery and homicide but those cases had all been liquor stores and filling stations. But what the hell, I told myself, how different could a bank be? Just more money, more people with a story, and more dead bodies.

I'd just do what I'd been doing all along.

Which was how I'd managed to achieve a won-lost record of 38-0.

I pulled out a chair at the end of the first folding table, the head honcho's chair.

It was time to get a description, time to find out what characteristics and traits the bank's customers could put together for us. I opened my iPad and flexed my hands.

"Who's first?" I called to the jumble of people. "Let's put someone on death row, shall we?"

Faces lit up and grins appeared on faces that moments before had looked defeated and afraid.

"I like you," said a senior who was wearing canary slacks, white shirt, and paisley suspenders.

"I like you too, sir. Pull up a chair and spell your name for me. We'll get you on your way in about ten or fifteen minutes."

"Fine. Then I like you even more."

"First name?"

# Chapter 11

Cops had been killed, my crew was dead, and I was on the run the night of the First Commercial mess.

I was alone, hiding out in a $30 motel room down by the waterfront, waiting for the heat to blow over. I became morose and helped myself to a pity party. After all, I had served in the Army, paid my taxes, and took my wife and daughter on a vacation to the mountains every July when San Diego's thermometer climbed. My work as a bank security alarm installer provided our family with enough money to buy a new car every third year and enough money to support our church's mission outreach at Christmas. I cheered for the Chargers and watched *Downton Abbey* with my wife. I was a good guy made to do bad things. Self-pity comes easy when you're alone and frightened.

I wanted to go home but was afraid, with cops scouring every nook and cranny for the one that got away from the bank job. Then I got bold and went to a payphone and put a call through to Joanna. Amelia was still very sick. According to *Time* magazine, the new owner of Convergent Pharmaceuticals celebrated his acquisition with a weekend in Monaco playing Baccarat and drinking Dom until he couldn't walk. He was down five million USD in less than twenty-four hours. He got up at three p.m. the next day, scanned the exchanges on his laptop, and saw he had made more money than he had lost. I thought about hunting him down and robbing him. Or shooting him. But he probably had armed guards up the ass. Sitting around in that room I dwelled more and more on the guy at Grand Canyon Insurance who had denied my claim. His name was Washburn Rambis. Two days of thinking about nothing but him, and I was ready to explode. Against all good judgment, I decided to take action.

I changed flop houses two nights running, just being sure no one was close behind.

It all became too much; I headed for Grand Canyon Insurance. I rode the big dog out of San Diego on a non-stop to L.A. The date was August 14, just four days after our failed robbery of First Commercial.

Realizing the head underwriter would probably refuse to see me, I decided that begging on my knees wasn't going to cut it. I needed more--I needed a threat. So I decided to take a gun along. I promised myself I wouldn't brandish it unless I was absolutely forced to pull it out and change the guy's mind about our case. One thousand dollars at a pawn shop not four blocks from the bus station in L.A. bought me a used Glock, still in its original box, neatly packaged with the original three magazines. I loaded the magazines with 9mm ammo and took a taxi to a Target store. I purchased a new outfit, all in brown, changed my clothes, had my traveling clothes folded into brown boxes, and rented a car. I drove to GCIA's offices in Bel Air.

The company occupied the top four floors of a building of cantilevered glass, reinforced steel, and concrete. GCIA's floors were overrun with GCIA employees keeping the wheels turning for the wildly successful insurance company. I walked inside and was greeted by pink marble floors and gleaming walls of marble and stainless steel. A Ted DeGrazia oil graced the west wall and a panoramic, air-brushed graphic of the Pacific set off the east. The sun was rising in both paintings, implying that GCIA was young and new and just beginning its quest to take over the insurance world.

Entering the lobby, with the Glock tucked inside my waistband, I passed by the security desk and proceeded to the building directory. The lobby was very busy as the clock was approaching lunch time and people were coming and going, connections were being made, and meals were carried to and fro. I was wearing the dark brown uniform of a UPS driver and was carrying three fake packages wrapped in brown paper. As far as anyone knew, I was there to deliver the packages. Even building security ignored me when I passed by.

But UPS drivers don't linger in lobbies so I hurried to the elevators and jabbed the button for seven, the main lobby of GCIA. Four other passengers lifted off with me, all eyes glued to the flashing numbers, while the smells of corned beef and fries enticed noses trained in noontime dining. Stops were made and most passengers were offloaded by the time my doors opened on seven.

I stepped off the elevator, carrying the packages ahead of me, looking to all the world like a UPS delivery man. I was ignored as I approached the reception desk. Phones were lighting up, the three receptionists fielding calls and making connections like air traffic controllers, until, finally, the Asian girl on the near end looked up at me and smiled.

"Who you got?" she said.

"Washburn Rambis. Signature required."

"Top floor. Then down the hall to ten-twelve."

"One-oh-one-two. Got it. Thanks!"

Back on the elevator and a short ride up to ten. This time when I stepped off I was greeted only with a small lobby connected to a hall at either end. I decided that the even numbers would be to my right, and off I went in search of Mr. Rambis.

Down to the end of the hall and there it was. Two glass doors. The name plaque said it all in three horizontal lines: Washburn J. Rambis, Vice-President, Underwriting. Even though I was balancing three packages, I was able to push open the nearest door with one hand. I stepped inside. The mandatory ficus on the right, two leather chairs and magazine-strewn coffee table on the left. Five steps and I was in front of the receptionist's enclave. She was on the phone and couldn't spare a smile or acknowledgment. So, I took a seat and began flipping through the coffee table magazines.

I was still grazing covers when the receptionist said, "You need a signature sir? I can sign that for Mr. Rambis."

"Nope. Special restriction. He has to sign in front of me then I certify it."

She let out a long sigh, letting me know how inconvenienced she was. But she jabbed the button on her phone nonetheless.

"Mr. Rambis? Delivery requiring your signature."

* * *

I did a strange thing when they let me into Mr. Rambis' office: I kicked the door shut behind me. Without turning to look, I then reached back and locked it.

"I'm not UPS, I'm Pritchett and you're refusing to insure my little girl."

He half-stood behind his desk and pointed at me. "Sir, I'm demanding you leave my office this instant or I'm calling security."

"Sure, you do that. But first agree to pay for my daughter's meds. I've made my insurance payments every month like clockwork and you owe us now."

Rambis shook his head violently and reached for his phone.

But then I dropped my packages to the floor, kicked them aside, and whipped that monstrous gun from my waistband in one move. The front sight was trained on Rambis; my mouth ground side to side as I was in a full-out rage. I was blinded by it.

"What?" asked Rambis, startled and the color draining from his face. "Can we talk about this?"

"I'm Carlos Pritchett. My little girl is the kid you're murdering."

"Whoa, whoa, slow down, Mr. Pritchett--"

"You slow down, Mr. Rambis. I'm here to shoot you. But first I'm going to give you a chance to call your underwriting supervisor and order him to cover Amelia Lynne Pritchett on my policy. Make it retroactive, too. You do that now and we'll talk about your future after."

Rambis sat down. He slumped forward in his chair and lifted the phone.

"Edward? Wash Rambis here. Need you to add an insured to the insurance policy of Carlos Pritchett."

He started nodding. His face relaxed.

"Yes, that's the one. The new insured is Amelia Lynne Pritchett. Put the policy rider in today's mail. Thank you."

I nodded and dropped the gun to my side. I walked backwards and unlocked the door. I walked back up to the desk and sank heavily into a visitor's chair.

"Can I have a bottle of water?"

"Sure."

Rambis punched the intercom and set Leona about fetching two waters. We stared at each other for several minutes without talking.

She knocked once, placed the waters on the desk, and turned and frowned at the packages discarded willy-nilly on the floor. Her sense of order duly insulted, she began asking questions.

"What's this?"

"Just leave, please. We'll take care of that later."

She shrugged and stepped up to the door. "Open or closed?"

There had been too much stress and I knew the policy change would only last until I was out of the building. The whole policy addition was a farce and I knew it. These guys weren't going to do the honorable thing and actually cover my little girl.

I raised the Glock and showed it to the woman. She stepped back, her hand frantically feeling for the door.

"Close the door when you leave," I ordered. "I'm going to shoot Mr. Rambis now. You'll want to call the police."

She turned back around, thought better of it, and left the room, slamming the door shut behind her.

I sat upright in my chair. I arched my back and unscrewed the cap on my Arrowhead water. "Aaah!" I said after a long swill and then wiped my mouth with the sleeve of my chocolate brown uniform. Then I returned the gun to a horizontal plane, its muzzle pointed directly at Rambis' torso.

"Do you want to be a pretty corpse?"

"What?"

"Do you want me to shoot you in the heart or the head?"

"Neither one. Can't we--"

"Discuss? Do you remember how much discussion you gave me? You hung up on me, you son of a bitch up here in your ivory tower. Hung up on me when my daughter was sick and needed medicine! My baby girl needing care that you alone could have made happen! And what did you do instead? Hung up on me!"

I realized I had lost it, but I didn't care any longer. They were going to cancel so I decided to get my payback in advance.

I squeezed off a shot which hit Rambis in his right shoulder. He flew back in his chair, his head hitting the executive headrest. Then he flopped forward, bent at the waist, staunching the flow of blood with his hand.

"I'm shot!" he cried.

"No shit," I said. "Let me write that down and put it in my file."

"Please. I was only doing my job. Ow-ow-ow!"

"Dear, dear."

Rambis got angry. "Did you never have a job that made you do unpleasant things? That's what I do!"

"Like screw people over? Not really."

"I need an ambulance." Rambis stood and leaned against his desk.

I took aim and shot him in the other shoulder. The shot tore into his shoulder capsule and hit bone, which slammed Rambis back against the leather chair. He slid down its high back until he was sitting again, bleeding from the shoulders, and blinking in disbelief.

"Tell your secretary that if the cops come busting in here I'm going to shoot you in the face."

"I can't work the phone."

I leaned across the desk. "What's her intercom?"

"Zero."

I pushed zero and a female voice answered. "Mr. Rambis? We're hearing gunshots!"

"Tell her!" I shouted.

"Don't let the police in here. He'll shoot me if they try to come in!"

"They're in the elevator right now!"

"Don't let them in!"

"I'll stop them!"

I sat back in my chair and twirled the pistol around my trigger finger.

"Look, it didn't go off," I said. I twirled it again. Again, it didn't go off.

Rambis moaned. He was in agony, bent forward at the waist clutching his hands to both shoulders and rocking up and back in his chair.

"Now you know how my Amelia feels," I said. "She hurts all day every day. And you let her!"

I drew down on Rambis, aiming the gun at his right hand where it was pressed hard against his left shoulder. I pulled the trigger and the muzzle erupted again. Rambis screamed, his hand shattered where the third bullet ripped through it then tunneled inside his shoulder.

"Ow-ow-ow!" cried Rambis. "Just kill me, then! Don't let me suffer, please!"

"Nope. It's not going to be like that, Rambis. We're going to wait this out."

"What's that mean?"

"We're going to wait here until my daughter gets her treatment."

"What's that mean?"

"It means get your secretary on the line. It's time to negotiate with the police."

I leaned across the desk and again jabbed zero.

"Officers, this is Carlos Pritchett. Mr. Rambis is calling to ask for a medicine for a little girl. Tell them, Rambis."

Rambis turned his face toward the phone and said the girl's name, her location, and that she would need to receive medicine or else she would die.

There was a long silence on the other end.

Then, "How do we know this is Mr. Rambis?"

"Ohhhhh--" groaned Rambis.

"Give them your social."

"My what?"

"Tell them your social security number. That's something only you would know."

Before he could do that, Leona's voice came on the line. "Never mind, Mr. Rambis, I told them that's your voice talking. You want the girl to get medicine or the UPS man will shoot you. Duly noted."

Before the line went dead, I leaned forward and shouted into the intercom.

"And gather up the board of directors. I want to address those sons of bitches!"

Of course, that didn't happen. But what did happen was I wired my gun to Rambis' throat and taped it to my hand. If I went down, the force of the fall would pull the trigger and Rambis would die. Then I blindfolded Rambis. In this manner, I managed to extricate us from the GCIA building and make our way to my rental vehicle. There, I cut Rambis loose, climbed into my rental, and made my escape. In the rearview, I saw Rambis sink to his knees and pedestrians run to his aid. He would be all right.

Even as I was making my escape, my mind was whirring.

Reason had failed.

The insurance company would again dishonor its promises.

Which meant I was back to square one.

# Chapter 12

After the First Commercial fiasco, we met at a Denny's just outside Ocean Beach. It had been selected pre-robbery as the place where our crew would gather if we got separated during the robbery. I arrived there at eight-forty-five on the fifth night after the robbery. I was fifteen minutes early on purpose. I wanted to see who Phaeton brought with him or if he even dared to show up. I suspected him showing up was somewhere around one percent, maybe less.

The waitress strolled up, snapped her gum, and stuck a fist to her hip without a word of greeting.

I looked up at her. "Menu?"

"Sure. Right back."

She returned with a Denny's menu protruding from a cracked plastic cover. It was greasy inside and out. Good, the place felt like home.

"Maybe just coffee right now." I didn't want her coming and going in case Phaeton showed.

The waitress studied me. "You look exhausted, mister. You look like you need a bite."

My head came up and I fully met her gaze. She wasn't going to just go away and leave me alone. "Perceptive, aren't we? All right. How about a chicken fried steak and mashed potatoes with green beans? Apple pie with cheese and coffee. Water for now."

"Now you're talking! I like a man who eats."

Now I looked her over more closely. Her eyes looked at me tenderly. She had seen right through my hard-boiled shell. I hadn't eaten since last night and then it was only a plate of peel-and-eat shrimp at South Coast in OB after I got back from L.A.

Suddenly I was famished and just as suddenly felt like I wanted to hang my head and cry-- something I would never in a million years do--at least not so anyone would see. I had lost Chris and the Gnome and the Wheel, and Ramsey wasn't answering my calls. It was very lonely just then, having survived that gunfight and then shooting Rambis and making yet another getaway.

Now I had cops after me in Los Angeles and San Diego counties both. Still, I had sworn I wouldn't go to prison and I had done what was necessary to keep the promise I'd made to myself about that. I wasn't going to die in prison, no matter how many innocent men and women went to heaven. "Better them than me," I swore under my breath, thinking about the cops and Rambis after the waitress had headed for the order wheel with my selections.

I had commandeered the last booth on the right. I was sitting with my back to the wall, facing the arriving diners as they were led in by the hostess. It allowed me to see Phaeton when he came in. Then the son of a bitch made me. I felt the Glock bulging in my rear waistband. Even the gun knew it was time.

"You were hoping I didn't make it, right?" was the first thing I said to Phaeton.

The man's face was anguished and his lip actually trembled. He reached across the table to shake hands. I ignored the gesture. "Sit the fuck down," I whispered grimly.

"Look, I'm just here for my cut. I know you're--"

"No, you don't know shit about me. But I know everything about you, you stupid bastard. You got my entire crew killed and that makes me a very unhappy man. I told you I would take you down if you fired that weapon and yet here you are. Do you have a death wish, coming in here?"

Phaeton shot a look over both shoulders and then leaned confidentially across the table. "I'm here to make it up to you. I know where there's an even better score."

I leaned closer. "Oh yeah? You get my best friend killed and you think you can make it up to me with money? Are you fucking nuts? Do I look to you like I just balanced a ball on my nose over at SeaWorld? Huh? Do I look that stupid to you? No, you've got thirty seconds to tell me why I shouldn't just put your lights out right here, right now. I'm waiting to hear."

"The guy was making threats. He said he was an Iraq veteran and he had a concealed carry permit! He said he was going to draw down on me the second I turned my back! It was dealer's choice, Ant! I did what I thought you would have wanted!"

"Me? Hold on, asshole, you're not seriously going to try to lay this off on me, are you? What *I* would have wanted? *Ser*iously?"

"All right, so I shouldn't have bought his story. Foresight is twenty-twenty."

"It's hindsight, asshole."

"What?"

"It's hindsight that's twenty--fuck you, Phaeton! You killed that guy because you wanted to. Not because he posed any kind of threat. Well, I told you, mister, if you fired that gun you were finished."

"So you're going to kill me? Is that it?" Now Phaeton was leaning away from the table and my right hand had dropped below the table lip. I was going for the gun in my waistband. I grabbed it out and jumped to my feet and and shoved it against Phaeton's throat before he could even react.

"On your feet, asshole. We're going outside."

"I'm not going anywhere with you!" Phaeton cried. He lunged away from me. I was an instant away from snapping the trigger, when I felt a hand press against the small of my back. I turned my head slightly to see.

"They're out of green beans," the waitress said softly. "Is corn okay?"

"What?"

"Don't do that in here," she whispered. "Three cops just came in and sat down at the counter on Tess's side."

I slid the firearm back inside my waistband. I shot a look at Phaeton, who realized he had been spared by the police. Then Phaeton was up and walking away, exiting the restaurant, and there was nothing I could or would do to stop him. I took one step toward the door but looked around in time to see one of the cops leaning back from the counter, staring my way. With that, I stopped and turned back to the waitress and said, very loudly, "Ma'am, where's the restrooms?"

She made a mini-production out of showing me to the men's room and turned and smiled at the police officers once her customer was steered along. The cops returned to ordering, ignoring the far end of the restaurant now.

I stood at the sink and felt myself shaking. I was on overload and way out of my element. I wasn't a killer and I'd never shot people before. At least not until Rambis. Yet there I was just minutes ago, actually ready to kill Phaeton. I shook my head. Way out of my league.

"Shut it down," I told my reflection. "It's only adrenalin. You're gonna make it."

I sat back down in my booth and moved the chicken fried steak around on my plate. I was nearly crying, I was so upset.

I got up, paid my bill, and walked out into the dark parking lot where my car was waiting. There was already a paid-up, fully furnished studio apartment waiting for me not six blocks from the San Diego State University campus. It was the kind of area where turnover was high and no one paid much attention to anyone coming and going. I had lined it up before First Commercial. I had known I would need to go there at some point. I decided that it would be good to go there tonight and take a long shower and stretch out on the queen size bed. There was beer in the fridge and vodka in the freezer. I would be fine and tomorrow would be a new day.

In the darkness of my car, I reached back and found the duffel bag on the floor behind the passenger's seat. I felt its contents--a kind of lumpy, undifferentiated collection thought valuable by many strangers. It was always fun to dig through the contents of safe deposit boxes and see what floated to the surface. Tonight would be no different. I would get into bed with a cold glass of vodka, dump the bag's contents onto the bedspread, and paw through everything I had managed to escape with. Maybe there was something there; maybe not. But at least there was *some*thing to show for all our efforts. There was no cash: that had gone down with Chris and my tool bag. By now the money was safely back inside the vault at First Commercial.

The money was everything. I felt the tears wash across my eyes as I thought about the one thing that mattered to me anymore: Amelia, my daughter, and her thousand dollar pills. Without the money I was to take in at First Commercial, she would suffer. And I had failed. Thanks to a man named Phaeton, I had failed. There would be no money, no more pills for Amelia. It was a predicament that I could visit in my head only momentarily. It was just too much to wrestle with. So I forced myself to push beyond. I didn't know how, I couldn't say from where, but the money would come. By all that was holy, it would come.

But first there was Ramsey. I would swing by there tonight. With the info Ramsey would provide to me, Phaeton wouldn't live to see another day.

I pulled onto the on-ramp heading south to Chula Vista. Ramsey had a condo there across the street from the beach and it was still early.

I sped up onto the I-5 and melted into the traffic flow. Then my true mission forced its way into my mind. I took the next off-ramp and curled back to San Diego.

My daughter needed money more than Phaeton needed killing.

# Chapter 13

"Leticia," Hanover finally said to me Sunday night, "your eyes look like hot coals. Get home and try to get a good night's sleep before tomorrow. You're going to need to be sharp for the legal side of this thing."

He was right. I was tired and I took heed. By nine o'clock Sunday night I was home and in bed. I'd had yet another fight with my boyfriend, Rudy Monsorre. Which was nothing new; we fought every other time we were together. Even though Monsorre had left me just two days ago, leaving me emotionally ripped wide open, I managed to go straight to sleep. There would be time to deal with all that later. For now, being in my own bed and drinking down a half glass of wine was enough. It was lights out and I slept straight through until this morning, when I jumped out of bed and headed for the shower.

Monday morning, back at the office, I checked my photographs of the people in the bank. I compared the faces to the close-ups I took of the people I interviewed. By doing this I could confirm that I was finished interviewing all of the bank employees and all of the customers present when the robbery took place. It was very unusual for an assistant district attorney to conduct the field interviews; that would ordinarily be done by the detectives. But this time, with four dead police officers and several dead bad guys, Hanover and I decided that I should take the lead, so I did. The interviews were done in tandem, me and another detective who was doing follow-up once I was finished. So all in all it was very thorough and I was happy with our work.

The robbery had taken place on the Navy's Friday payday. After all was said and done, all the men and women of the Navy who went to First Commercial and traded checks for cash, came away paid in full. By Monday noon, I was talking with a lieutenant of detectives who had just asked me whether I'd heard of the cop who said, "Sometimes I use words I don't understand so I sound more photosynthesis."

I was laughing when my phone buzzed. A man was waiting to speak to someone about the robbery. He was claiming he was present when it was being planned. Did I have time? Of course,

I said, send him right in. I waved to the lieutenant to keep his seat and listen in. The lieutenant was John Wainwright and he was a nineteen-year veteran on the cusp of retirement. By the end of the year he would be rocking and sleeping late, but for now, he would love to witness the execution of the armed robber responsible for the death of the five cops. In fact, he would insert the needle himself, he told me. I had promised to do what I could in that regard. While we both knew the lieutenant would never handle the needle or trigger the plungers that pumped the paralyzing agent, we also knew we might both personally witness the robber's execution. Already a count in the indictment against John Doe listed first degree murder in its sub-text. I was alleging special circumstances, which meant I was seeking the death penalty. I would settle for no less.

Into my office came the caller. He was an athletic looking man, maybe thirty-five or forty, strong, muscular arms and neck, bald on top with very long hair on the sides and in back. He wore a gold earring in each ear and constantly groomed his dark mustache with his fingers after he had taken a seat in a visitors' chair.

"I'm Leticia Cross," I told him. "This is Lieutenant John Wainwright of the San Diego PD. We were just talking about the case. You're saying you know something about the planning?"

He gave me a very sly dog look, telling me with his eyes and face that he had something to trade, something I would be very interested in hearing.

"I do. I was there."

He had my interest. Sly or not, I'd take whatever I could find at that point.

"Why don't you give me your name first?"

"Vincent Phaeton. But everybody just calls me by my last name."

"All right, Mr. Phaeton."

"Just Phaeton is good enough."

"All right, Phaeton, where and when were you in on the planning?"

"I met up with the crew not thirty minutes before it went down. I know everyone involved. But I need immunity before we go any further. Can you give me that?"

Lieutenant Wainwright looked away. This one was my call.

"Maybe," I replied, "and maybe not. Did you fire any weapon at the police?"

"No, I was gone before the police arrived. That's not exactly right. I was heading down the sidewalk in a normal walk when the cop cars started coming up the street. No one gave me a second look."

"So your answer is no, you didn't shoot at anyone."

A sly look came across his face again. We were playing a game. "Now I didn't quite say that. You asked me did I shoot at the police. I did not shoot at the police."

"Did you shoot at anyone else?"

"Well, that's just it. Certain individuals are going to say I did. Can I get immunity regardless?"

"Do you know the identities of the men who robbed the bank and shot it out with the police?"

"I do."

"Could you point them out in a book of pictures?"

"I sure could. Easy."

"Would you testify against them?"

"Well, that's just it. I already have a record for armed robbery. Wouldn't that look bad if you had me testify?"

He obviously knew all about impeachment of a witness with evidence of prior bad acts. If he did in fact have a conviction on his record it would lessen his efficacy as a witness. He would definitely be impeached. But, hey, the feds did it with mob guys every day of the week. I would have no problem in doing it with these lesser lights out here in San Diego. In fact, the argument could be made that you would expect one of the guys involved in the robbery to of course have a criminal record. You would be surprised if he didn't. The truth was, people without criminal records didn't usually just step up to the head of the line and rob a bank. They would start with mom-and-pops and liquor stores, not banks. Then they would get caught, get a record, do a nickel in prison and then come out and rob a bank in order to set things right, as most of them would put it. Getting even was huge with perps. So of course Phaeton would have a record and I could work with that well enough.

"It wouldn't look great, but it would be expected by any jury that you would have a record. But, first things first. Your priors aren't sex crimes, are they? Juries hate guys with sex crimes on their record."

"No sex crimes."

"No child molests, kiddie sex stuff?"

"Can't help you there. The sex stuff wasn't ever my thing. Sure, there were plenty of times I could have undressed a teller or a Korean behind a cash register in a liquor store, but I never did. Just wasn't my thing, you know what I mean?"

"Why don't you tell me about your priors?"

"I've been popped twice on armed robbery."

"You're ready for life without parole then if you get popped on this one."

He smiled. It was again a sly smile, but it was a smile meaning we were both on the same page. "That's why I'm here, Ms. Cross. I can't do life."

"Anything besides armed robbery?"

"Minor stuff. Oh, yeah, there was a GTA and a B and E, but those got reduced and I got credit for time served."

"So you had trouble making bail." It wasn't a question. I was just making a note to myself.

"Yes. I can't make bail this time, either. That's why I need immunity."

"Well, I'm interested. I'd be lying if I said I wasn't interested. I've got a street full of dead police officers, so I'm very willing to talk, Mr. Phaeton."

He looked at me without comment.

"Here's what I can do. If you can give me actionable information that results in an arrest and indictment, I can offer immunity."

"Use immunity or full immunity?"

My, the man certainly knew his law.

"I only ever give use immunity. Never full, as you put it, or transactional, as I put it."

"Use is good. I can roll with that."

"All right. Are you ready to give me a statement right now?"

"No. I need immunity in writing." Another sly smile. "Just so's there's no confusion on down the road."

Smart man. I'd want the same thing. I'd never trust a cop unless a promise to help was in writing. I'd never give a district attorney a statement unless my immunity was recited in writing. Phaeton must have gone to the same law school I attended.

I told him to go wait in the waiting room. I told him that I'd dictate and print out a use immunity agreement. We talked about other possible crimes with the same crew--of which there were none--and agreed what facts the immunity would address, and then I was ready to dictate.

While he cooled his heels in the DA's reception area, I went to work. Wainwright excused himself and went back to work, telling me that I obviously had things under very good control. I thanked him and he left.

Two hours later, I had Vincent Phaeton's statement and I had the file photo of the man named Carlos and had put it on the wire.

The hunt for Carlos Pritchett was underway.

Meanwhile, Phaeton left my office and toddled off down the street, a signed get-out-of-jail card in his shirt pocket. He deserved it. He'd told me enough about Carlos to enjoy his execution, including the fact that Carlos had summarily executed an Afghanistan veteran of the U.S. Marine Corps who had been waiting in the tellers' line.

Phaeton had witnessed the whole thing and was willing to testify and help put the needle in the killer's arm.

I could hardly wait.

Oh, he added at the end, one more thing.

Carlos was wearing a monkey mask.

# Chapter 14

I was fond of telling people I actually had two faces. There was my freeway face--lipstick and a glower--that I put on during the mad drive down the 5 into San Diego every weekday morning. And there was my courtroom face: a hint of blush, lipstick and eyeliner, that I applied before the first court appearance of the day.

I began life in my windowless office at the San Diego County District Attorney's office just before eight a.m. when I arrived on the scene of that day's accident-in-the-making and started fielding calls from cops and vics and lawyers. I was a lifer on the staff of the DA and I was on-call 24/7 so there was very little differentiation between my personal life and my professional life. What little difference there was between the two was probably best demonstrated by my interchangeable two faces. Either one was suitable for freeway maneuvering; either one worked with judges and juries; but neither one had been enough to get my ticket punched on the Happiness Express, not since taking up with Monsorre, who had made it very clear he would never marry. A very sore point between us most days.

Here's the algebra of our relationship: I was a plain Jane. I was. And he was a GQ model. Even in my best moments I would do just about anything to hold onto him. Which was bad, very bad, because Monsorre was a crook. I know, I know, district attorneys don't hang with crooks-- that's what the citizens think. But the truth is, some of us get kinky after we're around it enough. Some of us are actually attracted to bad boys. I know I was. Plus, my body wanted to squeeze out a few kids.

When my thinking wasn't skewed by my time clock, I considered myself totally insane for taking up with a thief. What the hell was I even thinking? I chastised myself. It was something I kept under wraps, always careful to leave no trail from me back to Monsorre. At least I did my best not to. With a long sigh and flicker of fear in my belly, I admitted to myself I hadn't done this perfectly and maybe never would. This admission alone had cost me many hours of sleep over the past week. I had called Monsorre and left a message on his answer machine and I'd never done that before. He had dropped out of my life for three days and I was in a panic. So the message wound up on his machine. If I could only take it back, but I couldn't. Now he had evidence against me should he ever need it. "Damnation!" I whispered glumly at my desk on Tuesday morning. "Damnation."

I checked my watch. 8:14. The others would begin arriving any minute.

No sooner had I taken my eyes off my watch, than here they came. Three prosecutors and four detectives drifting in; my four visitors' chairs weren't going to do it.

"Let's move it to Conference Four," I said, and began gathering my things to lead the way. "Too many bodies for my hole-in-the-wall."

They turned and followed.

I stationed myself at the head of the eight-foot table in Conference Four. Everyone else managed to arrange themselves somewhat comfortably around the table.

I launched into my talk, welcoming everyone to the First Commercial bank robbery team and telling them I was happy they were all onboard. Detective partners would meet up with those present now and get the skinny later on. Plus there would be others.

Then, "I want to arrange ourselves in four teams this morning, each team reporting to me. So let me start with Andy Templeton on my left. Andy, you'll have Team One. Your assignment will be the interior of the bank. Whatever happened inside is your case."

Andy Templeton, a cherubic-looking prosecutor with a dozen years under his belt, brightened. "Good. I like working bank robberies."

"Plus the homicide," I reminded him.

"Yes, there's that too. What about the FBI? What's their role?"

"They've declined the prosecution over at the U.S. Attorney's office. I just got the official call yesterday, which is fine. It will make for less coordination problems for all of us. The whole enchilada goes to you, Andy. So let's run with that. Now listen up, people. We'll be doing Friday reporting. Everything you have on the case goes in a memo, on my desk, before noon on Fridays. I don't want any late excuses. You can all do this, so let's go for it."

"Who are my cops?" asked Andy. "Do I get to choose them?" He was looking eagerly around the room at the eight or nine detectives. There were some very capable dicks on board, all selected by me.

"You'll have Sargas and Willoughby." I nodded at the two detectives, whom I knew personally from prior cases.

"Excellent!" said Andy. "Exactly my choices." He smiled at the detectives who, in grand detective fashion, didn't break from their poker faces. Not even a nod at Andy.

"Moving right along." I then assigned teams to the police homicides--the officers who had lost their lives during the violent shootout in the streets. Each homicide received its own team.

Then, "Edward Hanratty I'm assigning to me personally. Ed, I need you to work hand-in-glove with me on day-by-day."

Because Hanratty wasn't a street dick but rather was a full-time investigator for the DA's office, he could afford a nod of recognition at me. "Got it," he said. Hanratty was a Mormon with good family ties and a set of strong ethics that touched every case he worked. The last thing he would do on a case would be to manufacture or plant evidence, so I knew I was getting a man I could rely on absolutely. It would give me the comfort zone I required while working up the overview of the prosecution itself. Which reminded me, I needed to explain my role.

"And here's what Hanratty and I will be covering. First of all, we're going to ramrod the entire investigation and the five independent prosecutions that will actually be folded into one prosecution led by me. We will follow up on witnesses you may have interviewed from whom we need additional information or who we feel might take us down a new rabbit hole worth following. That's for openers. Questions?"

No one raised a hand.

"Good. Secondly, I'm going to be responsible for all court appearances and lead counsel at trial. In and of itself that should require two full-time prosecutors but you all know about the staffing shortage we have, what with the county hiring freeze. So it comes to rest on my shoulders. This doesn't mean the rest of the attorneys in the room won't handle courtroom duties yourselves. You will, and that's why I need reports by Friday noon so I can make court appearance staffing calls for the coming week. Everyone on board with this?"

Again, no raised hands.

Then Hanratty himself slowly raised a hand. "Who do we have so far we're going after?"

"Who are the defendants? Now that's an interesting question. Glad you asked, Ed. So far, we have Carlos Pritchett, according to our CI. We just landed him. Carlos was the mastermind. He's the guy who's going down for felony-murder. I want the death penalty on this guy."

"Who else?" asked another dick in the back of the room. "This seems like a lot of firepower for one guy."

I nodded. "That's just it. I expect you all to develop new leads for us, possible defendants, people who had a role in making this thing happen. In particular, there's a man named Ramsey that Ed and I will be working up. We're thinking he's the one who developed the plan and then probably sold the job to Pritchett. We're just guessing at this point, though. But get to the bottom of it we will. I can promise you that."

"What about the dead bad guys?"

"You'll follow up on those. Every team gets a dead bad guy. Family, friends, phone records, bank statements—everything gets eyeballs."

"Any defense lawyers snooping around yet?" asked one of the deputy district attorneys.

I shrugged. "Some guy from Chicago called me. Something like Grisham or Gresham. He said he would be associating local counsel and then enter his appearance officially once he got court approval to appear in California."

"What do we have on the guy? Is he a big name?"

I smiled a sour smile. "Are you maybe suggesting I might be outgunned here, Shep?"

The prosecutor named Shep shook his head violently. "No, no, no. Nothing like that, Letty. We all know about you. I'm just wondering if you shouldn't tell us your choice for second chair right up front so you have all the firepower you need, too."

I smiled a sweetly disarming smile at the room. "I'm working on that. More will be revealed so try to contain yourselves and try not to wet yourselves."

Chuckles all around.

"So, that's about it from me. Let's hit the ground running today and make this the most successful prosecution ever run out of the San Diego District Attorney's office, shall we?"

Everyone voiced encouragement and buy-in. I was left with a good feeling about my team of prosecutors and detectives. This was going to be one hell of a show.

Then they broke up and I returned to my office. A half-dozen yellow phone messages had been spread across my desk where I couldn't miss them. I sighed and picked up my phone. It was time to dial and interact.

But more than that, it was time to kick some serious ass.

# Chapter 15

MICHAEL

The daughter's brush-up against death seized my heart and squeezed. Squeezed so hard I decided I had to jump in and try to help with an angle where I hadn't been paid to intervene. That made no difference; I was in all the way with Amelia Pritchett. All the way.

On my next visit to San Diego, I called Washburn J. Rambis of Grand Canyon Insurance and Annuity that afternoon. I had obtained the bank vice-president's direct line from Carlos. I started in on Rambis.

The voice came across as forced, an attempt at projecting great authority.

"This is Washburn Rambis," it said. "Mr. Gresham?"

"Thanks for taking my call, Mr. Rambis. By way of introduction, I am the attorney for Carlos Pritchett and his family. It appears that you are the vice-president of underwriting where the decision was made not to cover Carlos's daughter."

"That's the bastard who shot me! We have nothing to discuss, sir."

The phone went dead. So I re-dialed and he came on again.

"Please, I said, this is a business call concerning your employer. Whatever else you think, Mr. Rambis, this is your employer's business I'm calling about. Please don't hang up. Now, it's true that you are the vice-president of underwriting where the decision was made not to cover Carlos' daughter, am I correct?"

"Well, that's not exactly what's happened here. We didn't choose not to cover her. Our position is that an application was never submitted for the daughter. So there was no decision in that regard. It was a nonstarter."

"I see. Well, let me ask this. How much would the monthly premium be for you to cover her from this point forward?"

"I'm afraid that's not possible."

"Why is that?"

"Because we've discontinued that particular package. It's no longer for sale by Grand

Canyon."

"And you discontinued it when?"

"Within the last six months, I'm sure."

"Which would have been *after* she applied?"

"Again, Mr. Gresham, she never applied. I'll be happy if you'll just drop that assertion. It's not factual."

"Let me approach this from a different slant. This young girl needs a cure. Insurance coverage would probably buy her a cure. Without coverage from Grand Canyon she doesn't get her chance. Does this make a difference to Grand Canyon?"

"Mr. Gresham, I have had enormous sympathy for this girl's situation. But Grand Canyon can't just cover medical cases willy-nilly. We wouldn't last in business if we covered people just because their plight was desperate. That's a best-world scenario. We don't operate in that best-world. I'm sorry."

"What would you say in response to the insurance bad faith lawsuit I'm preparing to file against you personally and against Grand Canyon this afternoon? Would that give you pause? Would you have second thoughts?"

"Sue away, Mr. Gresham. We have lawyers too, you know."

"I'll do that, Mr. Rambis. I'll sue you and your employer and everything else over there that wears a suit and left fingerprints on this file."

"Well, I think I've spent about all the time with you that I can. I'm hanging up now, Mr. Gresham."

"Thank you, Mr. Rambis. I'll be seeing you at your deposition."

We hung up.

I took a cab over to a Denny's to meet with Carlos. We ordered coffee and I reported the conversation to him.

"So you're saying they won't even consider settlement?" asked Carlos.

"That's what I'm saying. There are no options here but to sue them. What's worse, they're writing your daughter's case off as a business decision only. They will entertain no humanitarian perspective."

Carlos's eyes narrowed and he slowly nodded. "There are options. We just haven't talked about them because you've threatened to turn me in if I mention them again."

"Carlos--"

"Don't worry, Michael, I won't do anything rash. Your license is safe."

"It's not my license, Carlos. Your daughter needs you free and able to help her. To visit her. You can't be there for her if you're in jail."

"Right you are. So what do we do?"

"I have my associate, Randall Cowher, preparing the lawsuit as we speak. It will be filed this afternoon and served on the defendants before the end of the week."

"And will that bring rain?"

I shrugged and told him I honestly didn't think it would. Why, I was wondering for the ten thousandth time in my legal career, did men do these things to other men? Much less to little children? It angered me and reinforced my resolve to go after the insurance company and leave it in a smoking heap on the courtroom floor.

"It won't bring rain, no. The underwriters, which Rambis operates, probably will never have much to do with the case. Sure, we'll take Rambis' deposition and work him over a good deal, but he really has no skin in the game. He's virtually untouchable."

"I hate hearing that."

"I know you do, Carlos. But I'm only a lawyer and that's not much else I can offer."

Carlos slid out of the booth. "Then we're done here. I appreciate your honesty. I appreciate your help."

"What about your wife's brother, the surgeon? Will he help with the additional funding you need to become self-insured?"

"He says it's a bad time for him. His group just invested in a building for their practice and he's over-extended. He has no equity he can tap and make us a loan."

"Damn, I hate hearing that."

"So we're basically finished, Michael. There's no place else to turn."

"I am so sorry, Carlos. Words cannot express how this breaks my heart for your little girl. Please forgive me that I can't do more to help."

Carlos reached across the table and shook my hand.

"No need. No need. You've done everything possible, Michael. Thank you."

"We're looking at a preliminary hearing on your case next Tuesday. Please don't forget. Let's meet here at eight o'clock that morning. Does that work for you?"

"That'll work."

We said our goodbyes and Carlos left the restaurant. By the time I had paid the bill and exited the restaurant, Carlos was nowhere to be seen.

I returned to my hotel room and drew open the curtains so I could see the bay. I sat there on my bed, watching the clouds wash and re-wash the sky over Coronado in the distance. Always making weather, always changing the light on the waves, the clouds were always there, friendly colorists, light-benders, nature's grace. I allowed myself to feel the anger I had toward insurance companies that abused people--which included all companies, I guessed. Watching the sky and clouds, I found myself wishing there was some comparable art in human nature. Some comparable dynamic capable of humanizing people so that sick little kids got their needs met.

I watched the sky and wondered what would happen to her.

# Chapter 16

LETICIA

As it turned out, I was second-in-command of the San Diego District Attorney's Major Crimes Task Force. The notion of me working on "major crimes" was very appealing. It impressed me, and impressed those around me.

But there was another part to it, an equally important part, to my way of thinking. That part involved my boyfriend, Rudy Monsorre, a man whose days regularly crossed the line between legal and not-so-legal. A little more about my boyfriend: Monsorre ran a chop-shop ring, a notorious gang of thugs who engaged in carjackings, VIN obliteration, and re-sale. Hungry for a new Mercedes AMG or Jag with all the bells and whistles? Just call Monsorre and he'd have your dream car ready to drive away by morning. And the price was unimaginable: nothing in his Chula Vista warehouse cost more than ten thousand dollars. Nothing. Monsorre toiled away stealing cars and reselling them 24/7, but occasionally he took a few hours off and crashed at my condo, where we'd face off in bed and fornicate like rabbits. Questions were never asked and details never given in either direction. We were together because we liked sex with each other and because there was a chemistry between us that just worked. Sure, it wasn't a real relationship but it was the best I had going at that time.

Here's a little bit more on our relationship. Some of this is hard to admit. I had never been accused of being beautiful. Quite the opposite, in fact: starting in high school I had been branded as "homely" and "plain" and "dull." My parents tried everything: braces on my teeth, Lasik for my eyes, even an ear reduction, but what they were left with in the end was the same homely girl with straight teeth and 20-20 vision whose ears never attracted attention. Same Leticia as before--homely, plain, and dull. So when, in my mid-twenties, I unexpectedly attracted Rudy Monsorre, everyone was delighted if not just a little shocked. This was because Monsorre was breathtakingly handsome, turned-out, and accomplished. His father was an economics professor at San Diego State University and his mother was a cellist (second chair) with the symphony. Monsorre had matriculated college just after high school, but then had dinked around, preferring football games witnessed through the haze of the contents of wineskin bags to scholarly pursuits, much to the chagrin of mother and father. A fourteen-month stint in Afghanistan with the Special Forces turned him into a better physical specimen and a more knowledgeable firearms specialist. He returned to the states ready to earn his way and make his mark no matter what it took. But carjackings came easily to him and the money was there for the taking.

We met in court, actually. He was the defendant on a misdemeanor theft charge and I was the prosecutor. There was a brief meeting with his attorney as we discussed disposition, a meeting that both Rudy and I attended. I guess I caught his eye, because he called me at my office the following day and asked if we could meet up for coffee. He said he had something serious to discuss with me. Thinking he might have inside information about some kind of crime, I somewhat reluctantly agreed to meet with him. I say "somewhat" because there was also a part of me that thought he was darling and it would be fun to see him again.

So how would a ball-busting dynamo like Rudy Monsorre end up with a plain Jane like me? Because the true nature of his wanting to meet with me surfaced almost immediately over coffee and bagels.

I was Major Crimes at the DA's office and Monsorre was engaged in just that--major crimes. He ran a chop shop--not a victimless crime but at least there was no violence involved. It was a property crime and that made it smaller--in my mind. All of this I became aware of only after we had spent two nights together in my bedroom. Then he finally admitted what he wanted from me. Whenever the task force was moving on automobile theft and re-sale of stolen vehicles, he solicited me to get word to him just before it went down, whereupon he would close down operations for a week and vanish.

Don't get me wrong. I was a bold, aggressive, and fearless prosecutor. Woe to the defendant who found him- or herself on the wrong end of a Leticia Cross indictment. Woe to the unwary who went into court thinking a plea bargain with "time served" was just around the corner. These very same people would, in a matter of a month or two of court processing, find themselves looking at ten or fifteen or twenty-five year terms of incarceration at State Prison or San Quentin. In the twinkling of an eye I could transform a minor type of crime into a major stretch in prison. That's just how good I had become and everyone around the office knew that about me. No one was surprised, then, when I went to Major Crimes and no one was surprised when I was tasked with prosecuting the First Commercial National Bank robbery featuring

Carlos Pritchett.

A few fun facts about me after I graduated to Major Crimes, the big time. Yoga in the morning and Pilates at night. A frequent habitué at California vineyards. Nordstrom's St. John Collection and Armani office wear. Pot but no coke, thank you very much. Caribbean vacations where I would meet up with Rudy Monsorre and make underwater videos of bubbly lovemaking. Toughest and best prosecutor in the DA's office. Defense lawyers cringed when first spotting me at the prosecution table on a new case. Immediately they would begin preparing clients to expect long, tough sentences to prison. I never met a stone that I wouldn't turn over when I was after evidence of a crime. Witness statements and documents alike found their way into my briefcase and made their way into courtrooms where they were flaunted before juries who never hesitated to convict. So when the Carlos Pritchett file surfaced on my desk after that day at the bank, the day of the robbery, I was quick to exclaim, "Oh, look, everyone! Another asshole on the night train to Q!"

As in San Quentin.

I immediately made him out to be a cop killer and armed robber. I already had Phaeton in my clutches to finger Carlos for the murder of the veteran in the teller's line at First Commercial. That would have to be enough because, despite my investigators' best efforts, no video could be found of Carlos returning fire at the police as he made his getaway. Instead, he could be seen dragging his friend Chris Courtney by the arm as he tried to help his friend to safety. Chris didn't make it, of course, but Carlos did: all while never firing his weapon.

"Damn you," I exclaimed. "Damn you for not firing that TEC at my coppers!"

But he had fired at my coppers in the alley as he made his getaway. However, there were no cameras down the alley as there were bristling all up and down the street in front of the bank.

Over time, I spoke to all police involved that day and I learned that Carlos had, in fact, fired at the police in the alley but hadn't hit anyone. Carlos had killed or injured no one in blue. I weighed the evidence and thought I would have no problem convicting him of attempted murders...maybe, for shooting blindly at the pursuing cops. So there was that. Plus, the murder of the veteran inside the bank: with Phaeton's testimony, I had enough to send Carlos Pritchett to Death Row. On a good day, I would see the needle in his arm, while on a so-so day I would put him away for life plus 100 years. I was left hoping for a good day. I had witnessed executions that I had brought about before; this time would be even better: the man had killed a veteran, a true no-no in all courtrooms. The plan was to take his life, plain and simple. So I filed my indictments and alleged Special Circumstances, meaning I was after the death penalty. Then I shuddered. I desperately needed a smoking gun, which I didn't have. So I went to work.

I spent the day after I was tasked with the First Commercial case reviewing evidence sheets. Witness statements would come next. Having later been approached by Phaeton and giving him immunity from prosecution in return for his testimony against Carlos, I began looking for that certain piece of evidence to prove what Phaeton was saying was true, that Carlos had shot the veteran in cold blood. I had to have corroboration because Phaeton, with his priors, was impeachable. Without a solid piece of evidence to back up his story, Phaeton would be tagged by the defense lawyer with a foot-long list of prior convictions, jail time, prison stretches, and just all around bad acts--proof he was, at bottom, just another undesirable.

I narrowed my evidence review down to the gun found inside the bank, a TEC-9. It had been dusted but there were no prints. Fine, the perps were wearing gloves. But preliminary ballistics came back positive: the TEC-9 was the gun that killed the veteran. So the question became, how to tie the gun to Carlos? I went back over the police reports surrounding the weapon just in case I might have missed something. But it just wasn't there: the gun couldn't be placed in Carlos' hands.

Unless.

Unless the gun turned up in his custody. But how could that happen, I mused. The truth was, it couldn't. The gun was locked away in the evidence warehouse at SDPD. It was simply too late.

"Unless I somehow take it out of evidence and plant it on Carlos," I told Rudy.

Rudy rolled over in the bed beside me. "You get it out of evidence and I'll make sure it's connected to him. Deal?"

"I don't know. How would I do that?"

He shrugged.

I shook my head. "It's impossible. The police reports state it was found at the scene. I can't remove it and have it turn up in his car. Now, can I?"

"So what else could tie him to the dead guy?"

I thought and thought. Then, "Well, the witnesses say it was the monkey who killed the guy."

"What?"

"The robber wearing the monkey mask. *That's* who killed the veteran."

"So do you have the monkey mask?"

"No. It was never recovered."

"Then there you go. I pick up a monkey mask and let the cops find it in the car Carlos hijacked."

"That car has been located and searched and returned to the woman it belongs to."

Rudy smiled and ran his hand down my bare arm. Instant arousal.

"I'm the guy who can have that door panel off and back on in less than a minute."

I sat up in bed and placed my back against the cherry wood headboard.

"Wow. I'm liking this. What comes next?"

"An anonymous tip. Someone calls the cops and tells them where to find the mask."

"And the monkey is connected to Carlos!"

"Bingo!"

"OMG!"

# Chapter 17

## MICHAEL

My investigator, Marcel Rainford, joined me in San Diego. We took on a month-to-month lease in executive housing down by the San Diego Bay. I also expanded my single executive office into three offices to make room for him. Marcel would fit right in here. He was dark-complected and had spent years in the sun as an Interpol detective who worked the Middle East for a good portion of his career. He was also conversant in Spanish and that could prove to be very useful. Most of all, Marcel was a winner. If a case was just outright trouble for my client, Marcel had no problem digging in until he found just the right evidence we needed to raise reasonable doubt. So, I set him loose on Leticia Cross. While that wasn't a normal place to start, I needed to know everything I could about her. I usually did know everything about the prosecutors in Chicago, but California was a brand new game, like the song says.

Within two days, Marcel had his first report on my desk. Here's what it said:

*September 4, 2015.*

*Spent day staying close to Leticia Cross on orders from MG. Snapped 12 pix of her coming into Hall of Justice on Broadway and heading for elevators. Lost her there, office is in restricted area and I didn't want to be recognized. 12:35, she came downstairs with two other women, walked down a block on Broadway and entered a restaurant: Spike Africa's Fresh Fish. I followed on foot and wasn't made. I observed from outside. 13:20, they exited, proceeded toward and entered Hall of Justice, again headed for elevators. 17:54, subject emerged from basement parking in yellow Corvette; I fell in behind her.*

*18:25, arrived at condo, obtained address and unit number then surveilled until 21:00, when a good-looking young man approached Ms. Cross's unit and let himself in with his own key. He was inside until he emerged at 04:08. He was carrying a silver container and headed downstairs to the parking garage. I decided to follow.*

*I tailed the man down to the waterfront, always aware of the lack of buffer cars present during the day. He pulled up to a warehouse and a vehicle door opened. He drove inside and the door closed behind him. I now had two locations to scout out in more detail.*

 *\*\*\*\*\**

 *The following information is provided pursuant to the attorney work-product privilege and is not to be disseminated to any person, agency, or company.*

 *After ensuring Ms. Cross was at work (sighted in a courtroom beginning a trial), returned to boyfriend's warehouse and verified his presence. Earlier, I had followed him to his condo. Proceeded to his condo. Put on latex gloves. Entry was simple. Closed the door confirmed no one else on premises.*

 *[Attached: layout drawing of condo]*

 *Began in kitchen, examined drawers, cupboards and refrigerator: vodka in freezer, twelve pack of Coors beer in refrigerator. Reviewed phone setup, noticed blinking red light on answering machine, hit PLAY and listened. Message was from someone self-identified as "Letty," assume Leticia Cross. Told machine team of detectives and uniforms was headed for warehouse within next day and he should remove all vehicles. Then thanked him for Jimmy Choo shoes dropped off at her place. Re-recorded and secured message.*

 *Searched remainder of condo, found nothing incriminating. He lives a Spartan lifestyle except in his closet: he has forty suits hanging—I counted. His place is neat and tidy and there was no computer around for me to fire up.*

 *Next I will visit Leticia Cross's own condo (?) and continue this report. One more thing: I installed two video devices in boyfriend's condo. Motion activated.*

It didn't matter. My hands were shaking with excitement as I put the report back inside the Carlos folder. We had evidence that the district attorney's office was warning this particular criminal when the cops were getting close. It was astonishing and it gave me a totally different perspective on Carlos' case. I left my office to find Marcel. But then I got pissed once the thrill had passed. Marcel had committed a serious crime, according to his report, the crime of residential burglary.

He was cranked back in the highback chair in his own office, speaking on the phone. He motioned me to come on in, so I took a seat in one of the two visitors' chairs. The conversation continued for another few minutes and at the end I realized he was talking to Mrs. Lingscheit, our widowed office manager in Chicago. I had known he was sweet on her but it sounded like he was inviting her to come join him in San Diego for a week of "sun and sand." I was glad for them and not just a little surprised. I knew he'd made overtures to her before, but I didn't know it had come to the point where a night or several might be spent together. Farthest thing from my mind, truth be told. The conversation reminded me that I hadn't talked that day with Danny yet. We needed to develop a more regular routine while I was away. As for our kids, they were in Evanston with their nanny and with Danny's mother, who had moved into our spare bedroom in order to help out. The kids and I did FaceTime every day after school and again at night when bedtime prayers were said. They were thriving; I wished I could say the same thing for me. I was miserable being without my wife and without my kids, and there wasn't a damn thing I could do about it. So it wasn't with just a little jealousy that I overheard Marcel inviting my Chicago office manager to come visit.

He hung up the phone.

"See my report?"

"Burglary? Have we fallen so low we're committing burglary now, Marcel?"

I was hot. This latest jaunt could not only get me disbarred, it could put me behind bars. Pissed, was an understatement.

He shrugged and raised his eyebrows.

"That's the trouble with you lawyers. You want results but you won't accept risk. You can't have it both ways, counselor. Of all people, you should know that."

"B and E isn't mere risk, it's a crime. A felony. And recording her message? That's eavesdropping, another felony, for fucksake!"

"I know, it just doesn't get any better does it?" he said with a great smile. "We've got that lady by the short ones, Mikey. She belongs to you!"

This was Marcel at his best. He wasn't reckless--I had to give him that. So my anger ebbed slightly. Marcel could pull these stunts but he always covered his tracks. It was occurring to me that we could use Leticia Cross' phone message against her without ever really saying where we got it except to say someone had sent it to us. Someone unknown. What's more, we could use it to get something out of her we couldn't otherwise get. My mind went spinning along and I began to see how we might spare Carlos from the needle going into the case. Would that work?

Well, I don't like the felony-murder rule and that's where they had him hung up. Where Carlos didn't actually shoot the veteran or shoot any of the police officers he was nonetheless guilty of their murder just because he was involved in the bank robbery, the felony. I didn't like the rule because it gave an unfair advantage to the prosecution: they could in theory send a man like Carlos to the death chamber even though he hadn't fired one shot and even though he had told the others that he wouldn't be a part of any shots fired and that they were not under any circumstances to fire their weapons. But now we had Deputy District Attorney Leticia Cross herself committing what was potentially a very serious crime, in warning her boyfriend of an impending shakedown by the cops. Tit-for-tat and all that, I was thinking. So maybe Marcel had done us a huge. I began to rethink my initial reaction to his breaking and entering.

I lowered my voice.

"Yes, maybe we do have her by the short ones. And maybe you've just saved Carlos' life. Okay, let's leave it at that for now."

"And my next move is to get inside of her condo and see what turns up there."

"No, please, enough of this. I'm telling you to stay the hell out of her apartment. I won't be a part of that."

His face registered his displeasure. But I knew Marcel; he would comply with my order when he knew he was over the line.

"So where do you want me next, Boss?"

"Next, I want you to track down this Phaeton character and see what we can get on him. Surveillance first and then we'll get his statement out of him. I don't know how, but we'll cross that bridge when we come to it. Feel me?"

"Yes. Do we know where he's hanging out?"

"No. I'll leave that up to you."

He smiled. "Not to worry. He won't be hard to locate. Guy like that will leave a trail a mile wide."

"After that, go see this Ramsey character Carlos is talking about. He's the guy Carlos paid seventy-five grand for the First Commercial bank job. See what you can get out of him."

"What am I looking for there?"

"Well, for openers, he's the guy who put Phaeton in touch with Carlos in the first place. He might have a lead on where Phaeton's holed-up. Try him. But start with Phaeton himself before you give up and go ask Ramsey for help. We're not sure that Ramsey isn't in bed with Phaeton or, at the very least, friendly to him. Are we good on this?"

"We're good."

"All right then."

We stared at each for several minutes, then, until, at last, Marcel pulled out a cigarette, lit it, and broke off eye contact.

He was already long gone.

# Chapter 18

MICHAEL

Danny decided--with the blessing of her doctor--that she would come visit me in San Diego.

She arrived on a Monday. The sky was blue, the clouds non-existent, and the temperature 74° when she came into the airport. Perfect weather and a perfect opportunity to have my wife in my rental for however long I could persuade her to stay. She was wearing white shorts and a light sweater with a white Ralph Lauren underneath, and sandals on her feet. We retrieved her large roll-along and I placed her carry-on on top and we headed for short term parking.

On the way to my executive suite she brought me up to speed on a friend of hers whose son was arrested for drugs, and Danny, who is also a criminal lawyer like me, said she might consider defending him in court. I had the distinct feeling she was testing me to see what I'd say, but I just kept quiet. Her doctor had told me, privately, to let her set her own boundaries for what was manageable and what wasn't. When I didn't engage, she looked out her window and watched San Diego pass by.

Back at the executive suites hotel where I had a unit with two bedrooms, we got her stuff inside and then ordered a carafe of coffee from room service. We enjoyed our coffee, chewed our Danish, and made small talk about her potential drug case and about our kids. She had spent the previous afternoon with them and told me she had gone home totally exhausted and slept for twelve hours before awaking and catching the plane today.

It was time for me to return to the office and meet with Marcel. At first, I had thought about getting Danny's help with the case—she was tremendous at seeing defense opportunities—but I knew she was away from the firm on doctor's orders, so I called her a cab and instructed the driver to take her to Seaport Village on West Harbor Drive. I knew she'd love the place and I would meet her for an early dinner about four o'clock.

I was dreaming up defense scenarios with Marcel in my office just after two o'clock when my cell chimed. I whipped it out of my shirt pocket and was slightly concerned when I saw it was Danny calling.

"Do you think you could come here earlier, like maybe three?" She asked.

The day was a slow one, so I said sure I could.

"Good. I'm just missing you so much," she said in that tiny, faraway voice that anymore set my nerves on edge as I had come to associate that voice with her dissociative withdrawal from the us that was us. She was leaving, in other words, so I made myself hurry in getting to her in order to head it off.

As if that were even possible. It wasn't.

We went into a small cafe, ordered, then found a small table on the patio.

Our coffee came and Danny removed her sunglasses momentarily. It was then that I saw tears welling up.

"I made a mistake coming here," she said, "I'm scared to be in a place where I don't recognize anything."

"That can be nerve-wracking," I said. In my own travels I had once or twice become disoriented myself, I told her, which didn't change the expression on her face.

"And I'm scared, Michael, I feel like I'm letting you down and you're going to leave me."

By now there were tears rolling down her cheeks. She dabbed at them with her linen napkin but still they came. Other diners around us were taking note and I tried scowling at them to make them look away. Clearly, though, Danny had embarrassed herself and she suddenly wanted to leave. I threw a twenty on the table and let her lead us up the steps and out of there. Then I steered her to my car and we climbed inside.

We made our way through a crush of early rush-hour traffic and parked in the front lot of my long-term stay. I took her hand as we headed through the lobby and down the hallway then up two floors to my room. She didn't withdraw her hand, but neither did she return the pressure when I squeezed it once or twice just to let her know I was with her. Danny was becoming more and more distant with each step we took and, to be honest, it was making me uncomfortable. I'm not the type who is easily made uncomfortable, but her widening withdrawal was making me very sad and lonely for her. It felt like I could reach out for her but then she'd just manage to dance out of my grasp. Then I'd imagine life without her and that would make me so sad and depressed that it made me want to cry. Damned if I did; damned if I didn't--that's how it felt.

Back in the room we tried to act normal. She switched on the TV and tuned to CNN, where we watched a story about the mutilation of women's genitalia in the Middle East. I thought that was unwise to stay with, so I convinced her we should switch over and watch *Ellen,* which was always an upbeat show.

Ellen sallied forth and we watched for an hour. At the end of the show, I realized Danny hadn't begun unpacking her suitcases. So I said something, like, "Do you want me to find some drawers for your suitcase things?"

She turned abruptly around to face me. "I don't think that's necessary. I'm uncomfortable and I'm leaving to go home tonight."

Need I say my heart fell? Because it did, right on down through the floor. I was struck dumb by her words, as well. I couldn't think of a single thing to say to her that wouldn't sound clingy or angry, because actually I was both just then.

Then I said, "If you leave, you're not giving us a chance. Please stay."

"If I stay, I'm not giving me a chance. My doctor said he didn't think my coming here would hurt me but I should leave it got to be too much. Now I can see why."

"Is it something I'm doing that's hurting things?"

She looked deep into my eyes then looked away. "You couldn't be more perfect, Michael. This is about me. I'm just not doing real great right now. I need the familiarity of my own place. I'm sorry."

"Do you want me to call and make reservations?"

"No, I did that on my phone while you were watching *Ellen.*"

I hadn't even noticed. "What time's your flight?"

"With TSA junk it's about two hours off. I should leave now. I'll call a taxi."

"No, for God's sake, let me drive you."

"Please, Michael, I've put you out enough. You stay here or go out and get a nice dinner. Maybe you'll meet someone who isn't all fucked up like me."

"No! Don't say that, Danny! I love you and adore you. I don't want to meet someone else. I want you!"

"And I want you, too. But right now it's just not possible."

I needed her to give me some hope, something I could hold onto.

"Do you know when it might be possible? How long are we talking about before I get you back?"

"I don't know. Maybe next week, maybe never. I just have zero idea. My doctor doesn't know either."

With that, she pulled her luggage together and I moved it to the portico in front of the hotel. A taxi pulled in and Danny waved at him. She turned and kissed me lightly on the lips then hurried to her ride.

Then she was gone and I was alone.

I. I. I. I was trying not to make this about me.

But it was getting closer and closer to impossible.

# Chapter 19

## RUDY

Rudy Monsorre was cursing and mentally kicking himself as he drove his Mercedes AMG from his chop-shop across town west to Pacific Beach. His on-again/off-again relationship with Leticia was making him crazy. Still, today it was on again, so he was proceeding with monkey mask in hand.

Elva Reinhardt's address was on Nora. Rudy found the address and drove right on by. Then he made a U-turn and came rolling slowly back up the street, stopping a hundred feet short of Elva's driveway. Then he waited.

The woman's car had been recovered by the policed after Carlos had driven it to the San Diego airport, whipped into the parking structure, and caught a cab. He had taken the cab to within two blocks of his safe house, where he climbed out, paid the driver, and waited until the cab was out of sight before walking home. Elva Reinhardt had her Durango back the same night.

Within the hour, Reinhardt--a nondescript woman wearing an overcoat and beret--exited the house, climbed down the four steps, and unlocked the Durango SUV. She climbed inside without looking around and then backed out, swinging to her right and pulling ahead without bothering to look behind. So, she didn't see Monsorre pull in behind her and tail her from a safe distance. They wound back out to Garnet Avenue and turned south. She turned right and drove to Nimitz Boulevard. Sure enough, at a Point Loma turn-off she cornered at too great a speed and had to ride her brakes all the way up to the traffic light. Monsorre stayed three cars behind; he was sure he was invisible.

They drove up through Point Loma, stopping at the Waterfront Grill, where Elva pulled to the curb and parked at a forty-five-degree angle. She bounced out of the SUV and went directly into the restaurant. Monsorre, parked two cars beyond her, watched the mime inside as the hostess led Elva back into the dark behind the front windows. He gave it five minutes before slowly opening the driver's door on his Mercedes and coming out in a crouch. Bent double, he went behind his car and moved up to Elva's vehicle. Using a pick set, he was inside her SUV in seconds. With her door barely open, he crouched and expertly accessed the driver's door panel, slipping it open from the near side. Then the monkey mask was slipped between door metal and panel and the panel restored to its original condition. He gently locked and closed her driver's door and moved back to the rear of her vehicle, where he abruptly stood upright, snapped off his gloves, and strode boldly back to his Mercedes.

Monsorre backed out and pulled into the light traffic crossing on his left. With a whisper of acceleration, then, he was up to the corner and turning right on a yellow. Then he was headed back toward the freeway, smiling to himself as he went on his way.

Headed northbound on the 5, Monsorre took the off-ramp at La Jolla and drove up to the closest Conoco station where he knew there was a payphone. He threw it in park and jumped out and headed for the phone booth. Closing the accordion door behind, he dropped a quarter and made a call to the number he had memorized.

"San Diego Police Department," said a gruff male voice.

"I'd like to give a crime tip," said Monsorre.

"Okay. Please proceed."

"The First Commercial Bank robbery. One of the robbers wore a monkey mask. That mask can be found in the driver's side door panel in the Dodge Durango parked at the home of Elva Reinhardt in Pacific Beach."

"Can you give me that address?" said the man.

Monsorre provided the street address.

"Can I get your name?"

Monsorre abruptly hung up the phone. The deed was done.

But there was a problem and both he and Leticia knew it: there would be no DNA found on the mask. Obviously they didn't have Carlos' DNA and couldn't manufacture that piece of missing evidence, but they had proceeded anyway. The argument would be that the polypropylene balaclava worn by all robbers would have prevented a transfer of DNA. It was flimsy but it just might fly. At least the right jury would probably buy it, Leticia hoped.

Back inside his Mercedes and now headed southbound on the 5, Monsorre clicked speed dial on Leticia's name.

"Hey," he said when she answered. "It's done."

"No problems?"

"She didn't know a thing."

"And you called the SDPD?"

"Done."

"Ah, good, good. Come by tonight and I'll make payment."

He felt a stirring between his legs, he told her. He loved receiving payment from Letty. It was physically lush plus emotionally empowering, as he put it, just to know a woman of such power was receiving him in her mouth.

He checked his watch. She'd be home by seven and he'd be inside her condo by seven-oh-one.

Reflexively he accelerated into the fast lane and began passing slower traffic. He checked his speedometer. Eighty-seven.

The evidence just kept materializing all around.

# Chapter 20

MICHAEL

"They've got me on a new mood stabilizer," Danny told me on the phone three weeks after her aborted visit. "And it's really helping. I can honestly say that I want to be with you now. You and the kids, honey."

This whole thing had burned me an untold number of times. I was very cautious and probably standoffish to the extent that she felt it.

"Good," I said. "Well, time will tell."

"No, Michael, this isn't like the other times. It's nothing like that. This stuff doesn't change my ability to think but it makes my moods less low and less high. I'm pretty level for a week now."

"I'm impressed. Well, let me know when you want to try the new you with me. I'm always up for that."

"Is tomorrow morning too soon? I still haven't unpacked my big bag from last time."

"If you think you're ready, I am."

I wasn't really; I'm the type who can only stand so many broken hearts in one month. Naturally I keep this to myself, but I was really, really defensive at that point

"I'll be there in the morning. Just leave a key at the front desk. I'll take a cab over and see you when you get back from the office."

"That works for me," I told her, brightening somewhat at her self-sufficiency. That was new, to an extent. The Danny I married had been totally self-reliant. Her words had the echo of some of that. Good, I needed to hear it.

"Goodbye, Michael. See you tomorrow."

\* \* \*

She did come. And she stayed for five days until her decision was made. She was ready to go home and start packing. She was coming home.

Danny was coming home!

To me and to our children. It would turn their lives upside-down with joy. Especially Dania, who missed her mother terribly and talked about her every minute. Which was fine; I was glad she loved her mom so deeply.

She called again to tell me her landlady had agreed to let her buy out of the lease for two thousand dollars--a steal. The landlady had been gracious and she had now been paid, as well.

It was actually going to happen this time.

And this time I wouldn't ever let her go again, at least not so easily as before.

This time, I was hanging on with everything I had.

# Chapter 21

MICHAEL

In downtown San Diego I jumped onto the trolley and enjoyed a five-minute ride to a tall building with the correct number. Inside, I checked in with the security desk and was waved through to the elevator bank. There, I rode up to the thirty-fifth floor and got off.

I found myself looking at a glass wall etched with an undersea view of Neptune's Garden. In the middle of it all were double doors. They displayed in gold leaf the name of the law firm so I went inside and up to the receptionist. I told her my business and she buzzed her phone and spoke quietly into her headset.

"Mr. Gray says for you to come right on in, Mr. Gresham. Down the hallway to my right, then left and down to the corner office. You'll find Mr. Gray inside."

I followed directions and entered the office of Horatio "Racehorse" Gray, my local counsel on the Carlos Pritchett case.

He got up from his executive chair and extended his hand. His eyes met mine squarely and with a hint of real happiness just to see me. No wonder the guy was so incredibly successful, I thought, and then we exchanged names.

"Michael Gresham."

"Horatio Gray. Call me Racehorse. It's worked for fifty-five years and shouldn't quit working now."

"Of course, Racehorse. And please call me Michael."

"So, Michael, thanks for dropping by. It's great to place a face with a name."

"I just wanted to thank you for allowing me to associate you so I could practice *pro hac vice*. That was a kind thing for you to do. Not all lawyers are so gracious as to welcome in competition from foreign lawyers."

"Nonsense, I've got way, way too much business to give that kind of thing a second thought. Even a first thought. It never crossed my mind. So, now, I understand you're defending one of our city's better-known bank robbers, Mr. Carlos Pritchett?"

"Indeed, I am. Carlos is the father of a little girl whose meds are so expensive he couldn't afford them so he picked up a gun."

"What happened to his insurance?"

"Refused to cover her. Some notion of failure to list her on the policy application by her given name. It's a long story and I won't bore you."

"So, how can I help?"

The question took me by surprise, to be honest. In using local counsel, it's always just a formality. Neither lawyer--local or foreign--actually expects the local lawyer to be involved in the case in any manner. But here, Racehorse was wanting to know how he could help. I found it strange and I also found it a huge relief to think I might have someone of his stature throw in with me. He was a giant because his fifty-five-year career marked him as the most successful trial attorney on the West Coast since Melvin Belli in San Francisco. Before that, maybe Jake Ehrlich. But Racehorse outshone all of these great lights during his career and now here he was, asking how he could help on the robbery case of Carlos Pritchett. I was floored but tried not to show it.

"Seriously?" I asked. "You really want in?"

"I do. I've had my people do some snooping. It seems your client's daughter needs this money yesterday."

"She does. She did. I need Carlos out of jail so that he can work on getting the money to buy the medicines she needs. Legitimately, of course."

Racehorse sat back against his chair and pinched the sweet spot between his eyes. He blinked hard several times while shaking his head.

"You know," he said, "for two cents I'd advance the money out of my own pocket."

I didn't say anything. It would be unethical for a lawyer to give money to a client, and I said so.

He only looked at me. "Michael, who's talking about giving Carlos anything? I'm talking about giving the money to the *daughter*, not to the father."

I looked hard at him. It was a matter of semantics and we both knew it. The potential for being hauled up before the bar association on ethics charges still ran high, even if the daughter were the recipient of the funds.

"What do you say, Michael? Go half with me?"

To say he had caught me by surprise would be a huge understatement. Here was one of the most respected and successful lawyers on the West Coast ready to lay it all on the line for people he'd never met. *My God,* I thought, *if he's willing to do that for complete strangers, where was my chutzpah? The hell with it,* I decided then and there. He was willing; I had to be as well.

"I'm in," I said in a steady voice. "I can't say it's the first time I've thought of doing this."

"Tell you what. I'll have my people set up a trust. No one will know who the trustors are. We'll each put a hundred thousand in. The trustee-bank can then pay the funds over to the little girl."

"Amelia."

"To Amelia. Neither she nor her parents will need to know where the money is from."

My mind ran back to the recording we had of Leticia Cross tipping off her boyfriend that the heat was about to come down on him. As far as I could forecast, the district attorney would be the only office ever even remotely interested in how this little girl got her medications. And I had enough on Ms. Cross to shut her the hell up forever if she ever tried to make an end-run around us with the state bar.

"Count me in," I said. "One-hundred-percent in. I'm leaving a check with you."

I already had my checkbook out and was writing a check.

"What's the name of our trust?"

He rocked back. "How about the Two Birds Trust. That work for you?"

"That's who I'm making it out to, then," I said, still writing. "One hundred thousand to the Two Birds Trust." I tore the check from my checkbook and slid it across the desk to Racehorse. He picked it up and looked it over, nodding.

"We are two good old guys," he said. "You, not so old; me, really old. Whatever, we've done a good thing here, Michael. Now, what's this I hear about tomorrow's bail hearing? Are you ready for that?"

I spread my hands in surrender. "I'm ready, but you and I both know there's not a judge in San Diego County who's going to release Carlos on bail. He's got Murder One staring him in the face, plus an assortment of armed robbery and fleeing felonies. No way in hell he's walking out of jail tomorrow."

Racehorse fiddled with a fat Montblanc pen, working it through his fingers like a mini-baton.

Then, "Does he have the money for bail of, let's say, one million?"

"He does. Especially now that his daughter's needs are funded."

"And the judge is Evelyn Knightly. You know of her?"

"No. I know nothing about her. Don't forget, this isn't my normal stomping grounds, Racehorse."

He caught his pen in midair and grabbed it in his fist. "Well, I do know her. In fact, I chaired her last run for re-election. She owes me, Michael."

"Oh, my God."

"Yep. So how about letting me argue the motion tomorrow?"

"Done. I'm relieved to have the help, believe me."

"All right. Let's meet in Judge Knightly's courtroom maybe ten minutes before the hearing. We can talk and I can meet Carlos. Get him pumped up a little."

"Sounds great, Racehorse. Nine-fifty tomorrow morning."

I stood up and we shook hands. He measured me with piercing eyes.

"Good to meet you, Michael. But after tomorrow, you're on your own with the case." He touched his chest. "Very sick in here."

"I'm sorry to hear that."

"Yes, I've cut way back."

"Well, thanks for helping with what you've done. Carlos and I both are forever grateful."

"Needed to be done." He held out his hand toward the door behind me. "See you in the morning, then."

"Right."

I was walking on clouds. Amelia had her drugs; Carlos was about to pull down his freedom. Things were looking up.

Or so I thought.

# Chapter 22

"Your Honor," Racehorse began with Judge Knightly, "this is a very sad story, this man's case. He has been arrested for armed robbery and there's even a count for felony-murder. But please allow me to tell you why Carlos Pritchett should be admitted to the benefits of bail while this case is pending."

"Please do," replied Judge Knightly. She was a woman in her mid-fifties, snow-white hair and robin's egg blue eyes that drew you right in. Her features were all California girl and you knew at once that she had at one time been a heartbreaker. Maybe still was. I watched the interaction between the judge and Racehorse, looking for some indication of familiarity between them, but both covered it up very nicely. Then I heard Racehorse getting wound up.

"…because Carlos Pritchett's daughter lies gravely ill in a hospital bed today, standing just outside death's door, right here in San Diego, at UCSD in Hillcrest. And her father is here today because of a Judas named Vincent Phaeton. Phaeton is a man who was, admittedly, involved in the First Commercial bank robbery and who now has gone running to the district attorney claiming Carlos Pritchett was there. Even that Carlos Pritchett was the mastermind. But, truth be told, there isn't one other piece of evidence that puts Carlos at the scene. All bank robbers were wearing rubber masks and all CCTV had been disabled. There isn't a picture of Carlos on the scene. There isn't another witness who can place him there, criminal or law enforcement. Nada, none. So the case against Carlos is very tenuous at best, and non-existent from where I sit. For these reasons, justice cries out that Carlos be released on bail so that he can run to his daughter's bedside and give the comfort and care that only a father can."

Racehorse paused to take a swallow of water and, as he did, broke into a coughing fit that required him to pull out a white handkerchief and hold it to his mouth. Finally, the coughing passed and he took another swallow of water before continuing.

"Now, in San Diego County, we of course are guided by the bail schedule. But before we get into that, let me simply remind the court that capital crimes (i.e. murder with special circumstances), when the facts are evident or the presumption great provide for no bail. However, this isn't our case. No, our case is one where the facts are not only not evident, there are no facts before this court that implicate my client in any of the felony counts the district attorney has charged him with. Moreover, there is no presumption against him that can be based on any known facts. For this reason, bail should be set in a reasonable amount and Carlos Pritchett be given the full benefit of the presumption that he is innocent from the outset. Thank you, Judge Knightly."

With that, Racehorse sat down and broke into a muffled coughing fit yet again.

Leticia Cross then took to her feet. She paused momentarily, lips pursed, hands on hips, before beginning.

"Your Honor," she began slowly, "Carlos Pritchett is accused of gunning down a U.S. military veteran in cold blood. There are, at last count, ten witnesses to this incredibly cruel act of shooting an unarmed man who the defendant just decided didn't deserve to live. His name was William Turnstile and he was a family man with two children in high school and one in college. The defense wants to play on your heartstrings with talk about the defendant's sick daughter, but the court should equally consider the dead veteran's children whose father is never coming home, not when they are sick, not when they are in good health. The presumption is strong against the defendant. The state can produce an eyewitness, a man who participated in the armed robbery, who will testify at trial that it was Carlos Pritchett who masterminded the robbery and who pulled the trigger on William Turnstile. The evidence cannot be any stronger than that and the presumption cannot be any greater. For these reasons, we believe there should be no bail and that the defendant should remain locked up for the safety of the public. Thank you, Judge."

She sat back down and then Racehorse was again on his feet. He raised one hand and pointed at the district attorney.

"If what she says were true, then I would agree there should be no bail. But what Ms. Cross has failed to tell the court is that her so-called eyewitness has two felony convictions against him, one of which resulted in his incarceration for a term of ten years in San Quentin. He is easily impeachable and shouldn't be believed by any jury, not even for a minute. But more than that, this felon's word cannot and should not be allowed to keep a man in jail without bail who is presumed by the law to be innocent. Eyewitness, indeed. Phaeton is simply a man who's looking for the easy way out by turning state's evidence. His testimony should be given the weight it deserves--zero. Please, judge, let's not allow this case to be reduced to such rubbish testimony. Bail should be set."

Judge Knightly looked out at the participants and the onlookers when Racehorse was resettled in his chair. She put eyes on me just momentarily as well; why, I don't know. Then she began.

"Bail is set at one million dollars on the murder charge and one million dollars on the armed robbery charge. The court is stacking bail, as required by statute. Mr. Pritchett, we have bail bondsmen in this state and your get-out-of-jail card will cost you ten percent of two million or two hundred thousand. Other conditions include that you surrender your passport, avoid all contact with felons and known criminals, commit no crimes, not even traffic violations, and that you obey the law in all respects. I also have the right to cancel your bail without notice to anyone, and even to raise it without notice, so be advised, sir. That is all, court stands in recess."

"After you've made bail," Racehorse said to Carlos, "go to your daughter first. I've received an anonymous call telling me that her medical care is being paid for by an anonymous donor. That same donor is putting up your bail money. Why? She just feels for your situation. Godspeed, Mr. Pritchett. I've now done all I can for you."

Tears were formed in Carlos' eyes and he wept while being handcuffed so the deputies could return him to jail for processing-out. His wife came forward and touched him on the shoulder and told him she would be right behind with the money for bail that had come to her anonymously. She already had a bail bondsman who would help.

Then they took him away, leaving just me and Racehorse at counsel table.

"So," he said to me, "now you know."

"Know what?" I asked.

"You heard my paroxysms of coughing. I'm sick, Michael. I'm done here. Hell, I'm done everywhere. This case is now all yours."

"Thank you for what you've done," I said, my hand extended to shake.

We shook hands and then hugged. His assistant then came forward and gathered up his leather briefcase and assembled his notes and put them inside. Then she took him by the elbow and led him away.

We were done. Carlos was all but free and back on the streets, his daughter's medical care already underway, I was guessing.

Now to keep him operating inside the terms of his conditions of release.

Would he stay out of trouble?

We were about to find out.

# Chapter 23

Nobody realized Vincent Phaeton was a very intelligent man in addition to possessing all of the cunning of a Q-trained convict. So when the district attorney called him in and said she was considering rejecting his immunity agreement, he squealed and cried out. "You can't do that! It's in writing!"

DDA Cross smiled a small smile. "That's where you're wrong, Mr. Phaeton. You need to study paragraph fourteen. It allows me to cancel this agreement for any reason whatsoever as long as I believe your proffered testimony has been compromised beyond usefulness. This means I can cancel you if you've been impeached and I believe that has all but happened. The defense has already won a bail hearing, thanks to your rap sheet. Your testimony is useless at this point. We're going to have to find other ways to prove Carlos Pritchett guilty than through you. You are on notice, sir," she said, and ripped the agreement in half. "Your immunity is withdrawn."

Phaeton sat across from her, stunned. He had been so sure. But now it was slipping away— had slipped away. The next feeling was of fury, intense anger and hatred toward those who had made this happen, particularly the lawyers who were defending his target. The mind of the criminal is capable of making connections that ordinary people just don't make. In this case, Phaeton decided that if he neutralized the lawyers who were against him he would destroy the defense case and his testimony would be validated. Yes, it made no sense; but that is how many criminals operate, always on the other side of what's logical and sensible. So, he decided he would hit them and hit them hard.

Michael Gresham was at the top of his list for payback. Except he knew that Gresham was always in the company of his investigator and this meant he was protected. Phaeton wanted an easier target, so he decided to find out whether Gresham was married. It was a simple matter to examine the archives of the *Chicago Tribune*, where he learned that Michael and Danny Gresham were on the board of a women's shelter in Chicago and that they had made a sizable contribution in its support. Danny Gresham: here was his target. Now to locate her.

Phaeton paid a kid five hundred bucks to hack the bank account of Michael and Danny Gresham. From there, it was simple to filter out the payments that were made on a monthly basis for her apartment near Evanston. Why were they living separately? Phaeton had no idea, but one thing was for certain: it made her a much easier target. He paid fifteen hundred dollars for a set of false papers and driver's license and purchased an airplane seat to Chicago's O'Hare airport.

Her condo was in a tall building set on the bank of Lake Michigan. Scouting out the address and the interior, Phaeton immediately confirmed there was CCTV everywhere, just as he expected. So the last place he would want to murder her was in the building where she lived. He then went into the basement and located the parking slot for her apartment number. *How simple is this?* He thought, matching apartment number to parking slot number. *The security arm of this complex should be ashamed.*

Next he located a parking slot that was vacant two cars away and spent three days waiting there. When the owner of the slot returned home in the evenings, Phaeton would already be gone, as he waited there only until five o'clock p.m. before calling it a day and moving on. But the next morning at eight he would return and wait, ready to pounce on Danny.

On the third day she came downstairs and backed her car out. He followed her up the ramp and out onto the street.

Ten minutes later, they were in the parking lot of a Dominick's grocery store, looking for a spot close to the front entrance. Phaeton parked two rows away and watched as his prey went into the store. He didn't follow; there almost certainly was at least one camera covering the lot and he didn't want his face recorded.

He pulled a black eyemask down over his face and climbed out of his rental, a Taurus. He removed the license plates in under three minutes and tossed them on the back seat. Then he climbed back in, moving the mask atop his head. Twenty minutes later, Danny reappeared, pushing a grocery cart toward her car. Phaeton waited until she had the rear door open on the SUV and was putting her groceries away.

Again masked, he came up behind her and pressed the barrel of the .22 pistol behind her left ear. Two shots behind the ear and two shots into the heart once she was lying motionless on the ground. Then, for good measure, two shots into her forehead. Now he was done.

Ever so casually he turned away and strolled back to his car. Climbing inside, he removed his mask and started up, heading for the closest exit, where he paused for traffic and then rolled out into the stream. A block away he turned into a neighborhood. He parked and replaced the licensed plates so he wouldn't be pulled over for driving without plates.

Then he was gone.

He didn't see the startled shoppers come upon the still body and he didn't see them dial 911 and stand there, frozen, until the EMTs arrived and checked the prostrate form of the woman. Slowly, then, the CSI workers arrived and cordoned off the crime scene and began their labors. They would find nothing, of course, to implicate Vincent Phaeton, who was headed south to Arkansas, where he would then head east to Georgia before heading back north and turning west to Los Angeles. In Los Angeles he abandoned the rental at the train station and bought a ticket south to San Diego.

# Chapter 24

When he burst into my office without knocking, the look on Marcel's face said it all. I wasn't going to like what he had to say.

"Michael," he began, "I have the most terrible news imaginable. Mrs. Lingscheit just called me. Danny has been found shot to death."

At first I thought it was some sort of demented joke. But it wasn't. Marcel, who is normally a very calm and collected soul, was on the verge of tears, something I'd never seen before. He came around my desk and placed a hand on my shoulder. "She's gone, Michael."

What can I say? Every feeling a human being can feel at such times took over my body and caused me to shake and weep uncontrollably. But in the next instant I was asking about my children. What did security say?

"Our security team has your house covered. Dania has been picked up from school and taken home. Your mother-in-law and the kids' nanny have been advised. We're on complete lockdown back there. The kids are safe."

"I've got to get to them," I said. "I've got to see they're okay."

"I understand," he said. "Mrs. Lingscheit is already making travel arrangements. We can print out your ticket any minute now."

At just that minute, Mrs. Matlock, my secretary/receptionist in San Diego, buzzed me.

"Call you need to take, Michael. The guy is plain nuts!"

"Michael Gresham," I said into the phone. "This better be damn good."

"Mr. Gresham," said a rough voice that sounded distant and muffled, "you don't know me, but I'm a friend of Vincent Phaeton's."

"Go ahead."

"I'm the guy who killed your wife. And right now I'm two blocks away from your kids here in Evanston."

My blood turned cold and my heart clutched in my chest. It was my worst fear, that whoever had shot Danny would also go for our children.

"I'm listening. What are you after? You called me so I know there's something you want."

"Twist in the Pritchett case. I want your man to testify that Vincent Phaeton had nothing to do with the robbery-murder at First Commercial bank. Do that and your kids will be left alone, as will you. Refuse and everyone's up for grabs. Know this: I will get your kids. Whether it takes six weeks or six years, I will get them when you least expect. Now repeat after me, I will make Mr. Pritchett exonerate Vincent Phaeton."

"I will make Mr. Pritchett exonerate Vincent Phaeton."

"Good, then we have a deal. Renege on this deal and your first grader dies. Then the boy. And they won't be pleasant deaths, Mr. Gresham. That I can promise you."

The phone then went dead. Call over.

"Michael," Marcel said, "you're white as a sheet! What the hell?"

"A man just threatened my kids, Marce."

"Then let's hunt him down. Starting now."

"Get a trace on the call," I told him. I looked down. My hands were shaking--but it was more rage than fear. He had punched the wrong button on me.

"Done. But you know it's gonna trace back to a payphone in some gas station or Pizza Hut."

"So be it. We can go from there."

"Now, I've spent many years chasing fugitives, Michael. I can tell you that ten times out of ten that caller was none other than Phaeton himself. You a betting man?"

"No need to bet. I'm totally in line with that. Let's start there. Find out what you can about the son of a bitch and then we'll go after him."

"Everything on the table?"

I looked him in the eyes. "Everything's on the table."

"Then we're good. I'll have answers by early afternoon. In the meantime, you fly back to Evanston and do what you need for the kids. I'm gone."

He wasn't kidding; as he spoke he was backing out of my door and heading for the courthouse, where he would go through the Phaeton file with a fine-tooth comb. Knowing Marcel, the bad guy's lifespan was down to hours, not days.

By noon, I was on a plane nonstop to Chicago. By eight o'clock the taxi was dropping me at my house in Evanston. The security guards on duty insisted on seeing my ID--they hadn't seen me in the flesh before. I had no problem with that, in fact, I expected it.

I thanked them and went inside, where my two children came running into my arms.

"They know nothing, Michael," Danny's mother told me. "They need you now more than ever." She burst into tears and turned away. It was all I could do to hold it together for the kids.

I hugged my children and sat down on the floor and let them crawl all over me. It wasn't difficult--we hadn't seen each other in several weeks now. Mikey hit me on the side of the head and told me he was very mad that I had left them alone. Dania cried and wrapped her arms around my neck and whispered to me never to leave her alone again, that she had been scared out of her wits. I told her I wouldn't, that she would go everywhere with me from now on.

We spent ten minutes like this, talking and saying hello. Then came the inevitable drawings and readings to show me how far they had progressed in school and pre-school. They were amazing, my two little ones, and I was struck dumb at how bright they were. I still am.

At nine o'clock Marcel called. He had a line on Vincent Phaeton. What did I want him to do?

"Do you have eyes on the man himself?" I asked.

"I will. He's headed back."

Which meant that he was headed back to California. Marcel had his ways of knowing these things.

"Unless I miss my guess, there is no one other than him," Marcel added. "Do I take him out?"

"No. You stake him out, don't lose sight of him even for five minutes, and wait for me to catch up to you."

"When are you coming back?"

"Early morning. Me and my children with Danny's mom and our nanny. We're all coming. I've already called Mrs. Lingscheit and she has air travel scheduled for us."

"Then I can expect you to come around tomorrow?"

"Expect no less. We've got some cleanup to do."

"All right, boss."

"And source a good video camera and sound system. We're going to take someone's deposition."

"Deposition? Seriously?"

"Well, not exactly. It will be more in the nature of an ISIS video of someone losing their head."

"That's a relief."

"Plus we'll need him to exculpate our client, Carlos. I'm sure he'll cooperate."

"Excellent. I'll be ready. Where will this take place?"

"Where he lives."

"He crashes in a ramshackle house in Ocean Beach, not far from the ocean. He's not on the lease."

"Then that's where we'll depose him."

"Or behead him."

"As you wish, Marcel. As you wish."

# Chapter 25

LETICIA

It was driving me mad, the fact I had left a message on Rudy's machine. A message that could get me convicted of a very stupid crime. So I panicked.

I conceived a plan whereby I would invite myself into Rudy's house and then access his telephone answering machine. I would then erase the call I had made to him where I tipped him off about pending police activity, if it were even still on there. I really didn't know, and Rudy had never mentioned it to me.

After work on Wednesday night, I slipped into a little black dress, laced a pearl necklace around my throat and strapped on a pair of heels. The makeup I applied was meant for dark lounges and smoky places, attractive but smoldering. Now I was ready.

Without bothering to call first, I appeared at Rudy's door and knocked gently three times. No answer.

I knew he was home--I had checked in with him and he was going straight home after a long day following an even longer night. So I knocked again, louder this time. No answer.

I pulled my car keys from my purse and rapped the knot of keys sharply on the wood door. The racket and clatter could be heard up and down the hallway and I was certain it could be heard inside as well. Just as I was about to repeat, the door opened a crack. I pressed my face into the crack and smiled, my lipstick making a soft outline of soft lips, the lips he loved to tongue.

It was Rudy, but he was acting very strangely. The safety chain was still fastened across the door. I was unable to push my way inside.

"Rudy? Why aren't you opening the door?" I asked. I allowed my voice to project not just a small tinge of hurt.

"Uh-uh-I'm busy tonight, Letty. I've got company."

"Really? Who else is here?"

"My-my cousin from L.A."

"Oh, well let me in, please. I'd like to meet him."

"Actually, it's a her. My cousin is female, and she's not dressed just now. She's taking a shower."

"Oh, then let me on in and I'll make some drinks and we can all get to know one another."

"I don't think so. I don't think tonight's a good night for that. Why didn't you call me first?"

"I did call, remember? You said that you were going straight home after work."

"And don't you remember me telling you that I was exhausted and needed to go right to bed?"

"That's what I'm here for," I said coquettishly. "I'm climbing in beside you and sending you off to Neverland with sweet, sweet dreams."

"Well, I don't think so."

"Well, I do think so. You're pushing me away here, Rudy, and I don't like being pushed away. Remember our agreement?"

"I thought we were having sex together. I don't remember anymore of an agreement than that."

"Remember how I call you sometimes and help you out of a jam? And remember you and the monkey mask you planted? All of that's stuff that brings us closer."

"It does? I just thought we were helping--never mind, this just isn't a good night. I'm closing the door now, Letty. I'll call you tomorrow."

He closed the door and I heard the lock click in place.

Now what? I wondered.

Cousin? I doubted it. In fact, the more I thought about it the more I highly doubted it. He'd never said a word to me about a female cousin in Los Angeles. Not that I'd ever asked about family, but still. So I did what all pissed-off lovers do, I again pulled my keys out of my purse and began rapping on the door until it opened again.

"What?" he said angrily. I jerked back.

"What? I want to come in, that's what." I screwed up my courage. "In fact, I *demand* to be let in. You have no right to treat your lover like this. Now let me in and I'll make drinks, we'll have one, and then I'll go on my merry way and we'll still be friends."

"Well--"

"Come on."

I watched as the chain was released, and then I pushed against the freed door. It opened just enough for me to slide inside, which I did. Now I sniffed the air. Definitely something Chanel. I couldn't say what, but it was Chanel. My worst fears were confirmed; cousins don't wear Chanel to visit cousins.

"Where is she?"

"I told you, she's in the shower."

I pushed past Rudy and went straight into his bedroom. The bed was unmade, the sheets and cover rumpled, and there was an ashtray in the center of the bed with lipstick-smeared filters poked into a great pile of ash. *Exhibit One*, I thought.

"Cigarettes, Rudy? Really? You let your cousin smoke cigarettes in your bed? You don't smoke and you don't allow smoking in your condo. We both know that. But your cousin's an exception? You must really love your cousin, Rudy."

I went around the bed and unlocked the two windows that looked down on the community pool far below.

"Let some air in here, for God's sake."

"I--I really don't want you in my bedroom, Letty."

"Nonsense! You can never wait to get me in your bedroom, Rudy. Now, I'm going to ask again and then I'm going to be really pissed. Who the fuck is she?"

"She's nobody. Just someone I met." He hung his head and reached for the ashtray. Like a dutiful child under the angry eye of his mother, he emptied the container into a wastebasket next to his dresser. Then he turned back around, holding the ashtray and thumping it against his thigh as tambourine players might do.

"Nobody? You've been screwing in here, Rudy. I can smell it. Women *know* these things. How stupid do you really think I am?"

"It's not like you and me are engaged or anything," he said, grasping. "I'll bet you've had other guys."

"You just lost your money, sir! I have been faithful, Rudy, faithful!"

"I have too! At least until this evening! But we never agreed--"

I wanted no more of it. It was time to get what I came here for. I pushed by him and headed for the kitchen and his answering machine. It was the old type, the type with a small cassette for messages. I poked the eject button and the tape rose up. Snatching it from the small receptacle where it operated, I dropped it into my purse.

"What the hell?" he exclaimed from behind. He had followed me. "Why take my tape?"

"Because I want to! Because I want to know who else has called you!"

"No one's called me. Now, give it back!"

He seized my wrist and tried to pull my purse away. I resisted, pushing him back with my free hand. He seized my free hand too and shoved hard. I flew up against the kitchen island and bent over backwards, the purse now dangling from the crook of my arm. He reached over and ripped the purse off of my arm and turned away with it. Looking frantically around, I snatched up the iron breakfast skillet and smashed it down against his head. Rudy dropped straight down, down onto his knees, then crumpled over to the side. He didn't move.

I toed him with a patent leather pump.

"C'mon, Rudy. Quit playing around."

He didn't respond. So I toed him again, this time in the crotch, playfully pushing against his genitals. This never failed to excite him.

Still no response, however.

So I squatted down and felt around for the pulse in his wrist. No such thing. Without thinking, then, I reached for the pulse in his neck. Still no pulse. The lawyer within kicked in and I plucked a dish towel from a drawer and wiped my DNA and prints from his wrist and throat. I pried the cassette tape out of his hand and wiped his hand. Then I got serious and wiped his other hand, too, using the dish towel yet again, removing my own DNA from his hands. I did the same thing with the iron skillet. I turned the skillet over. It was covered in blood on the flame side. Which was when I noted the pool of blood spreading out from my lover's head. I stuffed the dish towel into my purse.

It occurred to me then: I needed to call 911. But before I did, I crept back into the bedroom and looked around until I found Little Miss Pussy's underwear. I snatched up the garment and went back into the kitchen, where I rubbed the inside crotch panel of the underwear against the handle of the iron skillet. I knew that the skillet was now covered with DNA. I returned the underwear to the bedroom and tossed the garment back onto the floor. Sure, they might contain my DNA, but I really doubted they would ever trace it to me. Then, having second thoughts, I again retrieved the underwear and this time wadded it into my purse. Now I was spotless. The old prosecutor knew what was what and I knew the crime scene was perfect.

So I crept into the living room and, using the underwear as a glove, picked up the phone and dialed 911. I didn't say anything when the voice answered--I didn't need to have my voiceprint at issue in the murder trial. But I did leave the phone off the hook, knowing that the cops would be scrambled to the location regardless.

Using the underwear yet again, I pulled open the front door and stuck my head out. All clear. So I stepped out into the hallway, again stuffing the underwear into my purse.

Back in my Volvo and pulling away from the curb, I had one thing on my mind: the underwear. That evidence had to be jettisoned and damn fast.

Two blocks away was a 7-Eleven. I pulled in behind it and found the mandatory dumpster, where I climbed out and deposited the underwear and dish towel into its maw. Now I could drive off, comfortable in knowing that the crime scene had been washed.

As I drove off, I failed to see Beatrice Easley, a street person with bulging garbage bags and a Safeway cart, nose her cart up to the dumpster and look inside. This would come out later. She evidently retrieved them and continued memorizing my license plate. She later told me she thought it just might be good for a few bucks.

Now, I was scrambling northbound on the 5, driving in and out of the fast lane in a terrific hurry to get home before any calls started arriving. Then the roof caved in on me when I realized I had forgotten to bring along his cell phone. The police would check his cell phone and make me and they would undoubtedly call at some point. So that was a given. What could I do about it? I wanted to be comfortably ensconced in my own home, answering the phone as sweetly and calmly as I could pull off.

I began imagining the conversations I would have with the cops, especially the second sentence, where I told them I was a deputy district attorney who had met the guy one night in a bar and might have given him my phone number and that's why his phone showed calls to and from me. We had met up once or twice, I would tell them, because he had a case he wanted me to investigate. They would know I had called Rudy that very day. Of course I had, I would say, he had told me that he had some information regarding a chop-shop, information that might lead to a prosecution. Our relationship was strictly professional and I was strictly following up with him on a police matter. Beyond that, there wasn't anything more I could say. That was it, that would raise a roadblock: it was confidential.

Always with the confidentiality. Lawyers always had confidential as their trump card. Tonight it would get played.

# Chapter 26

Detective Mitch O'Connell was Irish, overweight, abused alcohol on a nightly basis, and was the SDPD's go-to robbery investigator. He was medium-height with a history of ordering "portly" from Big and Tall, rheumy green eyes and ears that had no discipline when it came to growing wild hair. Staying trim and neat was a daily battle, he complained to his wife, who had ordered him an electric ear and nose hair trimmer two Christmases running. But, he was one of the best-liked among the detective bureau and his partner, Eleanor Howell, would have taken a bullet for him.

The items seized and put into a special to-do room at SDPD for evidence-yet-to-be-processed came up on O'Connell's to-do app on a Wednesday. With Eleanor close behind, he rode the elevator down to the basement of the building and supplied his ID to the sergeant-in-charge. That being done, he and Eleanor were granted passage into the huge room where evidence from the First Commercial robbery awaited them. The plan was to begin with the items seized and secured from the bank vault and work outward from there.

They examined the screwdrivers and hammers retrieved from the Hamilton vault first. The items had been dusted and returned negative: no prints, no DNA. Next came the bits and pieces of safe deposit boxes that had been drilled and opened by Carlos and Chris after the vault was breached. Again, nothing remarkable there and nothing remarkable had been expected. After all, the robbers were wearing latex gloves just like the dicks and techs wore when processing a scene so prints and DNA would be non-existent. Still, the two detectives continued in their review of possible evidence for trial of the case against Carlos and Phaeton and Ramsey.

Then came the oxy-fuel cutting torch. The tech tag was red on this particular item--meaning that useable evidence had been found and the item appropriately tagged for the detectives. O'Connell read the tag's number and matched it to the evidence inventory he had been handed by the desk sergeant on admittance. He read the inventory slowly so as not to miss anything. Eleanor came around and read over his shoulder.

"What do you think?" she asked O'Connell.

"What do I think? I think we've got a print and DNA on the coupling nut of the torch, that's what I think."

"Whose print and whose DNA?"

"That's what we're here to find out, my dear Eleanor. The samples are awaiting our orders in the crime lab. We'll stop by there after we finish up here."

"We catch a break and someone goes to jail," she said. "I like the concept so far."

He chuckled. "You sound like a cop."

"Funny thing," she mused.

They continued, then, spending the rest of that day and most of the next sifting through item after item until, in the end, they had found two dozen useable pieces of evidence. What did the evidence add up to? That would be the job of the DA to figure out. The detectives were careful not to draw conclusions in their reports--that would leave their testimony open to impeachment should the wrong conclusions be drawn, and juries hated impeached cops. Their job, then, was just to identify and report, nothing more.

On the third day, the duo proceeded to the crime lab and discussed their findings with the director.

"We've got a favor to ask," O'Connell began in an easy tone of voice with the woman.

"Sure, how can we help?" she asked.

"Item FCB-224 is a coupling nut on an oxy-fuel torch. A print was lifted and DNA sampled. We need hurry-ups on these."

"We need to know whose prints and whose DNA," Eleanor needlessly added. She had a habit of assuming most people knew less than they really did. So her approach with potential witnesses had long been off-putting, though no one had ever told her so. She would remain, at best, a mediocre detective who was known for having difficulty in securing the cooperation of witnesses, vics, and perps. But O'Connell could live with that, mainly because the woman knew no fear. She was totally, hands-down, the first to volunteer to go through a door first or up a stairway first and so everyone felt good about teaming up with her.

"How about five o'clock today? We can have it by then," the director said. "I'll pass the word down."

"Imogene, you have just made our day," O'Connell told her, resisting the impulse to hug the woman, whose demeanor was prickly and whose body language looked as if it was resistant to hugs.

"You and I go way back, Ocie," said the director, falling back on O'Connell's pet name. "I'll do what I can for my best bud anytime."

"My gratitude," said O'Connell, placing his hand over his heart.

They returned to the cubicle they shared with two other detectives, Harrison and Maldez, who appeared to be out for the day. They busied themselves with final reports on their evidence processing efforts on the First Commercial until 4:54 p.m. when the lab called.

"We've got your information," said the caller. "Are you ready?"

"Shoot," said O'Connell, his pen poised over his yellow tablet.

"The print and the DNA belong to the same person. His name is Carlos Pritchett."

The call ended after thank-you's and a few follow-ups on statistical accuracy.

O'Connell and his partner high-fived each other.

"We've got Pritchett in the vault with the cutting torch. Score one for the good guys."

"Oh, Leticia Cross is gonna give us a medal," Eleanor said half-sarcastically but half-truthfully, too. The woman would be ecstatic, no doubt about it.

"This is the first piece of hard evidence we have against the guy. We just earned our pay for this month."

"How do you think it happened?" Eleanor wondered aloud.

"My guess? He was having trouble connecting to the torch and he had to remove a glove. That's when he left the print and the DNA. Just guessing, though."

"Sounds reasonable. That's what we'll tell the jury, then?"

"Exactly. Let's go see Deputy Cross." Their own Deputy DA was in San Francisco for two days, so they were reporting to Leticia Cross.

They hurried to her office, fighting the early rush-hour traffic as they went.

Cross was still in her office and waved them right in.

She took her seat behind her desk and folded her hands before her. "So?" she asked. "What do my best and brightest have for me today?"

"Just the best possible result," said Eleanor.

"We can put your man Carlos Pritchett in the vault."

Cross's heart skipped a beat. "Seriously? I think I'm going to jump up and kiss you both.

What happened?"

"We got a hit on the cutting torch the robbers left behind in the vault."

"What kind of hit?"

"Print and DNA. Both Pritchett's."

"OMG!" cried Cross. "Merit badges for you both. That bastard's going down!"

"He is," said O'Connell with a self-satisfied smile spreading over his face. "He's dead in the water."

"Yes, he is," said Eleanor. "Do you know how we did it?" she asked Cross, who obviously would know they found a red tag in the evidence lockup and tasked the lab with a workup.

"Yes," Cross said with a warm tone. She knew Eleanor and knew of her propensity to over-explain. Her ears closed off as Eleanor launched into her recital. She was thinking only of Carlos Pritchett, the bastard whose head she wanted served up on a platter. Now she had the guy and now she could make not only the robbery but also the murder, the shooting of the veteran. It made her day.

"Kudos to you both," Cross told them then. "I'm putting you in for departmental merit citations. Pay increases to follow, unless I miss my bet."

"Fantastic," said O'Connell, who had only received one such citation in his eighteen years on the force.

"Suitable for framing?" asked Eleanor, who then laughed.

"Of course suitable for framing, Ellie. Of course."

Hands were shaken and more congratulations made all around.

Cross had finally caught a break. She drove home that night feeling much better about herself than she had for days now, ever since the murder of Rudy Monsorre. The memory of that sent a chill up her spine as she waited for traffic to clear on Washington.

The homicide detectives wanted to speak with her about that. They had leaked it to her that someone had emailed them an audio file that had been traced back to a computer at the public library. The file was said to be a phone call from Cross herself to Rudy Monsorre. Its contents were questionable and the dicks wanted her to fill in some answers they needed; nothing serious, they promised.

*Sure, nothing serious,* she thought. She knew how homicide worked.

And they wanted to talk ASAP.

Tears came to her eyes. She missed Rudy sorely. Missed his touch and his humor, missed the incredible sex that put her on another plane of ecstasy she'd never before known.

*Killed with an iron skillet?* She chided herself.

*Seriously?*

# Chapter 27

MICHAEL

"Talk about witness tampering," I said with an appreciative whistle. We--Racehorse and Marcel and I--were gathered around Racehorse's slate desk in his office.

Racehorse had just said that if he knew Phaeton had shot and killed *his* wife that he'd hunt him down, extract a confession to the wife murder and the murder of the veteran in the bank, then kill Phaeton himself. "Fuck him," Racehorse had said. "Fuck him and the horse he rode in on."

"You're seriously suggesting Michael kick down his door and finish him off?" Marcel said. I could see he was giving the suggestion some serious weight, something I wasn't. At least not yet. I needed him to take the stand in Carlos' trial and *then* I would kill him. Kill him dead for murdering my wife, my Danny. Wild horses wouldn't stop me then.

"Think of this, Michael," Racehorse continued, "waiting until after the trial to kill the bastard won't work. Why? Because he's going to be convicted at trial and taken into custody. Then where's your opportunity to shoot the prick? Huh?"

"Pay someone on the inside--I don't know," I said. The possibility had occurred to me, too. Still, as much as I wanted him dead, I wanted his testimony more.

"What about this, boss?" Marcel began slowly. "What if we go to his house, kick down his door, and record his confession? What if he then has an accident? Maybe he drowns in the ocean? We take him out in a boat and drown him?"

"I like that," Racehorse said without hesitation. "Drown the son of a bitch and let the sharks have their way. Then there's no evidence of anybody doing anything wrong. You wanna use my boat?"

"Seriously?" I said, the thought of drowning the man who killed my wife suddenly taking shape in my mind. "You have a boat?"

"Of course I have a boat. A forty foot Sundancer. Just for shits and giggles. But you're welcome to use it. Hello, Michael, you can have the damn thing if you want. I'm not gonna need it where I'm headed."

"Don't say that, please," I said. "You don't know anything for certain, yet."

"I know I'm inoperable, Michael. What more is there to know?"

"New medications are coming online every day. Keep praying, Racehorse."

"I'll leave the praying to you Catholics. Heathen like me, we just stretch out and let them kick dirt in our faces and that's good enough for us. Takes away the apprehension of having to answer to some guy in a long beard holding a list of my transgressions. It's the coward's way out, atheism. I can highly recommend it if you're a graceless sinner like me."

"Back to the boat," I said. "I'm thinking seriously about the boat now."

Racehorse opened his center desk drawer and removed a keychain. He tossed it to me and I caught it in one hand. "What?"

"Key to my boat. San Diego Yacht Club. Slip's on the tag."

"You weren't kidding," Marcel said. "Let's go collect up this guy," he said to me. "The fishes are hungry."

"There is a certain appeal there," I said. "Ever since Danny--"

My voice drifted away. I still found it profoundly difficult to talk about my love, weeks dead now, dead and cremated and preserved on my fireplace mantle. I cleared my throat and swiped a cuff across my eyes. "Well, now."

"Michael," Racehorse said in a slow, Southwestern drawl, "do yourself a favor. Do the world a favor before this man can hurt anyone else. Take him out, please."

Both men looked at me. I trusted them both implicitly. I knew they had my best interests at heart and I knew their judgment to be sound. Then it came to me: I wanted the man dead a hundred--no, a thousand--times more than they.

"What are we waiting for?" I asked Marcel. "Do you know how to operate a boat like this one?"

"Is the Pope Catholic?" Marcel said. "Oh, that's right, you Catholics always have an answer for that riddle, don't you?" He laughed.

I smiled.

"Racehorse, thank you."

"So, Michael, Saturday night, you'll be my witness?"

"I said I would and I will."

"Don't forget, please. UCSD Hospital in Hillcrest. Get my room number at the front desk."

"I will."

We said our goodbyes and Marcel and I rode the elevator down to the parking garage, where we climbed into his RAM pickup. He fired it up and the diesel loped and loped. He had driven from Chicago to San Diego, proclaiming that he couldn't operate without his own ride. No one argued with him.

"How do we get him from your truck to the boat?" I asked.

"Seriously? We walk him. At gunpoint."

"That's right. He's alive when we head out. Now I see."

"Michael, you're losing it on me, here." He gave me a hard look. "It's about Danny, isn't it?"

"Of course it's about Danny. I'm losing my place in the script. You're going to have to keep pointing me in the right direction on this one, Marcel. I'm too close to the problem to find the solution."

"I can do that. Just sit back and enjoy the ride."

"Will we both go inside?" I asked twenty minutes later when we pulled up before a nondescript house on Narragansett in Ocean Beach.

"You wait here. I'll be back with our guest in two ticks."

"Fair enough."

Sure enough, five minutes later, here came Marcel holding Phaeton by the scruff of his collar, a nickel-plated .44 magnum buried in the guy's ribs, next to his heart.

"Get out, Michael."

I did as ordered. Marcel cuffed the guy while I held the gun pointed at him. Then we traded back and Marcel manacled him to the seat post in the crew cab's backseat.

"Let's rock and roll," Marcel told me. "You drive, I'll keep an eye on our featured guest."

"What the fuck?" asked the voice of the man who killed my wife. "Who the fuck are you assholes?"

"Introductions will be forthcoming," Marcel told him as I started up the diesel. Soon we were headed south toward the yacht club. Along the way, Marcel teased and prodded Phaeton with the huge gun he had brought along. Phaeton couldn't avoid the taunts and pokes and prods. I must say, he took it like a man though he was anything but. He was a coward through and through and I hated him. At one point I even told him so and he said he didn't mind. I promised him he would.

The boat was dark and sloshing quietly dockside when we climbed aboard. First on was Marcel while I held the gun on Phaeton, then Phaeton while I still had the gun trained on him, then me. Marcel cuffed our guest on the rear deck, attaching him to a cleat. Then the engine rumbled to life after Marcel familiarized himself with the controls and dashboard. Within minutes we were cast off and backed out. Soon we were beyond the breakers and truly at sea. I went forward to talk with Marcel while we planed along.

"Where we going?" I asked.

He nodded toward the open sea. "Out there."

"How far?"

"Far enough. How's the chum?"

Marcel had gone into a bait store while I waited outside with Phaeton. He returned with a huge Styrofoam chest of ice and chum.

"Still with us. What's it for?"

He smiled and I could see his eyes glint in the dashboard lights. "Shark bait."

"We are going to attract sharks? Oh."

"Michael, please go below and strip the sheets off the forward bunk. Bring them into the lounge and hang them against the far wall as you're going down the stairs."

"Okay, but what for?"

"We need a backdrop for our movie."

"You brought a camera?"

He smiled and touched his shirt pocket. "iPhone. Best camera on the market."

"Oh."

"We want his confession, don't we?" he asked. But it was rhetorical. We both knew the answer.

We ran directly away from the shoreline for a good half hour. I went below and arranged the backdrop. Eventually, Marcel throttled back and the boat came to a pause in the calm sea. It rocked forward and aft but there was no pitch or roll.

"All right, take the pistol and bring the asshole downstairs. I'll be waiting."

I did as instructed, passing the gun down to Marcel as Phaeton made his way down. Before

I was all the way down, Marcel had Phaeton seated in front of the backdrop. The man sat listlessly, his face drained of color, staring dreamily at Marcel and his gun. Even handcuffed and far at sea, he managed every now and then to smile his insincere smile--his sneer--at whatever caught his eye. I hated him even more and was relieved and ready to move it along when Marcel raised his camera and peered through the lens. He then began videoing the conversation that was about to begin.

"State your name," he commanded Phaeton.

The man raised his head. He wasn't sneering now.

"Vincent Phaeton."

"Where do you live?"

"Uh--Ocean Beach."

"What is your occupation?"

"Handyman."

"You're a convicted felon?"

"Uh-huh."

"Say yes or no, please."

"Yes. I'm a felon. Still can't vote," he said with just the beginning of a sneer.

"What were you convicted of?"

"Armed robbery. There was also a rape and a burglary somewhere in there."

"You served your time at San Quentin?"

"Uh-huh. Yes."

"And when were you released?"

"Couple of months now."

"What have you done since then?"

"You know, just general handyman stuff."

"Like bank robbery kind of stuff?"

"I was in on that, yes. Not because I wanted. I was kind of forced into it."

"Tell us how that happened."

"Well, this guy I met at Q knew a guy named Ramsey who would help me start over when I got out. I went to this Ramsey guy and he hooked me up with Carlos the Ant."

"How were you forced?"

"Ramsey said he would take me down if he told me about the plan and I tried to say no. He said he would have me killed."

"Sure. Tell us about Carlos."

"Not much to say. He had a crew and I threw in and we hit the First Commercial. But I killed the soldier, not Carlos."

"What soldier?"

"There was a veteran in the tellers' line. He mouthed off, so I accidentally shot him."

"You were wearing a mask?"

"I was."

"What were you?"

"What was I? I was the monkey. I wore the monkey mask."

"If the witnesses in line said it was the monkey who shot the veteran, would you agree?"

"Yes, the monkey shot the customer. I shot him."

"So the witnesses would all be correct?"

"Hell, yes."

"You're sure you were the monkey?"

"Sure I'm sure. I even saw myself in the bank window when we went by. I was the monkey with the TEC-9."

"Why are you admitting it was you who shot the veteran?"

Phaeton shook his head and slowly drew a deep breath.

"Just need to get it off my chest. I've got immunity."

"Have you discussed your role in the robbery with the police or the DA?"

"I have. They want me to testify and I said yes."

"So you're going to testify against Carlos and Ramsey?"

"That's what they tell me."

"Who tells you?"

"Her name is Leticia Cross. Her detective friend is something O'Donnell or O'Connell--I don't exactly remember. Some overweight white guy with shit growing out of his ears."

Marcel turned to me. "That sounds pleasant. Glad I'm not eating my dinner, I'd puke."

"You would know what I mean if you saw the guy. Gross, dude. Hey, can I bum a cigarette or what?"

"I don't smoke," Marcel said. "You'll just have to wait."

"Oh. Well, that's about all I know about the bank stuff."

"What about Danny Gresham? Did you shoot her?"

"Who?"

"Dania Gresham--Danny. The wife of Michael Gresham. Did you shoot her to make Michael Gresham leave you alone?"

"Did I? No, didn't, never. Why would I shoot some woman I don't even know?"

"Same reason the monkey would shoot a veteran he didn't know, I suppose," Marcel said smoothly. Frankly, I was impressed. But then I remembered: a dozen years with Interpol and the New Scotland Yard? Of course he'd know how to take a statement. It was obviously child's play for him.

"Did anybody force you to say these things you've told us?"

"Force me? I doubt anyone could force me to say something that wasn't the God's truth. I'm not like that."

"Okay."

"So what's next?"

Marcel lowered the smartphone and replaced it in his shirt pocket. The recording was evidently complete.

"What's next?" Phaeton repeated.

"How good a swimmer are you?"

"I'm no swimmer. I did track and football. No swimming."

"So when we throw you overboard you're not gonna beat us back to shore?"

"Fuck you talking about, throw me over? Didn't I just cooperate?"

"All except for lying about shooting Danny Gresham. Michael recognized your voice tonight as the guy who called him and threatened his children after his wife was murdered. He's ninety percent sure it was you on the other end of that call."

"But it wasn't me!" Phaeton squealed. "I didn't murder anyone's wife."

"Sure, you did," I said, suddenly climbing to my feet and addressing Phaeton eye-to-eye. And even if you didn't, it's close enough. You're trying to put my client away, trying to hang a murder rap on him. I'm the kind of lawyer who won't allow that to happen to his clients. Shark bait."

"What's that supposed to mean? You guys aren't--"

"We are."

"Wait, wait, wait, wait, wait. Slow down! Now, let's talk. What if I can point you at the guy who shot your wife? Does that get me back to shore?"

"I don't know, ask Marcel. This is his show."

"Marcel? What do you say?" Phaeton cried. "Does cooperation get me home?"

"Too late for that. Just you knowing the shooter is close enough for me. You've admitted you know who he is. That's good enough. You're going in the drink, pal."

"You'll have to shoot me, then. I ain't climb--"

Marcel suddenly turned and swung his revolver up and shot Phaeton in the leg.

The gun's explosion below decks was deafening. I could even see the fire belch from the barrel of the gun in the dim light.

"Say what?" Marcel asked Phaeton. "You ain't climbing what?"

"All right, all right, all right, all right. I'm cooperating. I shot the wife, all right? But Ramsey, he--"

Blam! Marcel shot the guy in the left arm. This shot threw him back against the backdrop and now the sheet dropped from the wall and covered him. A red flower of blood quickly appeared where the man's arm hung uselessly at his side. The shot had all but rendered him unconscious.

Then he revived enough to tear the sheet away with his good arm.

"Okay, just tell me what we're doing. I know you don't mean to kill me. You still need me at trial."

"Michael," Marcel said, ignoring our prisoner, "you climb up on deck. I'm going to lift him from below and you're going to pull him from above. Got it?"

I hustled up the stairs as directed. The man was heavy but we got him up and out. We left him lying on the rear deck. Marcel stepped over him to the Styrofoam chest.

"Now for the chum," said Marcel. He emptied the contents of the Styrofoam chest on the starboard side of the boat. Then we sat and talked for ten minutes until we could hear the water around us stirring.

"Sharks," Marcel said with a smile. "They're here for a taste."

With that, he stood up and removed Phaeton's handcuffs.

"All right, ducky," he said, shoving his gun against Phaeton's ribs. "Up and over for you."

Phaeton responded by crying long and hard. But Marcel wasn't having any of it. He rolled the guy to the edge of the boat and shoved him over with his boot. Hearing a loud splash and a final cry, I knew the man was in the water.

Then the water around us suddenly erupted. There was no sound other than a great slashing and splashing and then, just as suddenly as it had started, all was quiet again.

I got up and stepped to the side of the boat. It was totally dark three feet out. Nothing to see.

"Feel better?"

"Much," I said. "Feel much better."

"Good. Let's head back, then."

There was nothing else to say. We had done what we came to do. Danny was avenged. Carlos was in the clear thanks to the monkey mask statement from Phaeton. Of course it was still a felony-murder case, but at least Carlos hadn't pulled the trigger that killed the veteran. That was something.

And Phaeton? He was in hundreds of pieces by now, skimming through the ocean.

I liked the image. Skimming in a hundred pieces.

But it didn't heal my broken heart.

# Chapter 28

CARLOS

Once I was out on bail, I spent every waking and sleeping minute at Amelia's bedside in the hospital. She wasn't improving as we first hoped she would. The doctors were concerned and her mother and I were frantic, though we hid it from our baby.

Through the dark of Friday night, I could hear her shallow breathing as she slept. It was a light sleep--she would awaken every twenty minutes or so and ask for water. She just couldn't get enough water.

At seven the next morning, Dr. Xu came around. He summoned me out into the hallway.

"What's the latest, doc?" I said in a strained whisper. I couldn't hide my panic and made no effort to do so.

"She's not responding to the medication as we had hoped. The fever is running away with her and we can't seem to stabilize her."

"Meaning what?"

"Meaning she's not doing any better. In fact, she's doing worse, I would have to say. I don't want to alarm you more than you already are. But I owe you the truth. We'll give it another twelve hours then we'll assemble the team and speak again. Keep up your prayers, please."

"We will," I promised. "We'll keep praying for all we're worth."

"Good. Thank you, Mr. Pritchett. Please send your wife out now and let me speak with her, too."

I returned to my daughter's bedside and sent Joanna into the hallway. I assumed she would receive the same message as me.

"Daddy," said the small voice from the bed, "I don't feel good. Can you tell someone?"

"Of course, angel," I said. I pumped the call button clamped to the bottom sheet of the bed. It lit up and stayed that way. Within three minutes the nurse appeared.

"How are we doing, pudding?" she said to her little patient. She adjusted sheets and placed a cool compress to the girl's forehead. "Dad, help hold this on here, please. This will help. Your head hurts, doesn't it, sweetie? Daddy's going to hold this on here. You press the button again if you need me, hear?"

"Okay. It feels cold, Daddy."

"It is cold, baby. I'm sorry."

"It's okay, Daddy. You're trying to help."

In that moment, in the early dawn light, I suddenly saw the face of Washburn Rambis, the insurance underwriter who had refused to cover my daughter's medical care early on. I would have given anything if Rambis could be there just then, just to see what his refusal had done to my child. The man wouldn't leave the hospital alive. Not while I was around, he wouldn't. I chased the thoughts from my mind. For now, my daughter needed me. Rambis could wait.

But his time would come around. There would be a reckoning.

# Chapter 29

### DETECTIVE O'CONNELL

Detectives O'Connell and Howell pulled into the underground parking at the District Attorney's Office and rode the elevator upstairs. It was late Friday afternoon and most of the DA's deputies--the warriors--had returned from court and were in various stages of decompression after another long, hard week pursuing justice at Justice Hall. The receptionist at the front desk buzzed Leticia, then told the detectives she was expecting them, they should go on in. They rounded the first corner, then stopped in the hallway where they were alone.

"I'm telling you, I have very grave concerns about Deputy Cross," detective Howell said to her partner. "I know what you said in the car but I'm still not convinced. She was involved with Rudy Monsorre. The audio file proves it. Maybe even tipping him off about police activity." She was referring to the audio file a mystery person had sent them, a file containing the recorded voice of Deputy Cross in which she was advising Monsorre of impending police activity.

"We don't know that," O'Connell scoffed. "That call could just as easily have been about the case she was working up with Mr. Monsorre. Maybe even about some chop shop he was spilling the beans on. I'm of the opinion he was a cooperating witness and she was working him."

"Think what you will," Eleanor Howell sniffed, "but I happen to strongly disagree. She's complicit and that's that. Call it intuition if you want."

"I'll tell you what I think. I think one audio clip isn't enough to build a case. And if you're going to ruin a deputy DA's career, you'd better have an airtight case. We are a million miles from that."

"Well, that's probably true."

"It sure as hell is, Ellie."

They continued down the hallway and turned left, where they stopped outside of Leticia's door. O'Connell rapped his knuckles against the wood and heard, shouted from inside, "Enter!"

They stepped inside, where they found Leticia dictating into her hand-held recorder. She set it aside and turned and smiled at her visitors.

"So," said Leticia, "you ready to update me on the bank robbery?"

O'Connell pulled uncomfortably at his necktie. "Not exactly, Ms. Cross. We actually wanted to ask you some questions about Rudy Monsorre's death. We know you were acquainted with Rudy."

The prosecutor leaned back against her chair and appraised her visitors with eyes that suddenly had turned anything but friendly.

"Knew him? I was investigating a case he brought to our office. That was all."

"Well," said Detective Howell, "we have a little more to ask you about than just that." She looked at her partner. O'Connell nodded at her to proceed. "So here's the deal. We have an audio file of you telling Rudy Monsorre that a team of detectives and uniforms was headed for his warehouse in the next day or so. Then you continue and thank him for a pair of Jimmy Choo shoes he evidently dropped by your place. Would you like to comment on this?"

Leticia's eyes flashed a cross look at the two detectives. She carefully chose her words.

"First of all, where did you get this audio file? I need to know who's recording me."

"It was sent to us anonymously," O'Connell said. "Sent directly to my office email."

"Do I get to listen to it?"

Howell looked at her partner. She shook her head. "We didn't bring it along. You'll just have to trust that we're not making this up because we aren't. Now, again, why would you be warning a police target of an impending search of his premises?"

"I can't imagine that I did. I'd have to hear the actual recording before I could comment."

"We can appreciate that," O'Connell said in great innocence. "But for now, if you did tell this person a police investigation was headed his way, why would you tell him to remove all vehicles from his warehouse?"

The deputy DA's shoulders slumped. "I wouldn't know. Maybe because he--"

The detectives leaned in. Howell was furiously taking notes of the conversation.

"Maybe he was undercover for me at that point. I honestly don't remember."

"Seriously?" O'Connell said, his eyes wide in disbelief. "You really want us to believe you don't remember whether a named person was working undercover for you or not? Ms. Cross, the audio file only goes back three weeks. It's very recent."

The color drained from the prosecutor's face. "You know what? I don't like your tone. Not one damn bit. And I don't like you two barging in on me while I'm thinking you're here about a bank robbery and you're actually here to accuse me of something."

"Oh, we're not--"

"Please," O'Connell said sharply. "No one is accusing anyone of anything. We're just looking to have this little audio blurb explained away. I know you have your reasons for saying those things. Maybe you were trying to entrap Mr. Monsorre by having him clear out his warehouse as evidence he was engaged in wrongdoing? I don't know. But I'm open to a possibility like that."

The prosecutor had managed to collect herself at that point. "Look. I'm going to have to retrieve that investigative file and see where my thoughts were at that time. So for now, I'm not going to answer any more questions about Rudy Monsorre or anything I might have said to him. I'm sure you understand that I want to be certain I'm giving you information that is correct and backed up by my file notes. Just give me a day or two and I'll run them down and call you. Fair enough?"

"Sure," O'Connell said. "That's more than fair. And believe me, we're not trying to spring anything on you here. We're just trying to look in every nook and cranny. As it stands right now, we have a young woman in custody whose DNA was found on the murder weapon that killed Mr. Monsorre. You are definitely not connected to that aspect of the case and I don't want you to get the wrong impression and think maybe that's why we're here, too. Because it isn't. It's just that silly little audio file. That's all, Ms. Cross."

"All right. Anything else I can do for you?"

"Well, actually there is," Howell said.

Leticia had just climbed to her feet, but now she sat down heavily and exhaled with a sound indicating she was running low on patience. "Yes?" she said.

"Your man Carlos Pritchett. He's--"

"So now we're switching gears and we're talking about the First Commercial robbery?"

"Yes. Carlos Pritchett went to Bel Air awhile back. While he was there he assaulted the chief underwriter of his insurance company. He shot him two or three times. Attempted murder charges have been filed but the Los Angeles District Attorney has agreed to back-burner the case until we're done with Pritchett down here. But also, I've talked to the underwriter myself. I think he's someone you need to talk to. He's got information that might be useful in your prosecution of Pritchett down here. So we were wondering--"

"We're here to ask you to join us for a ride up to Bel Air to interview this man. His name is Washburn Rambis and he's extremely willing to help. He believes he'd be dead today if Carlos had been any more accurate with his gun."

"Or maybe he's alive because Carlos was accurate," Howell hurried to add.

"Do you mean now? Today? Go with you today?"

"Yes."

"Yes. We were hoping. It's a very important aspect of the robbery case in San Diego."

"Well, I--I--I guess I can." Leticia was thinking that her innocence on the other matter would be reinforced if she cooperated with the cops on the Bel Air thing. In and of itself, the Bel Air connection sounded very tenuous, but she didn't want to seem like she was avoiding two of her chief investigators on that case, so she told herself cooperation was paramount. "Yes, in fact, I can leave right now."

"Good. It's only about two hours, with traffic."

"Give or take."

"Yes, give or take."

"Let me send this dictation off to my paralegal and I'll join you in the lobby. Fair enough?" The detectives stood and started backing out. Then they were gone.

Deputy Cross stood up from her chair and arched her back, hands outstretched, relieving the cramp she was feeling mid-back and below. It had been totally nerve-wracking. She'd never found herself under the gun before and she had found it horribly painful. She drew a deep breath and shook her body like a dog sheds water, trying to restore complete blood flow, as if it had been impeded by the cops. Then she sat back down in a rush, the air whooshing out of her lungs. "Wow. Son of a bitch."

* * *

It was late when they hit L.A., but Washburn Rambis had agreed to remain late at the office in order to help make the case against his assailant. He was only too happy to help, he said.

The two detectives and the prosecutor were rolling northbound on the 5. Then they cut over to the 405 and took the Sunset Boulevard off-ramp. Twenty minutes later they were parking in a restricted area downstairs in GCIA's building. It was a cop car on official business, so they didn't give their parking selection a second thought.

Upstairs, they entered through the darkened lobby and followed directions they had been given to his office. His door was open.

Rambis stood up when the trio entered his office. Deputy Cross noticed he was moving painfully as he shook their hands and resettled behind his desk.

"So," he said, "I wish we could offer you coffee or something but our staff is already gone. So forgive me, please."

"Not necessary," said O'Connell, who was clearly going to take the lead in what followed. "We'd just like to ask a few quick questions then we're out of here."

"First, is the bastard still behind bars?"

"Actually no," said O'Connell. "He made bail."

"Who the hell would allow bail in that case? Weren't cops killed?"

O'Connell spread his hands and sighed. "It's a long story. Short version, somebody knew somebody so he's out and walking around, a free man."

"Jesus, I hope he doesn't decide to drive up here and shoot me again."

"He's not allowed to leave San Diego."

"Well, that's a relief," the insurance man said, his voice full of sarcasm. He smiled at the other detective and the DA for buy-in on his sarcasm, but their faces remained blank. It was going to be a tougher audience than maybe he expected.

"Can you give us a brief synopsis of what happened when Pritchett broke in here?"

"Actually, he didn't break in. My secretary allowed him in. He was masquerading as a delivery man, boxes and everything. Only when he got inside, he locked the door behind him and told me he was going to kill me. Something like that."

"Is that when he shot you?"

"No. First, we went over his daughter's insurance claim. I told him we denied coverage on her, sad as it was, and as much as we hated to, because her name wasn't on the application for insurance. It wasn't her name on there, officers."

"What do you mean, not her name? Why would her father leave her off of an insurance application? It was for the whole family, right?"

"Right. And that's who we insured--the known family. It's like car insurance. You can't expect us to cover your Ford when you've only applied for coverage on your Chevrolet; same difference here."

"So there was no coverage. Then what happened."

"That's when the shooting began. He shot me three times, the lowlife bastard. Excuse my French, ladies."

"I've heard worse," said Detective Howell.

"Me too," Deputy DA Cross whispered.

Rambis then went on to recount the extent of his injuries and his hospitalization in quite some detail. Then he went over his physical and occupational rehab--he clearly wanted his visitors to know how terribly he had been injured by the man they were now prosecuting in San Diego, as if his own case would somehow increase Pritchett's problems in San Diego--which it didn't.

"One thing," O'Connell said when the insurance man was finished. "Would you come to San Diego and testify against Carlos Pritchett? Either at his trial or his sentencing hearing. I'm talking about evidence of prior bad acts."

"Sure I will. I mean, I'll ask my manager, but I don't see why not. Anything to put this gentleman away for a long time. And throw away the key, I might add."

Arrangements were tentatively made along those lines, with Rambis drawing a yellow line through the trial days on his office calendar so he'd remember to be available to San Diego then. A short wrap-up followed, and then the visitors were gone, leaving Rambis to his own thoughts and painful memories. Actually, the insurance man found it spooky to be left behind in the same office where he'd been almost killed, especially now that it was dark, so he hastened to leave the building as closely behind the police as possible. He made it out in record time and jumped into his car in the basement parking area and immediately locked the doors. *Thank heavens for power locks,* he thought with a grimace.

* * *

Just south of L.A., O'Connell pulled the police car into an Iron Skillet restaurant and parked in the first row of parking. "Let's grab a bite," he told his passengers. "I'm starved."

Leticia Cross looked up from the back seat. She had a terrible feeling that this unscheduled stop had been prearranged.

"I'm not hungry," she said. "I'll just wait here and work on my direct examination notes for Mr. Rambis. I have my laptop."

"Nonsense!" cried O'Connell. "It won't be the same without you. Come on inside and we'll talk it over all you want. I think he's going to be a great witness."

Deputy Cross didn't think that was necessarily true, but now O'Connell had come around and was holding her door open. So she surrendered to the moment and climbed out. *What the hell,* she thought, *you can certainly hold your own with these two hacks.*

"Sit anywhere," the hostess said and handed out three menus.

After settling in and ordering, Howell said, in all innocence, "You know what's just occurred to me? I'm thinking maybe you can't remember about Rudy Monsorre's phone call you made because you've been putting in long hours on the robbery. It makes sense to me."

"It's been difficult," Leticia was quick to agree. "My mind has certainly been focused."

"So let me understand just one thing," Howell continued. "You're not telling us you didn't know Mr. Monsorre, are you?"

"Oh no, I definitely knew him. In fact, I'm remembering now that he had something to do with a chop shop. Maybe he worked at a chop shop and he was a CI."

"That would stand to reason. That's very likely how you knew him," said Detective Howell.

Several minutes passed. Cross studied the other diners. Howell excused herself and hit the restroom. O'Connell fiddled with his watchband. "Catches the hair on my wrist," he smiled at one point. Then Howell returned and slid in beside Cross again.

"You know what?" Howell said. "I'll just bet you wouldn't mind if I recorded a little of our conversation here, just to help me with my report later?"

It was a pending question. All eyes were on Deputy Cross.

She smiled as best she could. "Actually, I would mind. No prosecutor wants to give out comments before a case has jelled."

"What case would that be?" said Eleanor Howell. "I don't have any case in mind. I just want to make a few notes on my recorder."

"Well--"

"It's harmless," O'Connell assured Deputy Cross. "We do this all the time with other DAs."

"You do?"

"Oh, sure. If it gets into some area you're uncomfortable with, just say and we'll turn everything off."

"Well--"

Howell whipped out her micro-recorder and hit the red R. Cross watched the digits start to count upwards as seconds passed.

"First off," Howell began, "your name is Leticia Cross?"

"It is."

"And Ms. Cross, you understand I am recording this conversation and you have no objection?"

"I guess not."

"We're here tonight to ask you about Rudy Monsorre. You knew Mr. Monsorre?"

"Vaguely. I think I saw him once or twice."

"Once or twice? You're sure that's all?"

"Sure? I'm certain it was only once or twice."

"And where would that have been?"

"Probably in my office."

"Ever at his home?"

"Definitely not."

"Or your home?"

"Same answer."

"Did Mr. Monsorre ever gift you a pair of Jimmy Choo's?"

"Shoes? Did he give me shoes? Is that what you're asking?"

"Yes."

"Definitely not."

"Did you ever thank him for a pair of shoes?"

"No. Why would I? I just said he didn't give me any shoes. You know what? Turn that damn thing off. This is way beyond just note-taking."

"You're refusing to speak with us any further about this matter?"

"You bet I'm refusing. You tricked me into thinking you were only going to be taking down some notes but instead you're interrogating me. I don't like it one damn bit, either, I want you to know. I'll be reporting this to your lieutenant."

"Our lieutenant said to speak with you about it. He said we should get your statement."

"Turn it off! Now!"

From the Iron Skillet restaurant all the way back to San Diego and her office, Deputy

Cross didn't say another word. Just to show there were no hard feelings, the cops tried to engage her, but the spell was broken. They were no longer allies; now they were working opposite sides of the same fence.

She opened her door and climbed out in the parking basement of her building. She slammed the door and abruptly turned on her heel and marched off.

"Wow," said O'Connell. "You hit a nerve there."

"I did, didn't I? So now what?"

"Now we get a search warrant."

# Chapter 30

CARLOS

I sat upright in the dark hospital room. Something was wrong: something--some piece of some machine--was no longer making its noise. It had been days--weeks--that I had spent at my daughter's bedside. Amelia had seemed to be gaining strength and maybe edging closer to going home, but then yesterday she had taken a downturn. The physicians were baffled; they were waiting for tests ordered by an internist who specialized in systemic infections. Test results were pending, we were told twice.

I looked around the room. My wife was home getting clothes for me. Realizing I was alone with my daughter, I listened for her breathing. Then I held my own breath and listened even harder. For the life of me, I could hear nothing from my little girl. Ordinarily her breathing was slow and steady though occasionally there were jagged fits of coughing. But even these had occurred less and less often over the past twenty-four hours.

I listened again. Definitely something wrong. I turned and looked at the machines over my baby's left shoulder. There were no less than a half-dozen monitors and LED's blinking and recording and evaluating and reporting. Except for one: there was no longer the mostly vertical, upside-down V's of the heart monitor. That's what was missing!

I leaned across my daughter and repeatedly squeezed the nurse's call button. Then I ran into the hallway and shouted down to the other end, where the nurses gathered and charted and chattered all night long. "Hey! My little girl stopped breathing!"

At that same moment, an alert appeared on the nurses' computer screens. Code Blue in the Pritchett girl's room. Code Blue!

People were surging down the halls, the crash cart leading the way. I was pushed to the side and told to remain outside the room. I complied, but leaned in head and shoulders until again snapped at to remove myself. So I withdrew. I could hear excited voices at my daughter's bedside. I could hear someone shout "Clear!" several times, maybe twenty seconds apart. Then, just as suddenly as the excitement and clatter had begun, it eased off. Amelia's nurse came into the hallway and placed a hand on my shoulder.

"We tried everything, Mr. Pritchett. But your little girl is gone. Amelia passed."

"*What*?" I howled. "Impossible! You all said she was better!"

I pulled the nurse closer and laid my head on her shoulder. I sobbed and sobbed and finally staggered away and went into where my daughter lay. Two aides were cleaning her little body. The nurse went to the head of her bed and removed the endotracheal tube. I watched the thick plastic hose snake up and out of my little girl. I hated the contraption, hated that it had failed, hated each and every tile in the ceiling that I had counted night after night. Then I threw my arms across my daughter's frail body and cradled her head in my hand. I kissed the top of her head and wouldn't stop until the same nurse gently tugged at me from behind.

"We need to finish with her now, Mr. Pritchett, if you're just about done."

She tugged a bit more emphatically and I finally allowed myself to be turned around, where I was asked again to leave the room so the aides and nurse could finish with the body.

I stumbled into the hallway and stood there, alone, weeping and gnashing my teeth, my hands clenching and unclenching while the tears fell from my eyes onto the tile floor. I pulled out my smartphone and called Joanna. She knew immediately from the sound of my voice. She came running.

Thirty minutes later, after Joanna had arrived and we had held each other and wept, we were again allowed back into the room to see our child. Joanna repeated the same things with her baby's cold body, cradling her and hugging her near. Tears fell from her eyes and she wept and rocked up and down while her body shuddered and shook. Then we were led away.

"We need to take her downstairs," the nurse whispered.

"What?"

"To the morgue. We need to take Amelia to the morgue."

"Oh, my sweet Jesus!" Joanna cried, collapsing in my arms.

I watched over my wife's shoulder as our daughter was wheeled away, receding down the long hallway until she turned the corner and headed for the bank of elevators.

"She's gone," my wife said. "Just like that."

"There will be revenge for this," I promised through clenched teeth.

"Don't talk like that. I won't allow it."

"Allow it or not, it doesn't change the fact that a certain man in Bel Air is going to die for this."

"Rambis? He didn't kill our daughter. The disease killed her."

"No! If she'd had her medicine on time she'd be home with us now, playing in her room and reading her books. This never would have happened."

"Have it your way."

"I will. I will have it my way. And I'll finish the bastard my way."

"Hush! Don't talk like that so soon after Amelia's passing. It isn't right."

I caught myself up short. She was right, of course, it wasn't proper.

Still, in my mind I was leveling my Glock at Rambis' heart.

I felt my finger pull.

# Chapter 31

"What did you think?" O'Connell said to Leticia as the clutch of police searched her condo. "That we wouldn't get your phone records? There are dozens of calls back and forth between you and Rudy Monsorre. He was a hell of a lot more than a confidential informant, Ms. Cross. Why don't you come clean with us and let's work this out? Tell us exactly what was going on."

The search warrant had been served at 7:03 a.m. before she left for work that Friday morning, and the search was still underway. O'Connell had asked her to wait on the living room couch and not move from there until they were finished. Now here he was, trying to get an admission out of her.

"I want to speak with my lawyer," said Leticia. "That's all I'm going to say."

"I was in your bedroom a few minutes ago. My officers are finding men's pants, black, men's shirts, also black, snakeskin boots, a man's Rolex. And the clothes are the same sizes as the clothes we examined at Mr. Monsorre's home. Medium everything. Except the boots. Those are a thirteen, which might be a little large for a man his height. And what about the Rolex? Did he just leave that here? Just forget it? How much money did this guy have, anyway?"

"I want to speak with my lawyer. You can stop now."

"But you know what? You didn't remove all his stuff before we got here. Why not? Didn't you know we'd be coming with a search warrant?"

"I want to speak with a lawyer."

"Or is that what the garbage bags were for that we found on your bed? You were just getting ready to dispose of his stuff? How much have you already tossed? Come on, Leticia, let's clear this up now. You know they'll go easier on you if you just cooperate. It's not like you're charged with killing the guy. We've got his girlfriend for that. We just need to know what you were doing with him, that's all. It's not a major crime and no one thinks it is. What do you say?"

"I say I want to speak with a lawyer."

"Okay. But it would sure go easier on you if you would talk."

"How many times have I heard that, detective? I want to speak with a lawyer, period. Now back the hell off before I sue you for harassment."

"Okay, okay. But there is one thing I needed to ask about, not related to you and Rudy and whatever was going on. I'm just wondering when you left your prints all over his condo. We've found your prints in the kitchen, bedroom, the living room, all over in the bathroom including the sides of the tub and the shower tiles. It almost looks like you were living there. Had you been there the day he was murdered? Stopped by for any reason?"

"You have my prints?"

"Sure, deputy. It's very clear to us you were more than just his control when he was informing."

"I want to speak to a lawyer."

"But I'm going to tell you this. If I see *any* indication you were involved in his murder, I'm coming after you and I'm coming down hard. Do you feel me, Ms. Cross?"

"I want to speak with a lawyer."

"Fair enough. But you better get one who can explain the phone calls over the past year, his clothes in your place, your prints all over his place. Someone needs to start talking."

"I want to speak to a lawyer."

# Chapter 32

"Mr. Gray, what time would you like to die?"

Horatio "Racehorse" Gray looked at the TV above his hospital bed and clicked a button. He waited a moment while the upcoming shows displayed before he answered. Then he clicked it off.

"Six-thirty-one. The minute *Jeopardy*'s over. Not a second before. Not a second after."

The nurse who would administer the life-ending barbiturate cocktail nodded and backed out of the room. She returned to the nurse's station just down the hall.

"Gray still on?" asked the duty nurse at the nurses' station.

The floor nurse nodded and brushed a clump of hair off her forehead.

"Yes. He wants to watch *Jeopardy*, then--"

"Ours is not to reason why--" said the duty nurse in a sing-song.

Back in his room, Horatio Gray pulled his head and shoulders up onto his pillows. The effort caused him to cringe with pain and I could see the sweat bathe his face.

"Michael," he said to me in a voice that was a cross between a croak and a rush of pure air, "thank you for agreeing to be my witness."

I shook my head. "It's the least I can do. I owe you, Racehorse."

He smiled at the nickname. We'd been friends and law colleagues the past several months, litigating here in San Diego. Racehorse was the greatest trial lawyer I'd ever had the privilege of watching in any courtroom over my thirty years. Before he was stricken and received his prognosis, we had just finished up the most recent battle with the district attorney's office over Carlos Pritchett's upcoming trial. That day, Carlos was walking around in normal clothes without handcuffs and waist chains, thanks largely to Racehorse. His ultimate resolution would come in the next two weeks when the jury would retire to deliberate. By then, Racehorse would be no more and I'd be standing with his associate at counsel table. We'd be without Racehorse's know-how, and the thought of practicing in a California court as a foreign attorney with very limited knowledge of California trial law and California evidence law was more than just a little frightening.

The next half hour flew by while Racehorse lay with his eyes closed. His shallow breathing filled the otherwise quiet room. I busied myself with my tablet, working on the next pleading to be filed in Carlos' case. I had several questions to ask Racehorse but I held off. Maybe it was better to just let him go and figure out my quandary on my own. Then the thought of proceeding without him gripped me like a cold fist and a chill snaked its way down my back. I shivered and kept typing.

His eyes fluttered open at precisely 5:59 and his long, bony fingers worked the TV remote fastened to his bed. He smiled at me and nodded at the TV.

"*Jeopardy*, Michael. Do you partake?"

"Can't say I do. My mother watched during her nursing home years."

His eyes narrowed at me. "You've been working on the brief?"

"I have."

"It's due tomorrow. Will you have it ready on time?"

He was ignoring that *Jeopardy*'s Alex Trebek had come onscreen and was launching into the game show's categories without fanfare.

"I will. I have some questions," I added selfishly, and immediately wished I'd let it go. *Let the man watch his show*, I chastised myself. *You're a big boy; you've got this.*

He muted the show.

"Well, ask away. You've got twenty-eight minutes to put it to bed," he said with a wry smile. Metaphors came easily and usually with a touch of irony with Racehorse.

"Well, for openers, we're arguing that Phaeton's disappearance had nothing to do with Carlos and that the DA shouldn't be allowed to connect their names during the time period after the robbery."

"Go on."

"And hospital records show Carlos was spending his days and nights in his daughter's hospital room during the time Phaeton disappeared."

"It's solid evidence in his favor," said Racehorse with a grimace. His already white face turned whiter still as any remaining color drained because of the pain he was enduring. I was certain the morphine had worn off and that he would give himself another jolt of it at any moment. When he did so, I would lose him for several minutes as he drifted away into semi-consciousness. I was hoping we could finish this final discussion before he needed the drug. Then I realized it wasn't right of me to put my needs ahead of his. He needed the comfort of the drug.

"Are you okay? Do you need a dose? Please go ahead with it, Racehorse."

He shook his head, rolling it back and forth on his pillow in a surprising show of strength. The guy continued to amaze me. And it was all about character. He had decided that he wouldn't let the pain rob us of these final minutes together. He was willing himself to rise above it.

"Go ahead, Michael."

"So do I put Carlos on the stand to testify?"

"Don't think so. Of course the district attorney will argue he was loose and that the hospital duty was not continuous. You overcome that by--"

His voice trailed off and his eyes closed. His hand uncurled from the pump he had been clutching. Which meant he had administered another dose of the pain killer and it had taken him away. I couldn't take my eyes away from him. He was a giant and yet he was dying like all humans must. His wife preceded him in death; his kids didn't come around, hadn't in twenty years, and no one else knew he was there. Not really. So I was it, as far as witnesses and loved ones at bedside. The witness part I could handle; the loved one role was far beyond my grasp. We were workmates and nothing more.

I watched closely for signs he was coming back around. But I knew I was pushing it. He was usually out of it for five, maybe ten minutes when he dosed. I checked my watch. 6:14. His soul would leave the earth in seventeen minutes and my oracle would be no more. I'd truly be on my own in this unfamiliar state and unknown courtroom with an unknown judge after that.

I wondered at his train of thought just before he self-dosed. He had been saying I could overcome the fact Carlos wasn't going to testify by--but he left off there. Damn! I checked my watch again. 6:16. He hadn't moved. His breathing had shallowed out again and his eyes weren't moving behind his eyelids. He was really out. I knew this from spending those weeks with him since the diagnosis and hospitalization.

I tore my eyes away from him and stared at my watch as the seconds ticked by. I was becoming frenzied inside. I *needed* what he had to say. At 6:22 his eyes fluttered open.

"What?" he said weakly.

"I'm sorry you're hurting, Racehorse. Let's let you just rest--" which was a stupid thing I was about to say. Why would he benefit from resting when he was going to die in nine minutes with a paralyzing agent in his veins?

"Michael," he said, "come close by me, son."

I got up out of the visitor's chair and moved two steps forward. I was standing over him then, peering down into what remained of his visage after the disease had drained away his flesh and fluids. The skin on his face was pulled very tight in a death mask and it had the sheen of a very thin, very pale face that was wholly unnatural in appearance. There was no flush, no color of any kind, no substance to indicate the skin held a living organism. He was all but gone and I knew it and his coming absence buckled my knees. I forced myself upright and locked my knees. I knew it was selfish to keep coming back to me-me-me even as he lay there dying, but I couldn't help it.

When we teamed up, he was a giant of a man, literally and figuratively. Literally, because Racehorse stood six-four and weighed probably 250. Since learning he was sick he'd probably dropped 100 pounds and walked stooped and bent, a whisper of his former self. While Racehorse had been first chair in the defense of Carlos' case, I had been a very quiet, very subdued, second chair. I probably hadn't said over ten words on the record and those were just to tell the court Mr. Gray was on his way to court with apologies for being tardy. When he became ill and too weak to move ahead, the court ordered a continuance before trial was to begin. We all knew the judge was continuing the case until Racehorse passed. Then we would be back at it full-bore and this time I would be expected to move into the first chair because the judge wouldn't countenance any further delays for new counsel to get up to speed and run the case. So there you were: the incredible lawyer I had retained to defend Carlos was dying and I was just inches offstage waiting until the court looked my way.

He unexpectedly took my hand in his and squeezed.

"I know you're scared. No lawyer should ever defend in a state where he isn't licensed. It's almost impossible to do."

"I know."

"So here's what I want you to do."

At just that moment, Racehorse's treating physician entered the room, a jovial bounce to his step, like always, and a bit of a smile on his face--forced there, because we all knew better.

We all knew that he was there to supervise the administration of the paralyzing agent by the nurse, Cindy--who also came into the room just behind him. So there we were, the four of us, prepared to help one of us have a good death.

My watch said 6:26. Alex Trebek announced it was time for final *Jeopardy*. To my astonishment, Racehorse seemed to be following that, for he raised a hand and indicated the TV screen. "Wait one," he said. We all turned to watch the contestant jump up and down gleefully as she discovered she'd provided the correct answer and now would do a week in Aruba with her earnings of $3400. Racehorse watched and then switched off the TV as the show faded away to commercial. He turned to me.

"What I want you to do, Michael, is--"

I was anxious to hear and prayed he got to finish this time.

"--I want you to be yourself. You have the magic to win. Now you need to trust it."

He turned to Dr. Willington and nodded.

"Let's do it, Doc."

Dr. Willington nodded at Nurse Cindy, who produced a long, fat syringe and plugged it into the IV access on the long translucent tube running into the back of Racehorse's hand.

"Anything you want to say?" Dr. Willington asked his patient, taking his other hand in his own.

Racehorse looked up at me. "Yes. Tell the jury Racehorse knows they'll do the right thing. You tell them that, Michael!"

I nodded. All eyes turned to Nurse Cindy, who looked down lovingly on Racehorse as she injected 200 cc's of death into his vein.

An irascible sinner, curser, cutup, and schemer, Racehorse was about to find out just how good he was with his final judge.

At least that was my take, as I gently returned his still hand to his chest. I turned, my eyes filling with tears.

I looked into no one's eyes as I took up my iPad and headed for the door.

Now he knew everything and I still knew only faith.

# Chapter 33

MICHAEL

After Racehorse was gone and we resumed our normal lives, it was quiet as night around the office. Very few calls, very little work to do except prepare for Carlos' trial, set to begin next Monday. I should mention that during this entire time, my wife, Danny, was uppermost in my mind. Yet, like almost all lawyers, the needs of my client and the pressing issues I faced everyday made me put all that on the back burner. When it was over then I, with my children, would do the appropriate thing with Danny's ashes and we would discuss what had happened and how we were going to think of her.

In the connecting suite I had added to my own digs, the kids were mostly okay during the daytime, Danny's mother reported. But we found them scared and clinging to us at night. Especially bedtime, when we said our prayers and acknowledged that mommy was looking down on everyone. That scared Mikey, who was just four, while Dania's eyes would sparkle and she would wave at the ceiling in her bedroom.

But still, there was much to be done and I was just treading water. Believe me, I knew that.

Racehorse died on a Saturday night and the Carlos trial started a week from the following Monday, with jury selection. So, Sunday just after noon I called Marcel into the office, along with Carlos and our support staff, and we began talking. Carlos, of course, was carrying his own grief over the loss of his daughter and at one point I didn't know whether we would be able to make preparations. The emotional tension in my conference room was just running too damn high. Eyes were moist and voices low and discussions of the facts of the case were very brief, telescoped, almost.

By three o'clock I was ready to call a halt to our meager efforts. Carlos hadn't really been present all afternoon, which was catching, meaning his virtual absence rubbed off on me and I played and replayed in my mind the fact that my wife was no more. It was gloomy and had to be ended, so I called it off at 3:05 p.m. and sent everybody home.

Marcel lingered behind after Carlos and my secretary and paralegal were gone. He wanted to talk--reading Marcel wasn't easy for me. Plus, he had been very quiet during our brief meeting with the staff and Carlos.

"What's up?" I asked him when everyone was gone and we were turning out lights.

"You're not going to like this," he replied. He was standing three feet away and as he said this he took a step back. Then he edged into a visitors' chair in my office where we were packing things away. He motioned that I should take a seat behind the desk.

"Okay, let's talk," I said. "What are you needing to tell me?"

"You know you told me to stay away from Leticia Cross's condo?"

"Of course I know. Why, what are you going to tell me?"

"I disobeyed."

"Meaning?"

"I went in last weekend and installed two video cams."

"Oh, fuck, Marcel! Tell me you're joking right now!"

"I'm not joking, boss. I wanted to get more on her. And I wanted to see if we could pick up on any planning against Carlos. I really like that guy, boss. I really want to help him."

I sighed. What was done was done. "What do you have so far?"

"I have a street person coming into Leticia's living room and cutting a deal with Leticia."

"What's that supposed to mean?"

"An old woman--I can't pick up her name from the video--comes into Leticia's house. She pulls something, underwear, out of her shirt and shows it to Leticia. Then they talk. The old woman tells Leticia she saw her put the underwear into a dumpster behind some 7-Eleven."

"What?" I say, incredulous. This was getting pretty far-fetched.

"Yes, and then Leticia hands the woman some bills--maybe a couple of twenties, maybe a couple of hundreds--I can't tell."

"Then what?"

"The old woman leaves. Then Leticia takes the underwear--whatever--into her kitchen and places it in her stainless steel sink."

"So I'm assuming you have the kitchen outfitted with a camera. Go on."

"She pours something flammable on the underwear and then lights it on fire."

"You must be joking."

"I'm not joking at all."

"Let me think a minute. What in the world would Leticia be hiding in a dumpster behind a 7-Eleven?"

"Evidence. Now you're going to love this next part. You already know I installed video in Rudy Monsorre's place."

"Yes, and I specifically told you no more B and E's."

He ignored that.

"Get this," he said excitedly. "I checked the feed last night. I didn't want to say this with the others here today. But you know what I've got? I've got video of Leticia Cross swinging an iron skillet at Rudy Monsorre and knocking him to the floor. He doesn't move after, so the camera stops filming after Leticia leaves the room. But then she returns maybe five minutes later and she's carrying a garment that looks exactly like what she burned in her sink. Only this time you can make it out. It's underwear--women's panties. She goes up to where she left the iron skillet and rubs the underwear against the skillet handle. Then she rubs it all over poor dead Rudy. She puts it on his face, his hands--everywhere his skin is exposed."

I am stunned and excited all at once. Marcel, this man!

"Anything else?"

"No, she then moves out of view and the video shuts down. Motion activated. But there is one more thing."

"This is astonishing you have this stuff, Marcel. You're very possibly saving Carlos' life here."

"That's what I'm trying to do, boss. But here's the kicker. The underwear she used on Rudy's skillet and hands? I've enhanced my video and guess what you can see? The underwear says, Friday."

"What? You mean a day of the week?"

"Yessir. These were Friday's underwear."

"Whoa, slow down, Marcel. Now don't tell me you can also make out a day of the week on what the old lady brought her?"

"No, I can't make it out. But my enhancement software can."

"Friday?"

"Yep. One frame when the old woman holds it up to the light to show it to Leticia. The light coming in the window behind her lights up the word Friday written backwards. It was the back side of the underwear we're looking at head-on, and the front side, farthest away, has the word written on it."

"I am totally blown away. This is astonishing."

"Yes. Did I do good, boss?"

"Come on, Marcel, you know you disobeyed everything I told you. You broke into two homes I specifically told you to stay away from."

"You didn't answer me, boss. Did I do good?"

"You did good. Wonderful, in fact. Now we have leverage with Ms. Cross. Or maybe with the DA herself. Yes, why not?"

"What, you're thinking of going over her head? I was thinking of going directly to Cross and forcing her to dismiss the case against Carlos."

"That wouldn't happen. She can't just dismiss it. Too many eyes on this one, FBI and on down. No, we take this to the DA herself and cut a deal."

"What kind of deal? Does Carlos do hard time?"

I smiled. "I'm thinking, Marcel. Hell, man, I just tied my horse outside and stepped in here for a quick drink. Don't be so pushy."

"Meaning you just found out and I'm being too aggressive?"

"Exactly. Let me mull it over for a day or two, Marce."

"Okay, sure. I'm not fired, am I?"

I laughed, actually threw my head back and laughed. It was the first time I'd done that in weeks. Months, maybe.

"No, Marcel, you're not fired. In fact, you're hired more than ever."

"Just don't tell the DA where the video came from, okay? Leave my name out."

"Marcel, give me some credit."

"I do, boss. I do."

"All right then, when do I get to see this video?"

"I emailed it to you, boss. You can play it anytime you want. Right now?"

"Sure."

He pulled his tablet out of his backpack.

"Now," he said, and we watched the video.

For the next hour we replayed the two video feeds over and over. Then we replayed them enhanced. It was exactly as he'd told me.

Someone was going down. Hard time. Someone named Deputy District Attorney Leticia Cross.

But first there was going to be a trial. I wanted to get her into trial, in front of a jury, before I played my trump card. This was necessary because going to the elected DA herself would certainly result in the removal of Deputy DA Cross, but it wouldn't get the charges against Carlos dismissed. I would have to go trial for that, and I would have to hunt down this unstrung female prosecutor to make it happen.

She deserved no less than the full treatment.

# Chapter 34

MICHAEL

We picked a jury on Monday and Tuesday, and by Wednesday morning the court was ready for our opening statements.

The jury seemed to be a fair one--seven whites, two blacks, and three Asians. Demographically they were all from San Diego and suburbs, and represented everything from a Ph.D. in chemistry who did research at UCSD, to a housewife from Kearny Mesa who sold Christmas cards in her online store, to a surfer from Point Loma, to an accountant--a CPA--who practiced forensic accountancy right downtown and who had, herself, testified in numerous trials as an expert witness. She was purposely left on the jury by me, and the state ran out of peremptories early on and so she squeaked by the state. I wanted her because she had worked exclusively for defense lawyers and likely would possess a certain skew in her thinking in our favor. After all, you can't testify against the state as an expert in any field without coming to understand how the state never fails to make evidence appear real that isn't really what it claims at all. Who better than a defense witness to know this? So we were locked and loaded with our jury when the judge turned to DDA Cross and asked that she give her opening statement.

Ms. Cross was wearing a plain black dress, pearls, and stubby heels that did nothing to belie the image we all had of her as dowdy and conservative. But then most prosecutors are very conservative in manner and dress--at least in court. What they're like at home, I have no clue (excepting Leticia Cross, who I knew more about than she would ever want). She strode boldly up to the lectern and laid her note cards face up before her. Then she cleared her throat and launched in.

"Ladies and gentlemen of the jury, my name is Leticia Cross and I am the deputy district attorney assigned to this case. This case is one of several arising out of a certain armed robbery of First Commercial Bank that some of you said you had heard about back when it happened. But here's some more that all of you need to know: the state will prove that Carlos Pritchett--" pausing to point at Carlos, sitting next to me, "--masterminded an armed robbery of First

Commercial last August and that, during the course of that robbery, he opened several safe deposit boxes with a drill and oxy-fuel torch, and then, without provocation and without remorse gunned down a customer of the bank, a military veteran, who had done nothing except exchange a few words with this vicious killer."

She paused for a sip of water.

"Two things right up front. First, we are going to prove to you that Carlos Pritchett was inside the vault and opened the boxes. We are going to do this in spite of the fact the bank's video feed had been cut off and despite the fact there were no eyewitnesses to what went on inside the vault once the guard in there had been forced out. The robbers were all wearing balaclavas and rubber masks. The defendant was wearing a rubber mask that looked like the face of a monkey--a chimpanzee, I am told. A number of bank customers and tellers will testify that it was the robber in the monkey mask who shot and killed our veteran. What happened to the mask and how do we know it was worn by Carlos Pritchett? Well, after the robbery, the defendant made his getaway by carjacking a vehicle owned and driven by Elva Reinhardt of Pacific Beach. It was a Dodge Durango. The vehicle was recovered after the defendant abandoned it, and was returned to Ms. Reinhardt. Following police searches of the vehicle, the monkey mask being worn by the defendant was found stuffed inside the door panel of the SUV on the driver's side. Evidently placed there by Carlos Pritchett because no one else had access to the vehicle other than Ms. Reinhardt, who is going to testify, if you will, that it wasn't she who placed the mask inside her driver's door."

She paused and stacked two note cards. Then she went on.

"The state will also prove beyond a reasonable doubt that the oxy-fuel torch left behind in the bank vault when the robbers fled was handled by the defendant. How do we know this? Because he inadvertently left behind his fingerprint and his DNA on the cutting torch itself. That's right, we examined the torch in the crime lab and we turned up this evidence that specifically and without any doubt places Carlos Pritchett in the vault with the torch. In other words, ladies and gentlemen, he was there and did his part to complete the robbery regardless of what he might try to tell you in the next few days. We're anticipating that he will take the witness stand and claim he was never there, because we have no video of him and no visual identification, but his prints and DNA place him exactly in the thick of it."

Another sip of water and another card stacked.

"Here's something else about the case you should know. We had another witness, a man who we know was a participant in the armed robbery, who has told us that Carlos Pritchett masterminded the robbery and that Carlos Pritchett shot the veteran down in cold blood. This gentleman cannot be located though we have scoured the city in search of him. However, we have his written and signed statement which we will introduce to prove these things--"

I shot up to my feet. "Object, Your Honor! The state is commenting on inadmissible hearsay not subject to cross-examination by the defendant in violation of his Constitutional rights!"

"What say you, madam prosecutor?" the judge said to Cross.

"It is what it is, Your Honor. Maybe the court should ask the defendant where his cohort went. He might possibly know."

"Objection! Totally improper commentary and insinuation! Move that all the prosecutor's last comments be stricken and the jury ordered to disregard."

"I quite agree, counsel. Ladies and gentlemen, the court instructs you to disregard the comments from the district attorney regarding both the testimony of an accomplice about anything having to do with this case and about the defendant perhaps knowing where the state's witness presently can be found. You are to disregard and give these comments no weight. Proceed, counsel, with your opening statement."

Somewhat chastened but plowing straight ahead regardless, DA Cross then went into what she expected other witnesses to say--the usual testimony I would expect from CSI, from the medical examiner, from the detectives at the scene, and from the bank customers and management. All of it not in great detail, just skimming the top of the waves as it were, giving the jury a taste of what all would go into making up the state's case against Carlos. At long last, she returned to her seat and the courtroom grew very still. The judge indicated it was my turn.

I ambled up to the lectern--without notes--where I met the eyes of each and every juror, acknowledging that I saw them and that they were all important to me.

Then I began.

# Chapter 35

MICHAEL

"Really, ladies and gentlemen," I told the jury as I launched into my dissertation, "this is the story of a man who is being framed. The sole issue in this case for you to decide is whether my client, Carlos Pritchett, did the things Ms. Cross has just accused him of doing."

The jury looked at me. My words had no meaning to them, they were just words. So far. But I was about to light them up.

"But during the course of my investigation of this case, and my staff's investigation of this case, we have made a truly astonishing discovery. And that is this."

I stood back from the lectern and pointed directly at deputy Cross. "This deputy district attorney is guilty of planting evidence in this case."

Suddenly the courtroom was in turmoil, the spectators gasping and shuffling in their chairs, the jury furiously scribbling down what I'd just revealed and, most of all, Leticia Cross flying up to her feet and all but screaming at the judge, who was pounding his gavel and demanding quiet in his court.

"Outrage, Your Honor!" cried the prosecutor. "Counsel should be admonished and the jury--we need a sidebar, Judge. I have a motion I need to make."

The Judge raised his hand for quiet. "Very well, counsel, please step forward and we'll discuss over here."

We moved forward, the DA and I, as directed. I had asked around and learned what I could about this jurist. Judge Nathan Sturdevant was a known assassin of lawyers. He was known for turning lawyers over to the Supreme Court for sanctions where he thought there had been attorney mischief in his courtroom that crossed a certain line. Which was the problem: from what I had been able to piece together, the lines that might be crossed were never particularly well-defined with this judge. This case had originally belonged to a friend of Racehorse's, a woman who was a friendly judge. But she had been rotated off the criminal calendar onto the probate calendar and our matter had fallen into the hands of Judge Sturdevant. I was cursing the bad luck that had removed Racehorse from the scene far too early, because, being from out-of-state, I really was all but clueless about the new judge. I would do my best but I would also need to be very careful. He was an unknown quantity except for his penchant for getting lawyers disbarred who offended his sense of proper lawyering, and by that alone, I had been made extremely wary.

We placed ourselves at the side of the judge's bench and began our whisper campaign to destroy each other's case.

"Judge," hissed DA Cross, "it is a lie and totally improper for counsel to claim I was engaged in wrongdoing. The jury has been unduly prejudiced and I have no alternative but to demand a mistrial!"

Judge Sturdevant turned to me. He was frowning, his brow deeply furrowed, and his eyes were furious when they settled on me. "Counsel, please tell me why I shouldn't hold you in contempt for this?"

"Because, Your Honor, we have evidence that the district attorney standing before you manufactured evidence in this case. I would ask the court not to force me to reveal what the evidence is at just this time so that the state cannot prepare for what we have, but I can promise the court that I will gladly go to jail on a contempt citation if I fail to prove what I'm avowing to the court at this moment."

"Counsel?" the judge said to Ms. Cross. "Anything further?"

"I can't argue against what he won't tell us, Judge. But he's already rung a bell that cannot be unrung."

"Mr. Gresham, if it turns out you have misled the court, you will go to jail. And I will personally see to it that you are disbarred from ever practicing law again. Do we understand each other?"

"I do understand, Judge. I will make good on my promise to prove that this DA, Ms. Cross, has planted evidence in this case to affect its outcome."

"Very well," the judge said, then, addressing everyone in the courtroom, "we will now continue with defense counsel's opening statement."

I returned to the lectern and took right up with it.

"Not only has this DA planted evidence, she has also conspired with her lackey to subvert justice."

The jury just looked at me. Subvert justice? Now what the hell did that mean?

"I'm saying this lackey of hers was a crook. She used a crook to plant the evidence. Then she warned this crook when the cops were coming after him at his chop shop. That's right, her partner in crime stole cars and cut them down and changed VINs and then turned around and parted them out or sold them as vehicles with VINs."

"Same objection!"

"Noted," said Judge Sturdevant. "Counsel, remember your avowal to me."

I ignored the judge before launching in again.

"Is that enough to make you not want to trust the state's case? Well, there's one more thing you're going to find out when the evidence is presented by my witnesses and that's going to blow the roof off this courthouse. You're going to have no choice but to set Carlos Pritchett free. Thank you for listening."

"Same objection!"

"Noted," said the judge. "Counsel for the state, you may call your first witness."

# Chapter 36

"The state calls as its first witness Detective Mitch O'Connell," Ms. Cross boldly announced from her seat.

The bailiff hurried up the aisle and out the double doors. He returned moments later with the portly, Irish detective in tow. He was clean enough, head-to-toe, I thought as he walked by on his way to the witness stand, though the brogans could've used a bit of polish. He took the stand and blinked hard as if to clear his vision. Then he looked to his left, at the jury, and gave a curt nod and half-smile. Now he was ready, having followed exactly the instructions the police academy gives all beginners for testifying in court: confident posture, spit-and-polish clothing, be seated and acknowledge jury, toss them a smile then back to the prosecutor, all ears.

"State your name."

"Mitchell O'Connell."

"What is your occupation?"

"Detective, San Diego Police Department."

"Assigned to?"

"Robbery-homicide. Five years now."

"Directing your attention to August ten this year, did you have occasion to respond to a call at the First Commercial National Bank in San Diego?"

"I did."

"Describe what you saw and did there."

"With my partner, Eleanor Howell, we responded to a two-eleven call from our dispatcher."

"Two-eleven being what?"

"Crime in progress. We were told to proceed to the bank, where we would encounter armed subjects in the process of robbing the bank."

"Tell us what happened when you arrived."

"We parked maybe a hundred feet from the bank's main entrance. We were the first unmarked on the scene, as I recall. The uniforms already on the scene yelled over to take cover, the robbers were still inside the bank."

"What did you do?"

"I exited my vehicle and went around to the trunk of the car, which I popped open. I distributed two M-16 military style rifles to Detective Howell and myself. We loaded and locked our weapons, then went to our respective front doors of the vehicle and crouched down behind them, waiting for the robbers to emerge from the bank."

"What happened next?"

"We waited what seemed like forever, but actually it was maybe three or four minutes, five at the most. Suddenly the door flew open and masked men carrying automatic weapons appeared. The close-by officers began firing first, most of them using handguns."

"What did you do?"

"I sighted the lead robber with my scope but couldn't get a clean shot. His partner began sweeping his gun back and forth at our cars. He sprayed bullets everywhere, including many into an apartment above the furniture store behind our vehicle. Luckily, no one was injured."

"What happened next?"

"They all came barreling out of their van. They were taking too much fire not to."

"What happened next?"

"Someone got a direct hit on the street sweeper--that's what we call perps who fire blindly like this guy. Someone nailed him but he was wearing body armor. He made it back inside the van. He dropped his weapon and I cried out for a cease-fire, but it was too late. Two made it to the rear of the van and we all of us started shooting. I know I killed the driver of the van because I saw his head explode back over the seat."

"Were you still at your vehicle?"

"Yes. Still crouching behind my door. The two perps who bailed out of the car headed for an alley that ran back alongside the bank. They got to the entrance and then paused, standing back to back, firing wildly at all cops. Several police were hit and I know that four were killed."

"By these two?"

"That's impossible to say."

"Why's that?"

"Because no one's keeping score now. You're just trying to stay alive and kill a bad guy or two."

"Did you hit one of them?"

"I did. Again, with my sniper scope. The guy slumped down to his knees and I stitched a burst up his legs, up his vest, and up his face. He toppled over and stopped moving. Clearly he was dead. His partner in crime began running down the alley so I gave chase."

"Did you catch him?"

"No, we didn't catch him. He escaped."

"Did you see him shoot anyone?"

"Did I personally see that? No, I did not."

"Was he wearing a mask?"

"Yes. An ant mask. I guess that's what it was. Some kind of big red bug face. With two antennae. I just assumed it was a red ant face."

"You're sure? It couldn't have been a monkey?"

"I don't think so. I mean, it might have been, sure. It might have been a monkey."

I was sure he added this after-thought comment to his narrative because he thought the DA was fishing for it. Ant mask, monkey mask, he was agreeable to either one. Which cost him points with the jury, as several put their pencils down and stopped writing.

"What happened next?"

"The running man made it out the other end of the alley and that's the last I saw of him. I later heard he wasn't caught. So I went inside the bank and began separating witnesses and staff into two separate groups. Of course staff could also be witnesses but that wasn't the point. We wanted two groups. The customers were then questioned by you, Leticia Cross, one at a time. I witnessed the statements they gave and helped out with that."

"What did Detective Howell do, if you know?"

"She went back into the vault. Later on she said they had recovered an oxy-fuel torch from the roof that had been used to cut through the vault."

"Tell us about that."

"Well, she said the robbers had built a small shack on the roof and used it at night to cut down through the vault. How she got the night part, I don't know."

I didn't object; it was hearsay but it was going to come in anyway. Why object to something and give it more weight with the jury, as if I'm afraid of it? So I took it in the shorts and it came in as pure hearsay. Okay for that, I could live with it.

"Did you later take that oxy-fuel torch to the crime lab?"

"CSI did, yes."

"Who or what is CSI?"

He looked at the DA like she was kidding—didn't she ever watch TV? Then he answered, "Crime scene investigators."

"And were tests done on the torch?"

"Yes."

"Do you know the results of those tests?"

Again, it's hearsay but if he doesn't get it in the CSI techs will. So I remain quiet.

"I do. The cutting torch had on it the fingerprint of the defendant, Carlos Pritchett, as well as his DNA."

"So would it be fair to say that the defendant had handled the torch on the roof?"

"Object, calls for speculation!" Now I was getting into it just a bit. Speculation is never good.

"Sustained. Please rephrase if you wish."

"Did you know whether the defendant handled the torch while on the roof?"

"Do I know that? Not personally, no, I don't know that."

"Fair enough. What else have you done with regard to the investigation?"

"Supervised logging into evidence the automatic weapon that killed the soldier. Personally delivered it and the spent bullet casings to the crime lab."

"What else have you done?"

"I've had the lead on the case. So I've been coordinating several other detectives in charge of bringing to justice the people who killed four of our police officers. That's been my main thrust."

"I believe that's all I have for this witness," said Ms. Cross.

So I popped right up for cross-examination.

"Did you or anyone on your team track down where the cutting torch came from?"

"Yes."

"Please tell us what you learned."

"The torch came from ACE Rents."

"What kind of place is ACE Rents."

"One of those places where they rent out tools and stuff."

"So this torch might have been rented at some time that had nothing to do with the bank robbery?"

"I'm sure it was."

"It's even possible that Carlos rented it at some other time that had nothing to do with the robbery, correct?"

"It's possible, but statistically unlikely."

"Do you have a background in statistical analysis?"

"No."

"Have you ever taken a statistics course?"

"No."

"So your comment that it was statistically unlikely, you just made that up just now, correct?"

"I guess. It just didn't seem likely to me, that's all."

"To you."

"Yes."

I paused to review my notes. I wanted the tension to build before I asked my next question. Then I plunged right into it.

"Detective, during the course of your investigation of this case, has it come to your attention that someone from the district attorney's office has committed a crime or crimes related to this case?"

"Objection! Foundation!"

"Sustained. Please lay your foundation, counsel."

"Very well. Detective, during the course of your investigation, have you talked to any deputy district attorney or attorneys regarding circumstances that had arisen not connected to the commission of the bank robbery and murders, but related instead to illegalities in how the case was being processed?"

"I'm not sure I know what that means."

"Have you also been investigating a deputy district attorney?"

"Yes."

"Give us that person's name."

He looked up at the judge. "Do I have to answer that? It's confidential at this point, Your Honor."

"Counsel," the judge said to me, "is this where you were going when we had our sidebar?"

"It is."

"Very well, you may proceed."

"Who was the deputy DA being investigated?" Now I was fishing and holding my breath in hopes I got the right answer. If I got the wrong answer, I was going to jail.

"That woman right there. Deputy District Attorney Leticia Cross."

Right answer.

"Objection!"

"Overruled."

"Your Honor, the state requests a ten minute recess!"

"All right. Court's in recess. Be back here and seated in ten minutes, everyone."

He rapped his gavel and pandemonium erupted in the courtroom.

I sauntered back to my table and chair to watch the exchange between Cross and O'Connell. But, no such luck. She simply approached him without any expression on her face and indicated he should follow her into the attorney conference room on the far side of the courtroom. They went in there together. Sheriff's deputies were posted on either side of the door, so there was no chance of eavesdropping. Not that I would have wanted to.

Then Carlos tugged at my sleeve.

"Yes?" I whispered.

"How did you know he was investigating her?"

"Because we know she's been doing some pretty bad things."

"How do we know that?"

"Because someone sent us a voice file. And someone sent us a video file."

"Shit, weren't you going to tell me about them"

"Need to know, Carlos. You're on a need-to-know basis with me."

"Oh."

"And that's not all. I was also lucky because, to tell the truth, I was fishing just now."

"Wow. You could've wound up in the soup," he said.

"Comes with the territory," I said, then reached around and patted his back. "Besides which, you're worth it."

"Oh. Well, same to you, Michael."

"Well, thanks."

Deputy Cross reappeared five minutes later and the judge called us into his office. She renewed her motion for a mistrial and again Judge Sturdevant denied her. But he did warn me that any further testimony about Ms. Cross better damn well have some connection to her trial, or I would possibly be sharing a cell with her. Everyone cooled down, we stared at one another with nothing else to say, and then the judge returned us to the courtroom.

I had planted my land mine with the jury. Now they wanted to know everything but I snatched the ball away and ran in a different direction. I confirmed the findings of the crime lab that the weapon that killed the soldier was the same weapon they examined. And that one of the spent cartridge casings matched up with the bullet that killed him. After that, I announced I was finished with the witness. There was no re-direct so the witness was excused.

"State calls Marvin Marquez," Ms. Cross stated. I knew her voice and knew its normal tone; this time her voice was shaky and lacked confidence. She had been wounded by my cross-examination, but she wasn't down and out. Not yet. The bailiff headed for the main entrance and witness waiting just beyond.

Thirty minutes later, Ms. Cross was finished with the witness, a bank guard. One had the feeling this was just another PR problem the DA was settling with the bank by calling its employees and letting them have their say. That was the only rational explanation I could come up with for why these bit-players were being thrown up in front of the jury.

# Chapter 37

Then it was my turn to cross-examine the bank guard.

He'd just told the jury that he, Marvin Marquez, was a guard positioned at the front of the bank just inside the main entrance. He had been at his duty station on August ten. Another guard was there with him. Were they armed? Yes, he was wearing his service revolver in his holster, a police special. What happened when the robbers came in?

"I got roughed up a little but I survived. There was nothing I could do. They were packing automatic weapons and I was packing a peashooter. No way was I gonna get shot to hell by interfering with these cowboys. Besides, they knew exactly what they were doing and I didn't want to be the dope that got in their way."

I started in on cross-examination at that point.

"Did you witness one William Turnstile getting shot?"

"The man in the teller line?"

"Yes."

"I didn't know that's his name. But I saw the monkey shoot him."

"The monkey?"

"You know, the perp wearing the monkey mask. That's who shot Mr. William."

"Mr. Turnstile?"

"That's what I mean."

"Describe what you saw."

"Well, the two of them had been exchanging words, though from my distance I couldn't tell you what they were saying. I didn't know if it was banter or threats. At last there was one more thing said by the dead guy and monkey man just gunned him down. Didn't hesitate, fired a three-round burst into his chest and smiled when the man died at his feet."

"How do you know he smiled? He was wearing a mask."

"I'm guessing. He didn't step away and he didn't come undone. He just stood there and watched the guy die at his feet. I'm only guessing he was smiling."

"Mr. Marquez, think this next question over carefully, sir."

"Okay."

"Did you at anytime see the monkey mask go back into the vault behind the tellers?"

"No, I did not."

"Could he have?"

"No. I was watching him. He kept his gun going from the tellers on his left to the customers on his right."

"Going?"

"You know, swinging it back and forth. Keeping them covered."

"Did anyone try anything?"

"Not that I saw. The tellers would have had alarms. I don't know if they tripped those or not."

"What about you? Any alarms?"

"Me? No, I'm just there for show. That's why I only carry a peashooter."

"You're not expected to shoot it out with robbers?"

"One rule they told me never to break: never discharge my firearm. Never even remove it from my holster. I'm just there for show."

"That's all for now."

I stood right up. "Mr. Marquez, did you see the perp wearing the ant mask?"

"The one with the big eyes? Yes."

"Did he ever fire his gun inside the bank?"

"He did not. There was only one shooting incident, the one I just described."

"Did you at any time see the ant inside the vault or entering or exiting the vault?"

"No. But I wasn't looking, either."

"But this much is sure: he didn't shoot anyone."

"He didn't shoot anyone, no. I mean that's right."

"That is all."

"No re-direct."

"We'll take our lunch break now. Back at one-thirty, everyone."

# Chapter 38

<u>MICHAEL</u>

Deputy DA Cross called a deputy sheriff who happened to respond to the bank robbery call for all cars. He walked into the scene and moved stuff around. The DA spent an hour with the officer, taking him through his movements inside the bank, what he touched, what he moved, what he put back. It wasn't helpful to the state's case--in fact it hurt it--but it was necessary because the guy's clumsiness had been recorded in the police reports and the DA knew I was going to raise hell with the CSI techs who responded.

The deputy sheriff was quite glum and spoke in low tones. There was no fight in him. His lack of experience had caused problems for him and for the case.

Then it came my turn to cross-examine. I stood and approached the lectern. I was shocked when I looked back up.

The deputy sheriff had screwed his face up into his meanest cop look, giving me daggers from the witness stand and I was thinking, *Don't start. You just don't know what can really happen in a courtroom. This isn't traffic court and my law license isn't still wet. This courtroom is the big time, the felony UFC, and all you brought was a cheap uniform and a stupid look.*

*Here we go.*

"Now, Deputy Sims, let me see if I understand your testimony."

No reply. Same mean look.

"You arrived at the scene of the robbery/shooting and walked up to the dead body, correct?"

"Correct."

"And the crime scene stretched from the entrance to the bank all the way to the rear wall, correct?"

"Correct."

"Yet, knowing that your duties were to help preserve the scene, the first thing you did was walk right into the middle of it and pick up a bullet casing, correct?"

"My duties were more than just scene preservation, counsel."

"So you were part of the Crime Scene Investigation team, is that what you're saying?"

"No."

"Had you just been promoted to homicide detective?"

"No."

"You don't deny that you walked into a death-by-shooting scene and picked up a bullet casing, do you?"

"No. I picked it up."

"Yes, you did. It says so right here in the police report, correct?"

"Correct."

"Not only that, you were shortly afterward confronted by Detective Benson, correct?"

"I don't know if confronted is the word I'd use."

"Well, tell us your word."

"Contacted. He contacted me."

"Deputy Rearsa, whose statement is part of the police reports, said he heard Detective Benson say to you, and I quote, 'Hey, numb-nuts, put the goddam bullet casing back where you found it.' Do you agree that's what was said?"

"Something like that."

"Oh, it wasn't exactly that? Then you tell me what words were used."

"I don't remember him calling me numb-nuts."

"How about dumb-ass? Did he call you dumb-ass?"

"No."

"How about fool? Did he call you fool?"

"No."

"You don't remember the pejorative word he used with you, but you don't think it was numb-nuts, is that your testimony?"

"I guess."

"No guessing. Is it or is it not your testimony that you don't remember what exactly he called you but it wasn't numb-nuts?"

"Yes."

"So Deputy Rearsa is wrong, he didn't call you numb-nuts?"

"That's right, Counsel."

"Now, let's talk about police talk. What does the word 'numb-nuts' mean?"

The deputy looked up at the judge as if to say, *Can you help me with this guy?* But I simply waited as the judge ignored him.

I pressed forward. "Sir? What does 'numb-nuts' mean to you?"

"Someone who does something stupid."

"Would you agree that picking up a bullet casing from a homicide investigation scene would be doing something stupid?"

"If you weren't with CSI, probably."

"So the word 'numb-nuts' might have been just the right word for you?"

"No--I don't think--I don't--"

"Object," said the District Attorney with very little enthusiasm. "Badgering."

"Counsel?" the judge said and looked at me.

"Judge, this is a felony-murder case. It's imperative that we understand a hundred percent what was said and done. *Exactly* what was said. And done."

"Overruled."

I went back to the witness, who was no longer staring daggers at me.

"So the word 'numb-nuts' might have been just the right word for you?" I asked again.

"I guess."

"Well, today you would agree that picking up that bullet casing was a numb-nuts thing to do?"

"Yes."

"Well, then, how numb-nuts a thing was it to then replace it where you thought it had been lying on the floor and then telling the police photographer everything was just like it was, that nothing had been touched. Was that numb-nuts?"

"I amended the police report later. I told them I did that."

"But you didn't admit it at first, did you? The first police report didn't say anything about you moving evidence of the shooting around at the scene before the dicks got there, did it?"

"No."

"What caused you to change your mind about telling?"

"Someone else," he said in a stage whisper.

"Louder, please. What caused you to change your mind and tell the truth?"

"Deputy Rearsa told the dicks I had moved stuff at the scene. Then they asked me."

"Let me see if I understand. Another deputy tells on you? Tells the detectives on you?"

"Yes."

"So only then do you tell the truth, correct?"

"Correct."

Then he slumped in the witness chair and there were definitely no eyeball knives coming my way. He'd become sweetly reasonable. It happens.

"Now, Deputy, let's see if you can tell us why the location of spent ammunition casings at the scene of a shooting is so hugely important. Can you help me do that?"

"Maybe."

"Maybe? Didn't they teach you at police school that the bullet casings might indicate the location of the shooter when the gun was fired?"

"They might have."

"Didn't they teach you that the manner in which an automatic weapon ejects shell casings can be used by a firearms expert to place the location of the shooter at the scene when the gun went off?"

"I think. I don't remember."

"Do you know why it's important in this case that we find out where the shell casings were located?"

"Yeah. Kinda."

"Tell us why the location so important."

"To know what happened?"

"Generally, but I'm asking specifically."

"So we know where the shooter was standing?"

"Getting warmer, Deputy. Care to try again?"

"Objection. Badgering."

"No," said the judge, "I think the witness opened himself to this on direct examination when he gave his theory of what happened that day."

"Why do we need to know his position, Deputy?"

"To--to--"

"Right. To know where the shooter was standing and then compare that to which robbers were in that area. Correct?"

"Correct."

"Now if Carlos Pritchett wasn't even in the area where the shooting occurred, it would be a stretch of the imagination to claim he fired the gun from clear down at the vault and killed a man clear back at the tellers' line, correct?"

"Correct."

"Especially since there was no bullet casing found that far away, right?"

"Right. Correct."

"But we have a problem. You moved the spent shell casing that could have helped the experts locate exactly where the gun was when it was fired. Do you remember moving it?"

"Yes."

"Do you remember you found that shell casing somewhere between the dead man, the tellers' ledge, and the far back wall of the bank?"

"Yes."

"A distance of about thirty to sixty feet?"

"Yes. Something like that."

"But you put it back where you thought it was, correct?"

"Correct."

"But we don't know how accurate that was, do we?"

"No."

"So the state cannot prove beyond a reasonable doubt whether my client fired the bullet that killed the dead man or whether someone else fired, can it?"

"I guess it can't."

"Thank you, Deputy. That's all for now."

"May the witness be excused?" said the judge.

"No," I said, without explanation.

Judge Sturdevant nodded and turned to the witness. "The witness will remain in the courthouse subject to recall to the witness stand."

I was going to let him cool his heels out in the hallway. I was going to give him the opportunity to tell all his buddies that it doesn't pay to stare daggers at the defense attorney,

Michael Gresham.

Beside me, Carlos stirred. He shuffled his feet. He was anxious. No, he was terrified.

He touched my arm.

"Does that change anything?"

I smiled at him and dropped my arm across his back for the jury to see.

"Well, yes and no. It's still the felony-murder rule whether you fired the gun and killed the guy or not. You're potentially guilty in either case."

"So why are we spending time on this."

"Because we want the truth."

"Oh. We do?"

"I know I do. Why, do you want to tell something that isn't the truth if you testify?"

He looked at me then. A smile appeared at the corners of his mouth. Then he was grinning.

"Lord, help us," I whispered.

"Hey," he said, leaning over to my ear. "If that numb-nuts deputy can move the furniture around, then I guess I can too."

I had no comeback. I knew that the truth got trampled by the prosecution's witnesses in just about every trial I'd ever defended. Why should this time be any different?

And why shouldn't we fight fire with fire?

The twelve-year-old kid deep inside of me was drawing near.

We just might win this case after all, I remember thinking.

# Chapter 39

MICHAEL

After lunch, Ms. Cross put two bank tellers on the stand. This was, again, more a matter of public relations with the bank than anything useful to the state. Then I realized they were treading water while machinations were going on behind the scenes. Probably, I decided, doing damage control to figure out what I had on their DA. Anyway, I cross-examined neither bank teller and they were excused.

Next up was the medical examiner. He and his staff had had a busy afternoon that day at the bank. A very busy afternoon. The jury was told about the M.E.'s staffing at the scene, how many bodies were examined, and what was done regarding William Turnstile, the deceased veteran. Nothing the M.E. said implicated Carlos in any way, so I didn't cross-examine. Sure, there were dead bodies at the scene, but whether Carlos had done the actual shooting wasn't known to the M.E.

I was also mindful of the fact that neither the M.E. nor any other witness had to prove that Carlos did the actual shooting of William Turnstile or any of the other dead cops. It just didn't matter, because this was a felony-murder case, where all it would take to convict Carlos of murder was the fact that Carlos had been involved in the robbery at the time Turnstile was murdered. He had been, so he was thus guilty--however the state hadn't proved this beyond a reasonable doubt. The state hadn't proved that Carlos was there at all, except for the implication of the fingerprint and DNA on the cutting torch. Phaeton's statement was something, but it could be dismissed, one, with impeachment, and two, by our version directly contradicting the state's version. He would be a wash. The fingerprint/DNA was compelling, of course, and could very well be enough to convict him, but, like I said, I didn't think it added up to beyond a reasonable doubt. Besides, we could explain how and when the print and DNA got on the torch. There was also the monkey mask found in Ms. Earnhardt's Durango, but I had plans to overcome that claim the state was making.

My cross-examination was short.

"Dr. Noonan, isn't it true that in all of your workup at the scene you found not one shred of evidence that my client had actually murdered anyone himself?"

"That's true. We only processed the scene. We never draw conclusions such as that."

"That is all, thank you."

Cross was finished, so she called her next witness. I had been waiting for this one, Washburn Rambis, with some trepidation because he was being called to prove prior bad acts. Meaning Cross intended to use him to show that because Carlos had shot him three times Carlos thus had the propensity to shoot people, that it was his nature, perhaps, to shoot people. I couldn't afford for this to come in. Research-wise I had my cases and points and authorities and was ready to argue the issue; it was going to be a close call.

Rambis, wearing a sports coat without his arms in the sleeves, took the witness stand. His arms were both yet in slings and the jury's eyes widened when they saw this. I didn't like the impression the guy was having already.

"State your name."

"Washburn Rambis."

"Your business?"

"I'm head of underwriting at Grand Canyon Insurance and Annuity."

"What kind of company is that?"

"Insurance. We sell life and health insurance."

"Do you recognize the defendant in this case?"

"I do."

"Identify him for the record, please."

"Sitting beside the lawyer Mr. Gresham. I recognize his lawyer, too."

"Did these two gentlemen pay a visit on you?"

"At separate times, yes."

"Let's focus down on the defendant's visit. When did that occur?"

"July third, this year."

"Where did it occur?"

"My office in Bel Air, California."

"What occurred during that visit?"

"Objection! Sidebar, please." I was out of my seat almost before the full question had been asked. The judge waved us to his perch. Cross and I crowded shoulder to shoulder to present our arguments regarding the testimony that was coming.

"Counsel?" Judge Sturdevant said to me.

"Your Honor, the state is going to offer Mr. Rambis' testimony that the defendant came to his office and shot him for refusing to honor his insurance policy on his little girl. The prejudice of allowing this far exceeds the testimony's probative value. The jury will quickly conclude that if Carlos would shoot Rambis he would also likely shoot a veteran in the First Commercial National Bank robbery. The evidence should be excluded."

"Counsel?" the judge said to Ms. Cross.

She launched in, her whispers growing louder the deeper she got into her logic.

"Prior bad acts are admissible. *Section 1103 of the Evidence Code* provides that in a criminal action, evidence of the defendant's character for violence or trait of character for violence (in the form of an opinion, evidence of reputation, or evidence of specific instances of conduct) is not made inadmissible if the evidence is offered by the prosecution to prove conduct of the defendant in conformity with the character or trait of character and is offered after evidence that the victim had a character for violence or a trait of character tending to show violence has been adduced by the defendant. Testimony to his effect has already been offered by the state. This evidence from Mr. Rambis is admissible."

The judge looked at me. "Anything further?"

"Again," I whispered, "the value of this evidence is outweighed by how prejudicial it is against my client. It shouldn't be allowed and probably is reversible error if you do allow it in."

"Objection overruled. You may continue, Ms. Cross."

"Thank you."

I returned to my seat and Ms. Cross returned to the lectern.

She launched in again. "Mr. Rambis, I was asking what occurred during the visit by the defendant to your office."

"What occurred? He shot me. Three times. Twice in one shoulder, once in the other shoulder. Damn near killed me. Then he used me as a human shield to make his getaway. He wired a gun to my throat and used it to get by the police. If they shot him the gun would go off and kill me. So they let him pass. They had to let him escape or I was dead."

"So he came into your office, walked up, and shot you?"

"No, we had words first."

"What kind of words?"

"He was angry. We argued. I tried to calm him down but it didn't work."

"So he shot you?"

"Three times. I mean, look at me. I still hurt. I still don't have my full range of motion back."

"That is all. Thank you Mr. Rambis."

Without being invited by the judge I hurried to the lectern and began my cross.

"What did you argue about before he shot you?"

"His insurance policy."

"It covered his daughter, Amelia."

"No, he said it did. But it didn't, actually."

"Did you know who Amelia was? Anything about her?"

"No."

"Did you know she was eight years old and suffering from Hepatitis-C and complications from the disease?"

"No. Yes, I guess he might have told me."

"Did you know she later died from the disease, from pneumonia complications?"

"I did--I didn't, no. But I know now."

"Isn't that why he shot you, because you refused coverage on his daughter and she was going to die without it?"

"I suppose he thought so," said the underwriter.

"What did you think?"

He spread his hands and looked at the ceiling, collecting his thoughts.

"I guess I didn't know much beyond the fact her name wasn't on the insurance application."

"Whose name was on the application?"

"Lynne Pritchett. But the daughter's full name was Amelia Lynne Pritchett. They left off the 'Amelia' and so she wasn't covered."

"Is there a rule that says that? Something in the insurance law that says you were right in denying coverage to her?"

"Not that I know of. It's just how it's always done."

"If a father doesn't include his daughter's full name, you always get to deny coverage, is that it?"

"Pretty much. But it's not just daughters, it's anyone."

"But there's no law that says that?"

"I'm not a lawyer."

"Objection, foundation," said Cross.

"Overruled. He deals with insurance law on a regular basis. He might know."

"So there's no law you're aware of that says you get to deny her medicine because her name wasn't fully given?"

"No specific law, no. It's tradition, I guess you could say."

"No, I couldn't say that, sir. Nor would I say that. You and your insurance company might try to say that in order to wriggle off the hook, but I wouldn't have said that."

"Okay. Whatever."

He smiled just then.

"Is this funny to you? That your acts directly resulted in the death of my client's daughter?"

"Objection! Speculation!"

"Sustained. Mr. Rambis, please don't answer that."

Rambis only shrugged.

"So you can just shrug it off? Her death is only worth a shrug to you?"

"Objection! Harassing the witness."

"Sustained. Move it along, Mr. Gresham."

In case anyone wasn't paying attention, I was seriously angry. The thought of a billion-dollar company refusing to pay a girl's medical bill just made me crazy. So I didn't "move it along."

"Wouldn't you shoot him if the situation were reversed and it was your daughter who was dying?"

"Objection! Speculation, inflammatory!"

"Mr. Gresham. I don't want to have to say this again. Move it along, sir."

"That's all I have," I said, and I slammed my fist down on the lectern.

Then I sat down in my chair. I was fuming and the jury could see it.

It wasn't an act, any of it. I would have shot the son of a bitch myself just then.

Judging from how the jury looked, several of them would have held him for me.

# Chapter 40

"The state has no further witnesses, but I would move to admit the state's Exhibit 144-C into evidence."

"What is that?" asked the judge.

"The written statement of one Vincent Phaeton."

"Counsel," the judge said to me, "are you familiar with the exhibit?"

I stood. "I am, Your Honor."

I knew that I also had a statement from Phaeton and that it contradicted and post-dated the one Ms. Cross was offering. I wanted mine to come into evidence so I made no effort to keep hers out. It wouldn't fly if I tried to have it both ways, keeping hers out and getting mine in. That just wasn't going to happen, not with this judge.

"Defense has no objection to Exhibit 144-C coming into evidence. In fact, the defense will soon be offering its own version of a Phaeton statement too. Hopefully the state will have no objection to our version."

The judge ignored me, which he should have.

"Let the record show that State's Exhibit 144-C is admitted into evidence."

I quickly read back through the written statement. It attempted to place the blame for the murder inside the bank directly on Carlos. Then I checked the California Statute 1111. In California, an accomplice's testimony is not enough to convict another without corroboration of what the accomplice is saying. So, the end result was that, legally speaking, the statement of Phaeton could not, in and of itself, ever be enough to convict Carlos. This is all predicated upon the California Penal Code, Section 1111. Plus, the corroboration is not sufficient if it merely shows the commission of the offense or the circumstances thereof. An accomplice is defined as one who is liable to prosecution for the identical offense charged against the defendant on trial in the cause in which the testimony of the accomplice is given.

"Your Honor, the state rests."

We then excused the jury while I made my motion for judgment of acquittal at the close of the state's case. This is a standard, almost mandatory motion that is never allowed, but I had to do it to preserve the record. It took up about forty-five minutes of time while I argued Penal Code 1111 and the state primarily basing its case on the testimony of Phaeton the accomplice who put Carlos at the scene as an actor. The court denied my motion when I was done, of course. We then went into recess for lunch. This was Thursday now, the fourth day of trial if you counted the first two days of picking a jury. The state's case against Carlos had been short but sweet. Unfortunately, it was enough to get to the jury and probably, as it stood right then, enough to convict him and possibly see him executed. So I had to pick it up in the afternoon and present a strong defense case.

I went to lunch with Marcel and Carlos. There was a diner a block down the street, a little hole-in-the-wall calling itself the All-American Diner. It featured a menu of what it called "men's food," a mix of stew, ribs and noodle dishes, hash, all-day breakfast, and the like. I'd eaten there before and found it not half bad. I followed Marcel and Carlos through the door.

We assembled, the three of us, around a two-person table at the rear, where the lights were low and the floor traffic was light. Except for the bathroom, which was just beyond. Every time the door swung open you were overcome with the unmistakable smell of disinfectant and urinal cakes. Nice.

We ordered and then fiddled with our water glasses and flatware while we tried to figure out what to say to one another at that point. Men are like that--no one wants to go first and get it wrong. Then Carlos took the lead.

"Well, are you going to put me on the stand?"

"Allow you to testify? I don't think so. At this point you'd have to lie and say you weren't there. I'd rather argue that to a jury in closing argument than have you take the stand and lie and somehow get caught in the lie. That would be the death penalty. No, I won't be calling you, Carlos."

"Besides," said Marcel, "the jury's not going to believe you anyway. They never believe the defendant. They know you're just trying to save your ass."

"It's true," I agreed. "Your testimony wouldn't be compelling at all."

"Well, nuts," said Carlos, "because I really wasn't there."

We hadn't had this conversation before. Truth be told, I never actually come right out and ask my clients whether they're guilty or not. Most defense lawyers don't. Still, I was shocked by what he'd just said.

"Weren't there? You serious?" Marcel asked him.

"As serious as a heart attack. I was someplace else."

"Yeah, where?"

"In my daughter's hospital room. I wouldn't leave her side back then. August tenth especially."

"Why August tenth?"

"It was Amelia's birthday that day. I wouldn't rob a bank on my daughter's birthday."

"Oh shit," said Marcel. "Boss?" Now he was looking at me.

I was flabbergasted, for want of a better word. Or maybe there isn't a better word. I was stunned that he actually meant to go down this road. Maybe he was kidding around.

"You're serious about telling this to our jury?"

"My wife has pictures on her cell phone. They're date-stamped August tenth and they clearly show me wearing one of those pointy birthday hats and blowing one of those noisemakers. Plus there's the cake on Amelia's bed sitting there waiting to be cut. Yes, I'm serious about telling them this."

Now my mind was racing. "Well, what do you say about the fact your prints and DNA were found on the oxy-fuel torch? Doesn't that actually put you at the scene?"

"Yes. But that was from a week before. By the time the actually robbery rolled around I had backed out. I couldn't go through with it. I attended my daughter's birthday party instead."

"You must be kidding," I said. "This is astonishing."

"Look at the pictures. I've got her smartphone right here. Look."

He held up the smartphone and began flipping through photographs. Sure enough, it was just as he said. Birthday cake, party hats, party favors, nurses holding small presents, pictures of Carlos himself playing a ukulele and singing happy birthday.

That last part was actually video.

His singing voice wasn't half-bad.

I prayed his testimony before the jury would be just as effective.

# Chapter 41

"Your Honor," I said we resumed after lunch, "Defense calls as its first witness Patrick Bendenetti."

Minutes later the witness could be heard behind me coming down the aisle and then pushing through the swinging gate. He was a man of medium stature, somewhat roly-poly, with a red-flushed face, dark beard beneath and bifocal glasses perched on his nose. He sat down in the witness chair and looked quite at home as he shot a quick nod and smile to the jury. Then he turned to me, all ears.

"State your name."

"Patrick J. Bendenetti, Ph.D."

"You hold a doctorate degree?"

"I do."

"In what field?"

"Biochemistry."

"Where do you work?"

"Persevere Labs. I'm a DNA analyst there."

"What do you do as a DNA analyst?"

"Test specimens for DNA and, if it is found, try to match it to a known or unknown person."

"Were you hired by me in this case?"

"I was."

"How much did I pay you?"

"Ten thousand dollars. My retainer plus prepayment for hours expended in travel and testimony."

"What did you do in this case?"

"A rubber mask was submitted to me for study. I examined it, tested it, and recorded my findings."

"What kind of mask was it?"

"A rubber monkey mask."

"I'm going to hand you what's been marked as State's Exhibit 77. Is this the mask?"

He studied the exhibit. "Yes, here are my initials on the inside. You can barely make them out."

"Okay. And you say you examined this mask and tested it. What did that consist of?"

"Taking swabs and samples and testing them for DNA."

"Did you find DNA on this exhibit?"

"I did not."

I paused, letting that sink in.

"There has been testimony in this case that this mask was worn by Carlos Pritchett, my client sitting at the defense table. Had Mr. Pritchett been wearing this mask on his face would you expect to find his DNA on it?"

"Definitely."

"Why is that?"

"Because when he exhaled that would have laid down minute particulates of spittle and other bodily secretions that would have adhered to the inside of the mask. No such evidence was found on this mask. Plus, I would expect to find his body oil DNA from merely handling the mask with his bare hands. Again, no such finding."

"So can you say that, to a reasonable degree of scientific certainty, Carlos Pritchett had never worn this mask before you tested it?"

"To a reasonable degree of scientific certainty, Carlos Pritchett did not wear this mask before I tested it."

I stopped and looked at the jury long and hard.

Then, "In fact, does anyone's DNA appear on this mask?"

"No. There is no DNA on this mask."

"Wouldn't the absence of any DNA indicate to you that this mask was not worn in this armed robbery?"

"Objection. Speculation."

"Sustained. Please move along."

"Let me rephrase. If this mask had been worn during the armed robbery, would it contain someone's DNA on the inside?"

"The chances of that are in the ninety-ninth percentile, to my thinking. Yes, it would contain, as you put it, someone's DNA if it were worn on a human face."

"Nothing further, Your Honor."

The judge looked down at Ms. Cross. "Cross-examination, Ms. District Attorney?"

"Yes, thank you. Dr. Bendenetti, there has also been testimony that the robbers were wearing balaclavas under their masks. Wouldn't this garment block the transmittal of DNA onto the mask?"

"Possibly, except for the mouth. There would be the air hole in the silk garment, which would allow spittle and bodily secretions to adhere to the mask. So I'm afraid the wearing of a balaclava doesn't change my testimony at all."

Cross then tried various other approaches, but the doctor was a pro. She got nowhere with him and finally limped away to her table and sat down in defeat. I had no further questions, so the witness was excused.

# Chapter 42

MICHAEL

"Your Honor, defense calls its own investigator to the stand, Marcel Rainford."

Marcel stood up from our table and stepped up to the witness stand. He buttoned his sports coat as he went, then took his seat and remained very erect in the chair, even statuesque. Like the police officers who had come through here, he had been trained to testify at the finest police schools too, but his were in Europe.

"Tell us your name."

"Marcel Rainford."

"Mr. Rainford, what is your occupation?"

"I am an investigator for Michael Gresham, LLC."

"That would be my law firm?"

"Yes."

"You are my investigator?"

"Yes."

"And you investigate whatever I ask you to investigate, true?"

"True."

"Did you three weeks ago or thereabouts obtain the statement of one Vincent Phaeton?"

"I did."

"And have you previously read through the written statement provided to the jury by the state from this same gentleman?"

"I have."

"Do they match?"

"They do not."

"Did you make a video of the statement you took?"

"Yes."

"And it also contains audio?"

"Yes."

"Would you play it for us now?"

Using a video controller that operated his laptop, Marcel brought the video up on a large screen that could be viewed by the participants, the judge, and the jury. He found the first frame and paused there.

"Where was this video taken?"

"In your office in San Diego."

"And why was Mr. Phaeton there?"

"I asked him to join us."

"Did he resist in any way?"

"He did not."

"Did you pay him anything to come in and testify?"

"I did not."

"Did anyone?"

"Not that I'm aware."

"Please play the video for us now."

Carlos clicked the play button and the screen leapt to life:

"State your name."

"Vincent Phaeton."

"Where do you live?"

"Uh--Ocean Beach."

"What is your occupation?"

"Handyman."

"You're a convicted felon?"

"Uh-huh."

"Say yes or no, please."

"Yes. I'm a felon. Still can't vote," he said with just the beginning of a sneer.

"What were you convicted of?"

"Armed robbery. There was also a rape and a burglary somewhere in there."

"You served your time at San Quentin?"

"Uh-huh. Yes."

"And when were you released?"

"Couple of months now."

"What have you done since then?"

"You know, just general handyman stuff."

"Like bank robbery kind of stuff?"

"I was in on that, yes. Not because I wanted. I was kind of forced into it."

"Tell us how that happened."

"Well, this guy I met at Q knew a guy named Ramsey who would help me start over when I got out. I went to this Ramsey guy and he hooked me up with Carlos the Ant."

"How were you forced?"

"Ramsey said he would take me down if he told me about the plan and I tried to say no. He said he would have me killed."

"Sure. Tell us about Carlos."

"Not much to say. He had a crew and I threw in and we hit the First Commercial. But I killed the soldier, not Carlos."

"What soldier?"

"There was a veteran in the tellers' line. He mouthed off, so I accidentally shot him."

"You were wearing a mask?"

"I was."

"What were you?"

"What was I? I was the monkey. I wore the monkey mask."

"If the witnesses in line said it was the monkey who shot the veteran, would you agree?"

"Yes, the monkey shot the customer. I shot him."

"So the witnesses would all be correct?"

"Hell, yes."

"You're sure you were the monkey?"

"Sure I'm sure. I even saw myself in the bank window when we went by. I was the monkey with the TEC-9."

"Why are you admitting it was you who shot the veteran?"

Phaeton shook his head and slowly drew a deep breath.

"Just need to get it off my chest. I've got immunity."

"Have you discussed your role in the robbery with the police or the DA?"

"I have. They want me to testify and I said yes."

"So you're going to testify against Carlos and Ramsey?"

"That's what they tell me."

"Who tells you?"

"Her name is Leticia Cross. Her detective friend is something O'Donnell or O'Connell--I don't exactly remember. Some overweight white guy with shit growing out of his ears."

A few more sentences amounting to nothing and the video ended.

"Your Honor," I said, defense moves this video, marked Defendant's Exhibit four, into evidence."

"No objection," said Ms. Cross. She knew better than to object: if my video shouldn't come in then neither should her written statement from Phaeton have come in. We were even in that regard.

"Without objection, Defendant's Exhibit four is admitted."

"That is all I have for Mr. Rainford, Your Honor."

"Cross-examination?"

"Yes."

Cross came to the lectern and I returned to my table. It was her turn to have a go at the witness. I knew Marcel would hold his own with anyone, so I gladly took my seat.

"Mr. Rainford, tell us what all you've done in preparing for this case."

"Well, Mr. Gresham told me at the outset this was going to be a tricky case and that I should keep a watch over my shoulder at all times."

"Why was it going to be tricky?"

"He said you were known as a prosecutor who tried to trick people, that I should be careful around you."

Her face drained of color. It had worked, our little trap. "Judge!" she cried out, "move to strike this prejudicial commentary."

"No can do," said Judge Sturdevant. "You cannot strike testimony you have adduced, Ms. Cross. Please continue."

"Again, what all have you done?"

"I've talked to the witnesses listed on your witness list, Ms. Cross."

"You've talked to all of them?"

"No."

"Which ones didn't you talk to?"

"The ones you told not to talk to me. That would include all police and detectives, most of the crime scene investigators and all of the crime lab people. Your gag order was very effective in preventing our client from fully preparing his case to defend himself."

This time her mouth opened and closed several times, but she knew objection was futile.

"One moment," she said, and returned to her seat at the prosecution's table. There, she flipped through her notes and whispered with Detective O'Connell, sitting beside her throughout the trial. He was very animated and shaking his head almost violently. Evidently he meant to shut her down and he must have gotten his way because she abruptly told the court she had no further questions.

Whereupon, Marcel returned to our table and resumed sitting beside me.

"Re-direct, counsel?"

"Your Honor, I would like to reserve the right to recall this witness for further direct examination after my next witness."

"Granted. Please call your next witness."

"Defense calls the defendant, Carlos Pritchett."

# Chapter 43

<u>MICHAEL</u>

At the mere mention of Carlos' name, the jury was electrified. Notepads were flipped open to clean pages, pens and pencils were poised, and everyone sat up just a little taller and straighter. There would be no sleeping through this one.

Carlos was dressed in the conservative navy suit I had purchased for him. Wearing his white shirt and red tie he looked like a candidate for the U.S. Senate. But he wasn't, sadly. He was a down-on-his-luck man whose baby girl had just died, leaving him in a hollow place in the world that he inhabited mostly by himself. He was depressed and just didn't care anymore. I knew this would all come across to the jury.

He took the stand and raised his eyes to look at me. He wasn't smiling and he hadn't even acknowledged the jury. Well, they'd just have to do without this time. This was the first non-professional witness to testify, not counting the bank employees, of course.

"Tell us your name for the record."

"Carlos Pritchett."

"Mr. Pritchett, what is your usual occupation?"

"Bank security installer."

"What does that mean?"

"In my past life, it meant that I would go to different banks where our company had been called in. I would do a security workup and make suggestions for improving the bank's security. Sometimes I would actually supervise the changes that got made. Not all the time."

"Directing your attention to August tenth of this year, were you in the First Commercial National Bank on that day?"

"No."

"Where were you?"

"At UCSD hospital in Hillcrest."

"What were you doing?"

"It was my little girl's birthday. I was helping her celebrate."

"Who was present?"

"Me, Amelia, my daughter, her mother, and different nurses and aides that came in and out."

"How old was your daughter?"

"Eight that day."

"Now, there has been testimony that you were part of a crew that held up the First Commercial bank that day. Were you?"

"Yes, earlier in the week I had been part of that crew. But then I dropped out three days before the robbery. I told the guys I just couldn't rob someone again. I was finished."

"Where were you when this happened?"

"On the roof of the bank."

"What were you doing?"

"Helping with the oxy-fuel torch that was being used to cut through the bank vault."

"You handled that torch?"

"Yes."

"Did you leave prints on that torch?"

"I guess I did. This would be when I first attached the hoses to the torch itself. I must have left a fingerprint and DNA on the coupling nut at that time."

"But that was long before the bank robbery occurred?"

"Yes, a good week. We had just rented the torch from ACE Rents."

"From three days before the robbery until the day of the robbery, did you take part in any further preparations to rob the bank?"

"I did not."

"Why not?"

"I thought I had made that clear, Mr. Gresham. I didn't do anything else because I had withdrawn."

"And you had communicated your withdrawal to all the other members of the crew?"

"Yes."

"Then who was wearing the ant mask inside the bank if not you?"

Carlos looked down thoughtfully. Then he looked over at the jury to give his answer.

"I don't know. Someone the ant, I guess."

On cross-examination there wasn't that much out there to attack. Amelia's birthday party became an item for ten minutes or less, then Cross saw she was getting nowhere with it and moved on. The key issue became the withdrawal from the conspiracy by Carlos. Did he actually withdraw? Did he actually communicate his withdrawal to the others? And if it wasn't Carlos wearing the ant mask, then who was it? Carlos stuck by his story and didn't try to embellish. As far as he was concerned the story was a simple one and he didn't try to add to it even when Ms. Cross tried to give him more rope with which to hang himself. Finally, she gave up and walked away, shaking her head. She talked it over with O'Connell for several minutes in loud whispers and then they evidently agreed: she should call it finished and leave it alone.

Which she did.

Carlos returned to his seat beside me almost a free man.

Almost but not quite.

# Chapter 44

I recalled Marcel to the stand and the judge reminded him he was still under oath. Marcel said he knew that, of course. I asked him about the audio tape he had of our prosecutor, Leticia Cross. She objected; we had another sidebar and the court again admonished me--privately, in whispers--that I was treading on very thin ice and that I could be sanctioned if I failed to connect-up what the jury was about to hear with an issue in the case. I said I realized that and we returned to our seats. Conferring with Carlos about the tape momentarily and getting his full approval to use it, I then went back to Marcel, who was still sitting in the witness chair, and I began.

"Please cue the tape and play it," I asked Marcel.

Then it played:

"Hey, Rudy, Letty here. A team of detectives and uniformed officers are going to swoop down on your warehouse before noon tomorrow. Be advised you should remove all vehicles before then. What else? Oh, yes, I wanted to see you and thank you for the shoes. All girls love Jimmy Choo and I'm up there at the front of the line when they're being passed out by sweet men like you. Call me. *Ciao.*"

The tape ended and the jury sat in stunned silence.

Then, "The state renews its objection and requests the court to direct the jury to ignore what was just played."

"Counsel, your arguments are already on the record and noted again. However, the defendant will now have the opportunity to connect up the phone call to our case. Counsel for the defendant, you may proceed."

I nodded and turned back to Marcel.

"Marcel, who was Rudy Monsorre?"

"He was the boyfriend of Leticia Cross, the prosecutor in this case."

"How do you know that?"

"He told me."

"When did he tell you?"

"The day before he was murdered. He knew I had been by his warehouse looking to talk to him. I had left my card and he called me that evening. He told me that he was fearful for his life. He begged me to install video surveillance devices in his house."

"Did you?"

"I did."

"Describe what you did."

"I installed two video cameras, motion-operated, in his house. One in his kitchen and one in his living room."

"Have you obtained video from either or both of those devices?"

"Kitchen video camera, yes."

"Your Honor, this video has been marked Defendant's Exhibit Six and we are about to move it into evidence. But first, we would like to play it for the jury as it will shed light on my investigator's interaction with Rudy Monsorre and will explain his role in this case, all in line with what the court has told me I must do in order to avoid sanctions. Second, the tape goes to the prosecutor's attempts to illegally affect the outcome of this trial, which is always relevant."

"Object, Your Honor," cried Ms. Cross. "The state hasn't seen this tape."

"Counsel, this video was turned over to you sometime ago," I lied. "If you haven't bothered to view it, that's your problem." I was beyond mere anger; they had tried to plant a monkey mask to send my guy to his death. At that point, it was open season on the prosecutor and her cops.

"Counsel," the judge said to both of us. "We're going to view the tape and the jury's going to view the tape with us. It is listed as an exhibit and therefore is admissible if it is relevant and probative. First let's watch."

"Please, Marcel," I said, "activate the video player in your laptop."

Marcel held out and clicked his laptop's video controller and once again the large screen leapt to life.

Except this time the subject of the video was Rudy and Leticia.

Here's what was portrayed from the video cameras in both the kitchen and the living room spliced together in sequence:

Ms. Cross comes into the kitchen, studies the phone answering machine, then pushes the eject button and the tape rises up. Snatching it from the small receptacle where it operated, she drops it into her purse.

Then Rudy comes into the kitchen and reaches around her as if to grab his cassette tape back from her.

"What the hell? Why take my tape?"

"Because I want to! Because I want to know who else has called you!"

"No one's called me. Now, give it back!"

He seizes her wrist and tries to pull her purse away. She resists, pushing him back with her free hand. He seizes her free hand too and shoves hard. She flies up against the kitchen island and is bent over backwards, the purse dangling from the crook of her arm. He reaches around, rips the purse off of her arm and turns away with it. Looking frantically around, she snatches up the iron breakfast skillet and smashes it down against his head. Monsorre crumples down onto his knees, then topples over to his side. He doesn't move.

She toes him with a patent leather pump.

"C'mon, Rudy. Quit playing around."

He doesn't respond. She toes him again, this time in the crotch. Still no response.

She squats down and feels around for the pulse in his wrist. No such thing. She reaches for the pulse in his neck. She plucks a dish towel from a drawer and wipes her DNA and prints from his wrist and throat. She pries the cassette tape out of his hand and wipes his hand. Then she wipes his other hand, too, using the dish towel yet again. She does the same thing with the iron skillet. She turns the skillet over. It's covered in blood on the flame side. She stuffs the dish towel into her purse.

She exits the range of both cameras. Then she returns to the kitchen, where she rubs the crotch panel of a pair of women's underwear against the handle of the iron skillet.

She creeps into the living room and, using the underwear as a glove, picks up the phone and dials 911. She doesn't say anything. But she does leave the phone off the hook.

Using the underwear yet again, she pulls open the front door.

She then disappears from camera view.

When the video ended, the courtroom was absolutely silent. Leticia Cross was frozen in her chair, staring straight ahead at the floor.

The judge announced a recess and the jury, in total shock and silence, was led from the courtroom by the bailiff.

Then Detective O'Connell stood. Without a word, he removed his handcuffs from his utility belt and fastened them around the outstretched wrists of Ms. Cross. She didn't resist and didn't speak. He then helped her to her feet.

Meanwhile, the judge and Marcel and I, along with the spectators, watched all this. It then became clear that the detective was going to remove the prosecutor from the courtroom. Holding her by the elbow, he took her away.

"Your Honor," I said even though we were off the record, "Defense renews its motion for judgment of acquittal."

"Please. Let's hold off on that until the District Attorney can assign a replacement prosecutor. We'll be in recess until one-thirty this afternoon."

He didn't bother to bang his gavel. The Judge, his shoulders slumped and looking exhausted, exited the courtroom. He was limping, which I'd never noticed before, and moving very slowly. The entire ordeal had taken its toll on him.

Meanwhile, Marcel stepped down from the witness stand and at the same moment, a TV news crew came charging through the swinging gate separating the attorneys and judge from the spectators. They demanded a statement from me. Microphones were pushed at me.

"I have no comment. The case is still pending," I said. "I'll discuss it with you after the case is concluded."

Marcel and two deputies then helped me and Carlos make our way up the aisle and down the hall to the elevators. The news crew tried to follow us onto the elevators but the deputies blocked their path. We were being allowed to escape.

Once we were alone on the elevator, I turned to Marcel.

"Did you really give her a copy of the video?"

"Did she plant the monkey mask to screw our client?" Marcel said by way of answer to me.

"Yes," I say.

"There's your answer."

And that's all that would be said about the matter. Tit for tat. She screwed us, we fought back.

It was going to be an interesting afternoon.

# Chapter 45

MICHAEL

We resumed with the replacement prosecutor standing in at exactly 1:30 p.m.

I renewed my motion for judgment of acquittal. The prosecutor had no idea what he should say and spoke about the need for a new trial or some such thing. In the end, the judge treated his words as a motion for mistrial and denied his motion.

But he allowed mine. He found on the record that the state hadn't proven his case and that the defendant was entitled as a matter of law to a judgment of acquittal. Carlos had won and the case was finished. From a judgment of acquittal there can be no new charges filed on the same facts. Carlos's case was done.

We were swamped by the media five minutes later. This time I answered all questions for the next thirty minutes while Marcel took Carlos downstairs to our car. Would I be moving my practice to California? They asked. No, I wasn't moving to California. Was I with Racehorse when he passed away? Evidently they knew the law well enough to know that a witness was required in assisted suicide. Yes, I said, I was there. What were his last words? He said to tell the jury to do the right thing, I told them. The media ran out of questions at just about the same moment when I had run out of answers. We parted, then, mutually satisfied that justice had been done and that the public's right-to-know had been thoroughly fulfilled.

I hurried downstairs, where Marcel's RAM truck was parked in a no-parking zone, hazard lights flashing, Carlos in the rear seat. I climbed in front and told Marcel to drive and drive and drive, that I needed to decompress.

We drove, then, out to Ocean Beach, where we parked on Newport Avenue and walked down to the beach. We sat on the seawall and removed our shoes and walked on the beach as far down as the lifeguards' station, where we sank down on the sand. For the next hour we talked about the case, about the deaths of Phaeton and Monsorre and Racehorse and Danny, my wife. Just as we were about to get up to leave, two uniformed police officers came across the sand.

"Carlos Pritchett?" said the lanky one. "Which of you is Carlos?"

Carlos raised his hand.

"We've been waiting back there to give you guys time to talk. But we have a hold on Carlos. The Los Angeles District Attorney wants him in L.A."

Sure they did.

With a sigh, Carlos held out his hands and was cuffed and then taken away. He told me later that they had stopped and allowed him to put his shoes back on. Nice of them.

So Marcel and I talked until the sun went down and the air turned cool.

Then we walked up to South Beach Grill and went inside and devoured peel-and-eat shrimp and downed a draft beer, followed by coffee.

"L.A. next, boss?"

"Yes. L.A. next."

\* \* \*

Before Los Angeles and all its problems, however, there was the pressing issue of my dead wife. What to do with her ashes? What would the kids want to do?

The night after the trial, I called Mikey and Dania to the dining room table before their grandmother served up her famous fried chicken and mashed potatoes.

"Guys," I began, "I want to talk to you about Mommy."

"Mommy's in a vase," Mikey said urgently, as if I might have forgotten.

"Urn, dummy," said Dania. "It's called a urn."

"All right, Mommy's inside--or her ashes are, so we need to decide what to do with them."

"Keep her!" cried Mikey. "She's our Mommy!"

"Take her home to Chicago," Dania said, her eyes welling up. "I want her with us too."

"All right, then," I agreed, "we'll take Mommy home with us. I like that idea, too. Now, do we want to have a memorial service for Mommy?"

"What's that?" Mikey asked.

"It's where people get up and talk," Dania explained. "You've seen it on TV before."

"She's right," I said. "People get up and talk and say nice things about Mommy."

"I love Mommy," Mikey said, dropping his chin onto his hand. "I miss her. Mommy, come home!"

"We all miss her, sweetheart," I told my son. I tousled his longish brown hair, which, I noticed, was in need of a cut. He was wearing it in a bowl cut and it was almost into his eyes.

Time to do the barber shop. Maybe that weekend, I remember thinking.

"I think a memorial service would be nice," Dania said thoughtfully. "Mommy needs to be remembered by lots of people."

"Who?" Mikey demanded.

"Uncle Jack, Aunt Margie, Grandma, Daddy, Marcel, Mrs. Lingscheit, Daddy's other wife--"

"No, I don't think other wives get to come," I said. "Not to this." The reference was to my ex-wife. She definitely wouldn't make the cut.

"Okay. Well, Cindy. Our nanny, Cindy. She has nice things to say about Mommy."

"She does," I agreed. So why don't we do this; now that the trial's over, let's go home to Chicago and we'll have a memorial service there. I'm thinking of something at our house, just Mommy's close friends and our family and people like that. We can sit around and have coffee and reminisce, remembering her. Does that sound okay?"

"Yes," Dania said. Her vote was the deciding vote as far as I was concerned. So I left it at that.

"Fine, then we'll have the service back in Chicago."

It didn't take long for us to pack and get our goods and clothes headed back to Chicago.

We followed, non-stop charter business jet, three days later, our suitcases and toys and carry-ons all but filling the hold to overflow. Cindy, our nanny, and Danny's mother, plus me and the two kids made for a whole bunch of luggage and belongings. But at last we were airborne and saying goodbye to the West Coast. Marcel, a speck somewhere below, drove.

We landed at O'Hare just after noon on a Saturday. Then we chartered two vans to haul our stuff up to Evanston.

Home, at last, though I still had Carlos pending in L.A.

It could wait until Monday. Then I would call the Los Angeles deputy district attorney assigned to the case.

I had some ideas for its resolution.

# Chapter 46

## MICHAEL

More often than not, in my criminal defense practice, cases are resolved with a simple phone call or two between me and the prosecutor. Sometimes business gets done even faster, at the prosecutor's courtroom table before court begins. Usually it's a few sentences both ways, then a deal gets done. It becomes rote because we've all done it so many times.

The Los Angeles prosecutor was a Stanford grad by the name of Eric Himmler. I noted from the yearbook he had played football at Stanford and graduated *summa cum laude*, so he was going to be very very bright. But he was also going to have a crushing caseload, being in L.A. I worried about Carlos and tossed and turned that Sunday night in my own bed. Carlos had been through enough out there.

Of course he still had the Chicago charges staring at him, but so far no one had fingered him as the perp, at least not from the photos they'd been shown. I had this from a reliable source out of the Cook County DA's office and I was anxious to address that case. But first, L.A.

So I called Mr. Himmler at noon CST, which would have been ten o'clock a.m. PST.

"Mr. Himmler, Michael Gresham calling. I'm the attorney for Carlos Pritchett."

"Hello, Mr. Gresham. Who's your client again?"

"Carlos Pritchett. The man who walked into Grand Canyon Insurance and shot the underwriter who wouldn't cover his child's medical problems. She was dying without the meds and my client was frantic and--"

"Hold on. I've got it right here. Yes, I know this case. I've talked to the victim and explained to him how I work. He didn't like what I had to say, but he went away without much of a fight. Here's what I'm thinking. Your guy was in a panic. His daughter was dying, so he commits attempted murder."

"But--"

"Hold on, Mr. Gresham, allow me to finish. The other side of the story is this Washburn Rambis character. You'll come into court and claim he was also guilty of attempted murder in trying to withhold important drugs from your guy's daughter, am I right?"

"Actually, it was a completed act. It was murder."

"Don't tell me your guy's daughter died?"

"She did. It was painful and very slow. The jury will hear all about it."

"Jeez, that's terrible. I was going to say something about a plea to felony assault, but now I don't know. Look, I'm buried in files here. So why don't we do this: Your guy pleads to misdemeanor assault, credit for time served, and we cut him loose."

I was stunned. Reflexively I said, "My thinking, exactly."

"I just need a copy of the death certificate for my file, in case the press or anyone else comes snooping. Is your guy going to sue the insurance company for bad faith?"

"We're talking about that."

"Off the record? I hope you sue the living shit out of them and bust their nut for at least a million. You've got my blessing."

"Thank you, Mr. Himmler. That's very kind."

"You're in Chicago, according to your entry of appearance. Why don't you send someone out here five hundred bucks and let them stand in for you? I'll send you a copy of the plea agreement and you can review it with your guy long-distance. We can do this on tomorrow's calendar call and get him out of jail. Fair enough?"

"Yes. That would be fair."

"All right. I'm emailing the plea to you this afternoon. Give your guy a call and he can sign it in court tomorrow. Tell you what. I'll just have the public defender stand in for you. Save you five hundred bucks. Is that okay?"

"That works for me. Thank you, Mr. Himmler."

"Thank you, Mr. Gresham."

And, presto, it was a done deal. Two down, one to go.

# Chapter 47

## MICHAEL

The Assistant U.S. Attorney was adamant.

"We have a truck driver telling us he picked your man up in Chicago. We found over two hundred thousand dollars in his backpack. He refused to identify the source of that money. After we booked him in, we found out he was a suspect in three other armed robberies."

"Three?"

"Yes. Didn't he tell you?"

Actually, no he had not. And I had asked him, too. But I plunged ahead.

"The only charges pending against Carlos Pritchett right now are the Chicago charges. No other case has been brought that wasn't either dismissed, rolled over to a misdemeanor, or had a judgment of acquittal entered. You have no priors on my guy and no reason to continue to hold him. As for the money, last time I looked it wasn't against the law to possess cash money in the United States. Last time I looked it also wasn't a rule that a citizen has to explain to the police where his money comes from. Last time I looked, you also engaged in an illegal search and seizure when you opened his backpack."

This last point was one I wasn't absolutely clear on. It would take some research. But I said it anyway, as lawyers will say just about anything when they're bargaining for someone's very freedom. It's been known to happen more than once.

The AUSA paused. I could tell he was reflecting. He was a man I knew, Thomas Jefferson Montoya, and he knew me. He knew I would go to trial with him and he knew it would be a dogfight. I was in Chicago now, where I had earned somewhat of a reputation as a pretty competent criminal defense lawyer.

"Michael, I need to share something with you. You'd find this out in discovery if the case went ahead, so I'm going to just short circuit that. The bank's manager, personal banker, and head teller all couldn't pick Carlos Pritchett out of a photo lineup."

"What?"

No, I didn't know. This changed everything.

"They all saw his picture, they all saw him in person, but no one could or would identify him. That's pretty damn telling."

"So you have no witnesses my guy was even in that bank."

"Pretty much."

"So what do you want to do?"

"All right. Why don't we do this," the AUSA said in a clipped voice, enunciating carefully as if giving full and thoughtful consideration to every word he was saying. "Why don't we put this case on the back burner. Let's continue it for, say, six months."

"A federal judge would never allow that."

"Oh, yes, he would, the one I'm thinking of, if--and it's a big if--your client will waive time."

He meant would we waive Carlos' right to a speedy trial. Of course we would. I could answer that without even bothering to consult Carlos.

"He'll waive time," I hurried to say. "Why don't you draw up a stipulation?"

"I will. Let me say this, Michael. If you're guy is not in any new trouble in six months, then I think we can quietly make this go away. I have no eyewitnesses who can identify him, so my case is very thin. No one can argue with what I'm proposing."

"I think it's the right thing to do," I agreed. "If this case went to trial I'm thinking a motion for acquittal might be very compelling to any judge."

"Unfortunately, I have to agree with that. So, do this, please: Pass along a message to your guy. Tell him that I'd love to throw his ass in jail but whatever he did to silence the eyewitnesses has evidently worked. Tell him sometime I'd like to know how he did it. Just for future reference."

"I don't think any such thing happened, Thomas, but I'll pass along your comments."

"All right, then. The stip will be on your desk tomorrow morning. Goodbye for now, Michael."

And just like that--snapped fingers--the case was disposed of.

Of course, Carlos would have to stay out of trouble, but he'd have no problem doing that, right? Especially with his pressing need for money gone by the wayside.

He'd easily stay out of trouble now.

Wouldn't he?

# Chapter 48

MICHAEL

Carlos the Ant got his nickname after serving in Afghanistan with the Army Corps of Engineers. The Corps had him moving massive M1 fighting tanks and bridge spans with giant machines. The men around him said he resembled an ant carting off a colossal load a hundred times its own size.

The army skills easily transferred back to the world. Caught up in a blind rage against Grand Canyon Insurance, Carlos thought nothing of stealing a crane and attacking. So, he went for it. With a Cuban cigar clenched between his teeth, Carlos worked the levers and steered the monster machine into the courtyard that lay at the front of the insurer's building. He was assisted by a new crew: two men at either end of the street keeping a lookout, another man in the getaway vehicle parked on the concourse out front and listening in on the police band, and a man positioned in the building across the street where he could shine a powerful light on the top floor of the GCIA building. As he worked the crane's mighty demolition ball, the tenth floor where Washburn Rambis' office was located, disappeared. It took less than seven minutes to level the floor. Then the men were gone, off into the night. They would meet up the next night at a local Denny's and lay plans for their next conquest, a bank in Seattle rumored to have a bimonthly payroll for Boeing employees and Amazon employees in the neighborhood of eleven million dollars.

But nothing eased the pain in his heart from his loss of Amelia.

So he took that pain and re-directed it, creating a not-for-profit organization fully funded with enough money to assist those in need of medications they couldn't afford.

The fund was named, simply, *Amelia*.

# Chapter 49

Leticia Cross avoided spending any time at all in prison. She avoided that punishment on a technicality that surfaced when discovery was exchanged. It seems the actual video recording of Leticia crowning Rudy with the iron skillet was, as discovered in its metadata, the work of the San Diego Police Department. Leticia went directly to court. She argued that the police had burgled Rudy's condo in planting the video equipment that had recorded her and was therefore the fruit of the poisonous tree and inadmissible under *Wong Sun v. United States.*

I thought not, because it wasn't Leticia's Fourth Amendment rights that had been violated but Rudy's—if we ignore the fact that Marcel planted the camera and the police had nothing to do with it. But…that wasn't exactly how it all settled out and somehow the police department's fingerprints were all over the video as metadata. So maybe it was a legitimate ruling when the court refused to admit the video; or maybe it was the bias of the judge on Leticia's case, a loyal jurist who had once served in the District Attorney's office and had even supervised Leticia when she first climbed aboard there. Local politics can be an intrigue and a complete hijacking of justice. But this much became known on the street: the judge herself thought Rudy Monsorre deserved to die. During his many carjackings, people had died and even children had been kidnapped and cast aside as so much detritus if they had unluckily been strapped into a rear passenger seat when the carjacking went down. It was unanimous: Rudy got what he had coming. Leticia had done a public service by cracking his head wide open with a chunk of iron. So be it.

It utterly astonished me, then, when one day I arrived at my office in Chicago only to find Leticia in my outer waiting room, casually thumbing through a recent edition of *Vogue.* Her face brightened when she saw me and she stood and extended her hand.

"Michael Gresham," she said, all cool and collected, "we meet again."

"You're not armed are you?" I asked her, only partially joking.

She unbuttoned her suit jacket and held it wide for me to see. No guns, no weapons of any kind.

"I'm not armed but I'm wondering if you can spare me five minutes of your time?"

I looked around the waiting room. Other clients and visitors hadn't arrived yet. *Why not?* I remember thinking. *Let's see what's on her mind.* I had Mrs. Lingscheit—our receptionist—buzz Marcel into my office and I took Leticia in tow and we joined him there. I definitely wanted him with me both as a witness and a bodyguard because I had zero clue what the lady was up to.

We gathered around my desk, one of the paralegals just outside my door brought coffee and water, and we prepared to have our discussion.

"So," I began once coffees were treated with sugars and creams, "what can I do for Leticia Cross today?"

She sat back, crossed one leg over the other and demurely tugged her hemline down to her knee. Then she spoke.

"I wanted to thank you and Marcel personally."

I didn't understand.

"Thank us? For what? We tried to put you in prison. Or worse."

She smiled, looking directly at Marcel.

"No, no you didn't," she said, sounding very sure of herself.

I still didn't get it and had no idea what she was talking about. But then Marcel spoke up.

"You're welcome," he said. "I did it because you nailed a very bad guy."

Now I was totally lost. "Did what?" I asked. "What did you do, Marcel?"

Leticia answered. "He left a governmental signature on the video. That was enough to keep it out of evidence."

"I'm sure I still don't get it," I complained.

She turned to Marcel and smiled as she spoke to me. "He left behind an artifact on the video that identified it as the work of the San Diego Police Department. That was what kept it from coming into evidence."

Then the light bulb went off in my head. "You did that?" I asked Marcel.

"I did it once I saw who we had captured on the video. Once I knew it was Leticia, I appended a digital signature to the end of the video file."

"But why?"

"Why? Because I thought Rudy was a bad guy and deserved to die. I had learned he paralyzed a two-year-old passenger during one of his grab-and-runs of a Chevrolet Suburban. Evidently he didn't know—or didn't care—that the child was in the very back of the vehicle when he grabbed it and then crashed while trying to get away from the pursuing cops. I was overjoyed when she cracked his skull with the skillet. Nothing could have made me happier." He turned to Leticia. "I'm still proud of you."

She laughed and took a sip of her coffee. "Well, thank you again. You literally saved my life by giving my lawyers a foothold to keep the video file out of evidence."

"It was nothing," Marcel said. "I would have done it for anyone who swatted that miserable excuse for a human being."

So there we sat, me thinking, through my astonishment, what an ingenious investigator I had working for me. Marcel never ceased to amaze me. But then he amazed me even more.

"So," she said, "how can I pay you back? I owe you big time."

Marcel shocked me then. "Join me for dinner tonight. Have you ever been to Ditka's?"

"No, I haven't. But I'd love to give it a whirl."

They left my office, then, I assumed to make their plans. Whatever, they had paired off and left me behind.

It was no small surprise, however, when Marcel came to me the next day with a request.

"She would fit in well here in our practice, Boss," he said. "She's brilliant, you know."

I gave him my most astonished look. It was all legitimate.

"Come again?"

"The woman needs a job. She's ruined on the West Coast. She wants to start over and I thought Chicago might be a good next step for her."

"You're serious about this?"

"Dead serious. I really got to know her last night. And this morning."

"Spare me the details, please."

"There are no details, Boss. It's all commentary and it shall remain private."

"Now I have no effing idea what you're talking about. And no, we're not hiring a murderess for this practice."

"I just thought that with Danny gone we were a hand short. If nothing else, Leticia would help us fill that vacancy while you found someone permanent."

He had me there. I *was* underwater. Work was pouring into the office—much more work than I wanted to take on, but I had always found it near-impossible to say no to people who came to me because they were hurting. It was my own fault that we were bursting at the seams. It all directly led back to me.

I tried another approach to quench his idea.

"She's not licensed in Illinois."

"Doesn't need to be. She can take the bar this winter and prepare cases for trial up until then. She can sit beside you in court as your investigator."

"Good grief."

"Boss, I'm very serious about this. I think we need it."

One thing about my relationship with Marcel: I trusted him totally. If he saw the good in Leticia Cross, then who was I to argue with him? And there was no denying it, she was a top-drawer criminal lawyer.

So, she joined my law practice.

Three months later, she passed the Illinois Bar Exam, coming in third out of several hundred candidates. By then, she had proven her value to the firm. She was nothing short of amazing in her ability to find the holes in the prosecution's cases and exploit those for our clients.

She came on permanent.

Which wasn't a minute too soon, I found out March 1 when a call came in from Seattle.

It was Carlos the Ant. He had been arrested in Seattle on charges of armed robbery. This time the feds were after him. Would I defend him?

"No," I told him, "I have my children to stay beside now, with their mother gone and all. But I'm sending an old friend of yours to take you on."

"Who's that?"

"Oh, you'll recognize her when you see her."

"I give up."

"Patience, Carlos."

I called Leticia into my office after Carlos and I had ended our talk.

"Pack a bag," I told her. "You're off to Seattle."

"I am? What for?"

"For Carlos the Ant. Remember him?"

She laughed. "I can leave tonight."

"Alaska Airlines. Be there."

"Yessir, Boss. Yessir."

I wouldn't see her again for three months.

But, last I heard, Carlos was a free man, found not guilty, on his way to Vancouver, Canada.

Who could blame him?

He'd definitely overstayed his welcome in the States.

Oh, one other thing. I found a buyer for my boat in San Diego. The money from the sale was donated to my favorite charity, $550,000.

*Amelia.*

I won't ever stop giving.


THE END

# Also by John Ellsworth (Avail. on Amazon)

**THADDEUS MURFEE SERIES**

Thaddeus Murfee

The Defendants

Beyond a Reasonable Death

Attorney at Large

Chase, the Bad Baby

Defending Turquoise

The Mental Case

Unspeakable Prayers

The Girl Who Wrote The New York Times Bestseller

The Trial Lawyer

The Near Death Experience

**SISTERS IN LAW SERIES**

Frat Party: Sisters In Law

Hellfire: Sisters In Law

**MICHAEL GRESHAM SERIES**

Michael Gresham

Michael Gresham: Secrets Girls Keep

Michael Gresham: The Law Partners

Michael Gresham: Carlos the Ant

For Debra Ellsworth and Noel Harrison and Mark Matlock

# About the Author

John Ellsworth was born in Phoenix, Arizona, and moved to Illinois thirty years ago. For thirty years he defended criminal clients across the United States. He has defended cases ranging from shoplifting to First Degree Murder to RICO to Tax Evasion, and has gone to jury trial on hundreds. His first book, "The Defendants," was published on January 15, 2014.

John Ellsworth lives in Ensenada, Mexico. He rescues guinea pigs, and plays classical guitar when he's not on his Mac dreaming up his next book.

## New Books - Email Signup


Sign up for my mailing list to get notified of new books. No spam, only new book notifications!

—John Ellsworth

# Afterword

Today I make my living by writing and I am very happy about that. For 30 years I was a practicing trial lawyer and the practice of law can wear you down in a hurry. But like most self-published writers my business thrives on readers' recommendations posted on Amazon. I would sincerely appreciate if you would take a few moments and give your thoughts about this book.

Made in the USA
Middletown, DE
18 June 2018